Praise for

SUICIDE NOTES FROM BEAUTIFUL GIRLS

"Twisted and intense in all the right ways, *Suicide Notes from Beautiful Girls* will keep you guessing (and your pulse racing) until its stark, shocking conclusion."

—MICOL OSTOW, AUTHOR OF THE NYPL FAVORITE SPOOKY TALE *AMITY*

"Simultaneously a pulse-pounding, breathtakingly twisty thriller and a complex, unflinching, heartbreaking examination of female friendship, *Suicide Notes from Beautiful Girls* is a story of love, damage, and an all-consuming relationship with the power to save or destroy—and it's unforgettable."

—ROBIN WASSERMAN, AUTHOR OF *THE WAKING DARK* AND THE COLD AWAKENING TRILOGY

★ "A taut, sophisticated thriller."

—*BCCB*, STARRED REVIEW

"Thoughtful and provocative, this will be a hard book for teen readers to put down until the thrilling, twisted end."

—*SCHOOL LIBRARY JOURNAL*

"Older readers looking for gritty, heady intrigue and suspense will find plenty to sink their teeth into here."

—*BOOKLIST*

suicide notes from beautiful girls

Lynn Weingarten

SIMON PULSE
New York London Toronto Sydney New Delhi

This book is a work of fiction. Any references to historical events, real people, or real places are used fictitiously. Other names, characters, places, and events are products of the author's imagination, and any resemblance to actual events or places or persons, living or dead, is entirely coincidental.

SIMON PULSE
An imprint of Simon & Schuster Children's Publishing Division
1230 Avenue of the Americas, New York, New York 10020
First Simon Pulse paperback edition July 2016

Also available in a Simon Pulse hardcover edition.

For information about special discounts for bulk purchases, please contact Simon & Schuster Special Sales at 1-866-506-1949 or business@simonandschuster.com.
The Simon & Schuster Speakers Bureau can bring authors to your live event.
For more information or to book an event contact the Simon & Schuster Speakers Bureau at 1-866-248-3049 or visit our website at www.simonspeakers.com.
Cover designed by Regina Flath
Interior designed by Tom Daly
The text of this book was set in Adobe Caslon Pro.
Manufactured in the United States of America
2 4 6 8 10 9 7 5 3 1
Library of Congress Cataloging-in-Publication Data
Weingarten, Lynn.
Suicide notes from beautiful girls / by Lynn Weingarten. — Simon Pulse hardcover edition.
p. cm.
Summary: They say Delia burned herself to death in her stepfather's shed, but June does not believe it was suicide because she and Delia used to be closer than anything, but one night a year ago, everything changed when they and June's boyfriend, Ryan, let their good time get out of hand, and now, a year later, June owes it to Delia to know if her best friend committed suicide or was murdered.
[1. Best friends—Fiction. 2. Friendship—Fiction. 3. Suicide—Fiction. 4. Death—Fiction.] I. Title.
PZ7.W43638Su 2015
[Fic]—dc23
2014039698
ISBN 978-1-4814-1853-9 (hc)
ISBN 978-1-4814-1858-4 (pbk)
ISBN 978-1-4814-1859-1 (eBook)

suicide notes from beautiful girls

Chapter 1

I'd forgotten what it was like to be that alone.

For the ten days of winter break, I drove. I made my way past the crumbling houses in my neighborhood, the mansions a few miles away, out toward the hills and then back again through stretches of cold, flat land. Up and down the Schuylkill River and up and down the Delaware, I cranked the radio and sang loud. I needed to hear a live human voice, and I was my own best hope.

But now break is over. I'm walking up toward school from the far lot, and I'm happy because I'm here, because it's done. I know you're supposed to like vacation, but it was lonely, that's the thing, like I was floating off into space, tethered to nothing.

My phone buzzes in my pocket. I fish it out, a text from Ryan who I haven't seen yet because he only got home last night: by the way got somehting in vermont I want to give you. Then a second later another one: not herpes.

I write back: good because it would be really awkward if we got each other the same present.

I click send with one frozen finger. Warm puffs of air escape through my smile.

I walk into homeroom, and Krista looks up like she's been waiting for me.

"Oh my God, June," she says. Her eyes are half open, and she's wearing a pair of red plastic glasses instead of her usual contacts. "Is it possible, *medically*, that I'm still hungover from Tuesday? That was two entire days ago!" She takes her big orange purse off the chair next to her so I can sit.

"Given everything, yeah, that seems likely," I say. She grins as though I mean this as a compliment.

The only thing I did over break, other than drive, was go to a party at Krista's boyfriend's house, which is a little weird since we're not close friends or anything. But we talk in homeroom sometimes, and neither of us has a lot of other options, is I guess the truth of it. When I got the text about her boyfriend's party, I'd been alone for so many days that I just said yes.

Her boyfriend, Rader, lives thirty-five minutes away, right at the edge of Philly, in a run-down apartment that he shares with friends. He's older, and his friends are too, some of them in their twenties. The party was mostly guys and the air was hazy with a few kinds of smoke. When I walked in, Krista was already trashed and going upstairs to Rader's bedroom. And I felt all these guys turn and give me the up-down. And I suddenly understood why I'd been invited—not for her, but for them. I spent the whole night leaning against the wall, not really talking to anyone, watching the party like a movie.

"Rader asked me to get your number for Buzzy," she says. She rubs her eyes.

I have no idea who Buzzy is. Maybe he's the tall guy who kept coming out of the bathroom sniffling and wiping his nose, or the guy with *A S S S* tattooed on his knuckles, or the one in the velvet shirt who kept asking if I wanted to touch it (I didn't) and who tried to put a shot of tequila in the fish tank (I stopped him).

"I have a boyfriend," I say.

"Wait, you *do*? Who?"

"Ryan Fiske."

Krista raises her eyebrows like maybe I'm joking.

"Seriously," I say.

She tips her head. "No shit."

I shrug. I'm not surprised that she's surprised. We've been a couple for over a year, but mostly no one knows about us. I guess we don't exactly seem like people who would be together.

"I wouldn't have thought you'd be dating someone so . . . *normal*." Krista means this as an insult, to him.

"Well, you don't know him," I say. But the truth is, he *is* normal. And it is comforting, somehow.

Ryan is one of those people who slides effortlessly into whatever social group he wants without even thinking about it. He is comfortable everywhere, and tall and handsome in the sort of way where even if he isn't your type, you can probably appreciate the bones in his face and the fact that they're all exactly where they're supposed to be to make a face pleasing.

He's a little bit of everything, I guess is what it is. And I'm not sure what I am. I don't think most people give me much thought at all, which is fine by me.

"I hope he's at least secretly into something freaky," Krista says. And then she winks and lets out a pained little moan. "My eyes are not ready for winking yet."

A second later the announcements begin. "Good morning, North Orchard students and faculty. Can I please have everyone's attention?" Vice Principal Graham. There's something strange in his tone. I sit up and listen. "It is with deep sorrow and a heavy heart that I must deliver some very sad news. A member of the North Orchard High community passed away over break." He pauses to clear his throat. And in that moment, I stop breathing. I think everyone does. In that moment it could be any of us. "Junior Delia Cole passed away yesterday. Ms. Dearborn and Mr. Finley and the rest of the counseling staff will be available for anyone who needs to talk, and my door is always open as well. Our thoughts and prayers go out to

Ms. Cole's friends and family during this difficult time."

The loudspeaker clicks off. And then there is silence, and the ding of the bell. The school day has officially begun.

My head detaches from my body. It rises right up into the air and floats toward the door, and so I follow it.

"He didn't say how," someone whispers. "What could have happened?" They sound confused, as though her death was so unlikely.

But I can so easily imagine a million ways Delia might have died. Maybe she climbed up onto the old closed-off bridge that stretches over the reservoir and went out onto the rotted part beyond the DO NOT PASS sign. Or she was up on someone's roof looking up at a big bright moon and teetered onto the delicate edge, even as they begged her not to. Maybe she walked across the road with her eyes closed, playing a game of chicken like she used to, her final moment the howl of a horn, a rush of adrenaline, and sudden blinding light.

Ryan is waiting for me outside homeroom. We lock eyes and he stands there staring, frozen, like he isn't really sure what to do with his face. And I'm not sure what to do with mine, either, because it doesn't even feel like my face anymore. I start walking toward him and he pulls me against him into a hug. His arms are strong and warm like always, but right now I can barely feel them.

I say, "This is . . ." And I stop because my brain has run out of words, and there's nothing in my head but air.

"... completely nuts," he says. He is shaking his head. And it occurs to me that this is the first time either of us has mentioned Delia, referred to her at all even, in over a year. I thought we would at some point—that it would be so strange when we finally did.

We make our way across campus, and he drops me off at the door of the English building, where my next class is. He leans in and hugs me again. The nylon of his jacket is smooth and cold against my cheek.

When he lets go, he looks down at the ground. "I can't believe this happened."

But the thing is, now that it has, it seems like it was always going to. Like somehow all along, Delia was far ahead of us, dead, and we are only just now catching up.

"I don't know if it's weird to say this now," he says, "but I really missed you."

And I know in a different version of the world than the one we are in, this would send a jolt of pleasure up my spine. So I say, "Me too," but being apart from him and winter break and everything that happened before this moment seems very far away. I can't really remember what missing feels like, or any other feelings either.

Chapter 2

I went to classes. My brain registered nothing. It mattered even less than it normally did.

It's right after lunch now. I'm in the bathroom standing at the sink. There are two girls, juniors like me, three sinks away. I don't know them well, but I know their names: Nicole and Laya. Nicole always wears big silver hoop earrings and Laya always wears a ponytail so tight it looks like her face might split. They are passing a stick of eyeliner back and forth.

I'm not really paying attention to them, to anything, until there's a buzzing sound—Laya's phone receiving a text. And then a half second later there's Laya's high-pitched voice shrieking, "No fuh-reaking way."

I look up. Nicole is lining her bottom lid, pulling at her face so you can see the pink around her eye. "What?"

Even though I don't know what Laya is going to say, my heart is psychic and decides to start pounding.

"So you heard how Hanna's older brother is training to be a police officer, right?"

Nicole nods, her head bouncing like it's too heavy for her neck to hold up.

"And you know how they didn't say how she died, right? Well, she said he said that's because"—Laya pauses, getting ready to say something juicy—"it was suicide."

Through the fog of feeling nothingness, my stomach drops, my heart stops beating. I lean forward, like I've been punched.

Nicole turns to Laya. "Whoa."

"Yeah. On New Year's Day."

"Oh my God, that is so sad!" Nicole sounds excited. "How?"

Laya shrugs. "Hanna's brother didn't tell her."

"I read a thing once that women, girls, whatever, are more likely to use pills, but I don't know, I could sort of see her, like . . ." Nicole puts her two fingers together and sticks them in her mouth. Then she jerks her head to the side and lets her tongue hang out.

The water is pounding down into the sink and splashing onto my shirt. Maybe I am going to throw up.

"She always seemed sort of off the rails . . . ," Laya says.

"Totally. Like one of those famous people who do insane things, except not actually famous."

"Yeah, like, famous only in her own head, though."

My sink has filled up. Water drizzles out onto the floor.

I face them now, something inside me sparks and catches fire. "Stop talking about her like that," I say. I try to keep my voice from shaking. They turn toward me, like they're only now noticing that I'm here at all. "Just fucking stop it."

"Um, hi?" Nicole says. "Private conversation. Besides, were you even friends?"

She looks at me, lips pursed slightly.

"Yes, we were," I say.

"Oh," says Laya. "Sorry." And for a moment she almost kind of sounds it. Laya and Nicole exchange a quick look and then head toward the door without another word. They are best friends, which means they don't always need to speak to understand each other. I watch them go. There's a squeezing in my chest, and my eyes tighten. The tears are starting to come, but I grit my teeth and I blink them back.

The thing is, when I said Delia and I were friends, that wasn't really true.

If we were still friends, then when I saw Delia's name flashing on my phone two days ago for the first time in over a year, instead of clicking ignore and not even listening to the message, I would have picked up. I would have picked up and heard Delia's voice, and would have known something was wrong. And then, no matter what Delia said, no matter what Delia was planning, I would have stopped her.

Chapter 3

1 year, 6 months, 4 days earlier

It was a relief to know she didn't have to explain. Not about the ache in her chest, the pit in her stomach, where it was coming from, and how much she didn't want to talk about it—Delia would just get it. She always did.

June imagined what Delia was about to say, maybe something along the lines of, "Parents. Fuck 'em," or "Only boring people have perfect lives." Delia could make you feel like the things you didn't have were things you didn't want anyway. She changed the whole world like that.

So that's what June was expecting, standing out there in the summer sun, waiting for Delia to fix this.

Delia tipped her head to the side as if she was considering something. She raked her curls behind her ear, hiked up her low-slung cutoff shorts, then reached out and took June's hand. She squeezed it tight, but still she didn't say anything at all. She just grinned and waggled her eyebrows.

Then she started to run.

And because she was holding June's hand so tightly, and June's hand was attached to June's arm, which was attached to June's body, June had no choice but to run with her. She stumbled at first, adrenaline coursing through her veins as she plunged toward the ground, then righted herself. Delia was ahead of her, arm stretched back, racing across the empty field, legs pumping, pulling June right along.

"Wait!" June begged. "Please!" June was in flip-flops. They were flapping against the grass until she accidentally ran right out of one of them. "I lost my shoe!"

But Delia didn't wait or stop.

"Fuck your shoe!" Delia called out.

So what could she do? June kicked off the other one and pumped her legs. When was the last time she ran as fast as she could?

"But where are we GOING?" June shouted.

"WE'RE JUST RUNNING," Delia shouted. Trees zipping by them, they were flying through the air.

The pit in June's stomach dissolved, sweat broke out along her back, her lungs were bursting. But still they ran, giddy and breathless, the pieces of June's life dropping away bit by bit, until she was nothing but legs in motion, arms, a heart, a hand, held. A body, stumbling, tripping, almost falling. Except she wouldn't fall, that's the thing. Delia wouldn't let her.

Chapter 4

After school I meet Ryan out front and follow him to his house like it's any other day. That's where we always go, even though no one is ever home at my house after school and someone is almost always home at his, and we're supposed to want to be alone.

Ryan puts his arm around me as we walk inside into the enormous open foyer. Ryan's family is rich. For some reason I didn't even understand that when I first started coming over. I knew that his house was nicer than mine, that it felt much better to be in here in this big beautiful space than it ever did to be at home, but that wasn't saying much. Delia was the one who explained it to me the one time she ever came here. Ryan was out of earshot and she'd leaned over the edge of their giant leather sofa and stared at me in this really intense sort of googly-eyed way that she only did when she was already drunk. “Shit, J,” she said. She was holding one of their very soft throws, stroking it like a bunny. “Why didn’t you tell me that your *love-ah* was *loa-ded*?” But things were already kind of weird between us at that point, so I didn’t say, “Wait, he *is*?” which is what I was thinking in my head. Instead I shrugged like it was nothing.

Now I’m on the sofa and Ryan has gone into the kitchen area. I can still see him from where I sit.

“Are you sure you don’t want anything?” He opens the freezer. “You might feel a little better if you eat something.”

I shake my head. I’m underwater.

While Ryan puts things in the microwave, I look down at the phone in my lap, at the tiny icon on the screen—the message from Delia, which I still haven’t listened to. Which I can’t even bring myself to mention.

The microwave dings and Ryan takes out his plate, carries it to the couch, and sits down beside me. He pulls his laptop onto his lap and opens up the Kaninhus website, which is Swedish for “bunny house.” Basically there’s a guy in Sweden who has these two rabbits who live in a penned-in area in his backyard, and the guy keeps a webcam on them all day long. Ryan showed me the site when we first started seeing each other. “I really, I mean, I really, *really* like these bunnies,” he said, almost like he was embarrassed about it, which was what made it so charming. He told me his friends would think it was super weird if they knew. (His friends have an extraordinarily low bar for what weird is.)

The bunnies mostly sniff around and wiggle their noses and eat stuff. We talk about them a lot, as though they are real and have hopes and dreams and complicated interior lives.

"Hi, Adi. Hi, Alva," he says to the rabbits on the screen. He is using a terrible fake Swedish accent, which is another one of our couple things. "How are you today, bunnies?" One of the bunnies is eating from a little dish. The other is asleep.

I guess he's trying to distract me, to keep my mind off things, as though somehow that's possible. Or maybe it's that he doesn't know how to talk to me about her, to have this conversation at all. I sure as hell don't either.

But I'm thinking how it feels wrong to be sitting here staring at these rabbits while Delia is dead.

And I'm thinking how Delia would say, *I'm dead, what the fuck do I care? Watch the fucking bunnies if you want to.* And then she'd curl up the corner of her mouth the way she did when she knew she was being sassy.

"How's your screenplay going, Adi?" Ryan says.

Normally I'd join in, ask Alva about her slam poetry or something (because we pretend they're both frustrated writers on a writing retreat in Sweden). Instead, I'm bursting with everything that I'm not saying about Delia.

I can't hold it in anymore. My mouth opens up and the words tumble out. "I heard it wasn't an accident."

Ryan turns slowly, the smile gone from his face. "Wait, like, are you saying she . . . ?"

I nod. "Did it herself."

"Jesus. How?"

"I don't know. But . . . there's something else." My heart is racing. I need to get this out. "She called me two days ago." I hate hearing myself say this. I hate so much that it's true. "But I just let it ring. She left me a voice mail. I didn't listen to it at the time because I . . ." I stop. I didn't listen to it because I couldn't. Because I had worked so hard to try and put her out of my mind.

"What did she say?" he asks.

"I still haven't played it yet."

Ryan exhales slowly. "Maybe you don't need to," Ryan says. "Maybe it will only make things worse."

"But how can things be worse than they already are?"

He just shakes his head, looks down, then leans back and holds out his arms in this way that I love, when I'm capable of feeling anything. Which right now I'm not.

I lean against him anyway, and he squeezes me tight. We stay that way until the front door opens a few minutes later and Ryan's mother and sister Marissa come in. We spring apart. I stand up.

"Junie, sweetheart!" Ryan's mother smiles. "We missed you over Christmas." She puts her keys and her fancy purse down on the counter.

His sister waves to me as she walks up the stairs.

"Marissa told me what happened at your school today,"

Ryan's mom says. She frowns. "Such a terrible shame, a tragic waste. Did either of you know the girl?"

I don't want Ryan's mother to make a fuss, the way I know she will if she finds out the full truth. "I kinda used to, a while ago," I say. "Not anymore."

"Oh, honey, that's still awful. I'm so sorry."

She reaches over and gives me a hug. I know if she holds on too long, I will break apart entirely, because all of a sudden it turns out I am just barely holding myself together. I have to get out of here.

I pull away awkwardly. "I need to use the bathroom." I can feel Ryan watching me go.

Once I'm safely inside, I turn on the faucet and slide down to the floor, my back against the door.

I cannot wait any longer. I fish my phone out of my pocket and dial voice mail. I hold my breath.

First the automated recording. "Message received Tuesday, December thirty-first, three fifty-nine p.m." And then Delia. "Hey, J, it's me, your old pal." Her voice sounds at once completely familiar and like I've never heard it before in my life. "Give me a call, okay?" She pauses. "There's something I need to tell you."

That's it. That's all there is.

Suddenly, I feel the edge of the door pressing into my back. Someone is trying to come in.

"One second," I call out. My voice cracks.

I slip my phone back into my pocket, pull myself shakily to my feet. I splash water on my face and pat it dry with one of their soft towels.

I'd assumed there would be something in her voice to make this all make sense, but all that's here is Delia sounding exactly the way she always did. She doesn't sound like a girl who is getting ready to die.

Except . . . she was. It was the day before; she must have known. Did she call to tell me? Did she call so I could stop her?

I open the door. Marissa is standing there in the hallway, smiling at her phone. "Sorry," she says without looking up. "I thought you were with Ry. He's in his room."

I walk down to the end of the hallway. He's waiting for me on his bed, his blue plaid comforter bunched up behind him.

"Did you listen?" he asks.

I nod. "She said there was something she needed to tell me. But that was it. She always did like to keep people in suspense. Guess I will be forever now." I try to choke out a laugh. Delia would have liked that joke. But the laugh gets mangled on its way out and comes out like a cough and a sob. I won't let the tears come. I can't.

"I don't understand," I whisper.

Ryan shakes his head, he clenches his jaw. "It's beyond understanding." And he looks like he is going to cry too.

* * *

"Junie?" Ryan's voice jolts me out of my trance. It's later. We haven't been sleeping, just lying in bed, holding on to each other. The sun has gone down and the room is dark.

Now he holds something out in front of him. "Your present."

It's a tiny snow globe, a perfect winter ski scene behind glass. When I look closer, I realize the person on the slope is a rabbit.

"It's Alva," he says. "Or Adi." He smiles. "When they went on vacation."

I try to smile back, but my mouth won't work right. "Thank you," I say. "It's perfect." And I think about the rabbit wallet I have for him back home, how I ordered it custom from an Etsy shop and was so excited when it came. How I spent a long time wondering whether buying him a present referring to our private joke was somehow too *much*, too *serious*. And I thought for a long time about whether to get one rabbit or two.

I remember the girl who only had that to worry about. It all seems like a million years ago now.

We make our way back downstairs. The kitchen is warm and bright and smells like sweet cooking onions. There's music coming out of the sleek speaker on the counter behind the sink—happy instrumental stuff with lots of percussion. Marissa sits at the kitchen table with her laptop open. Ryan and Marissa's older brother, Mac, is there now too, standing at the kitchen island. There's a tangle of peppers and onions sizzling in front of him in a pan.

Mac is nineteen and is different than the rest of his family. They all fit so easily into this world of happy family dinners, easy smiles. Even Ryan does, though on some level I think he probably wishes he didn't. It's a really good world to visit, but I've always only felt like a visitor. Sometimes it seems like maybe Mac kinda feels that way too. He graduated high school last year, and then went to Europe with his band. He came back a couple months ago and is starting a company with his friends, something to do with technology and filmmaking that's supposed to be a secret. He lives in an apartment in downtown Philly with a few other guys, but he comes here sometimes for dinners and things. I always get the sense that he has some kind of secret life, maybe part of the world I used to belong to before I met Ryan when my whole life was wrapped up with Delia.

"Mom's at some exercise thing and Dad's working late," Mac says. "Here's food if you guys want it." He hands us each a plate piled with grilled shrimp and peppers and onions. He puts a platter of tortillas in the center of the coffee table and surrounds them with sour cream and homemade guacamole. Mac is a good cook, but the idea of eating seems absurd to me.

But not as absurd as the idea that Delia could be dead, which makes no sense at all.

I sit with my plate in my lap, barely moving.

Delia devoured life in greedy, gulping bites. She never had it easy—there was hard stuff with her family, and hard stuff maybe wired into her brain. But no matter how bad things got, she would never have chosen to leave the world when there was still the chance that things could change, and things could *always* change. There's *always* hope. And the Delia I knew knew that.

So what the hell happened?

No one talks much at dinner. Ryan takes the onions off my plate and gives me the guacamole off his. I eat one bite. When the three of them are done eating, Ryan takes our dishes to the kitchen to load the dishwasher, and Marissa goes upstairs to her room. Then it's just me and Mac. He comes over to the couch where I sit, and leans in, voice low. "They're having something for her tonight," he says. "Her friends from Bryson, I mean."

I stare at Mac. I wonder if he is purposely not saying this in front of Ryan. I wonder, maybe, if somehow Ryan told him what happened all that time ago.

"Where?" I ask.

Mac shakes his head. "Sorry, I wish I could tell you. I only heard that they were meeting at her favorite place. And I don't know what that is."

But I just nod and almost smile, because the thing is, I do.

Chapter 5

2 years, 5 months, 24 days earlier

By the time Delia and June got to the reservoir, the boys were already there.

Delia linked her arm through June's. "Don't be nervous," she whispered. "It's not too late to change your mind." She was using this gentle, sweet tone she only ever used with June and her cat.

But June shook her head. "I want to get this over with." It was the summer after eighth grade, and June had decided it was time.

Delia snorted a laugh. "Well, that's one way to think about it."

They kept walking down toward the water, and June could hear the others now—laughter, the clink of bottles, and music coming out of someone's phone. According to Delia, they were out there almost every night during the summer. They all went to Bryson, which was the school Delia would have gone to if she hadn't convinced her mother to tell the school district that they still lived in their old house even after they'd moved in with Delia's stepfather.

"Guys at Bryson are generally hotter," Delia had told her once. "More skateboardery than soccer player, which is why it's better not to go to school with them. Then you don't have to see them in the morning and look at the oozy zits they popped when they got out of the shower, or smell their coffee farts, and have no choice but to find them disgusting forever."

And so when June mentioned not wanting to start high school still not having kissed anyone, Delia made a joke about kissing *her*, then laughed and said, "Well, you'll just make out with one of the Bryson boys, then." Like it was no big deal and already settled. Delia, of course, had kissed lots of people. Eleven at last count, according to her list.

They made their way toward the tiny flickering campfire and stopped. Delia reached over one of the guys' shoulders and snatched the bottle of beer from his hand. Then she backed up and sat on a rock. Delia stayed far from the fire. She always did. Fire was the only thing on earth she was scared of.

"Hey, D," the guy said without turning. He had longish floppy hair and a black-and-white striped T-shirt.

"Hello, boys," Delia said. "This is June." She turned to June and handed her the beer. "June, I can't remember any of their names. It doesn't really matter, though." Delia grinned at June. She was doing her Delia Thing, which guys always seemed to love. June held the beer tightly to keep her hands from shaking. She pretended to take a sip and looked at them more closely.

There were four: one shirtless with wiry muscles, two in black T-shirts who looked tough and cool, and the one whose beer she had. She watched as he raked his hair away from his face. He had a tattoo on the back of his wrist where a watch would be, a figure eight maybe, but she couldn't say for sure. He caught her staring at him, and by the light of the fire she thought she could see the tiniest hint of a smile.

"Tell us honestly, June," Shirtless said. "Is Delia paying you to hang out with her?"

"No," June said. "I'm her imaginary friend."

June hadn't known what she was going to say until the words popped right out. When she was around Delia, she was a better, more clever version of herself. Like she really was someone Delia had made up.

All the boys laughed. And for a second June felt bad; maybe it wasn't nice of her to join in with the boys' teasing. But Delia laughed too and slung her arm over June's shoulder, proud.

"Then how come we can see you?" said Shirtless.

"She must have a very powerful imagination," Striped Shirt said. "A dirty one." He was staring directly at June then. She felt herself blush, and she was glad it was dark. She liked the way his voice sounded, sexy but playful, like he was saying that but also making a joke about someone who would say that, all at the same time.

June glanced at Delia, who was looking back and forth between them. Delia gave June a tiny nod. *Him.* A minute later when the boys asked them to sit down, Delia arranged it so that June and Striped Shirt were sitting next to each other. And then a minute after that Delia walked toward the water. "Hey," she shouted. "Come with me if you're not a pussy." They all watched as she stripped down to her bra and underwear, climbed to the top of the tall rocks, and threw herself off into the reservoir.

"We better go down there and see if she died," Shirtless said. Even though they could already hear her splashing and whooping below. Shirtless and the two in black stood up. Striped Shirt stayed behind.

"Next time you take a drink from your sink," Shirtless said, "remember: my balls have been in your water." He leaped off the edge, and the others followed.

And then it was June and Striped Shirt all alone, just the way Delia had planned it. He leaned over and put his elbows on his knees. She could see the tattoo on his wrist again. It was covered in plastic wrap. He reached out to rub it like he wanted her to notice.

"I only got it a few days ago," he said. "So it itches."

"Does it mean something?"

"Yes," he said. And she couldn't tell if she was supposed to ask more questions or not. So she just picked up a skinny stick and poked the end of it into the flame.

She wished very much that Delia were still there next to her instead of far away in the water. June's heart was pounding. She felt small and scared. She closed her eyes, pictured Delia nodding. *Him.*

June took a deep breath, then turned toward Striped Shirt, and in one swift motion she grabbed the neck of his shirt and pulled him in toward her until their lips were touching.

For one horrifying second he just sat there, lips slack. His mouth was cold and tasted like beer, and she thought about the fish at the bottom of the reservoir that sometimes nibbled at their toes when they went swimming, and how this was what kissing one of them might feel like. But a half second later he started kissing her back, and a second after that he pushed his tongue against her lips. She opened her mouth and let it in.

This is my first kiss, she thought. *I am having my very first kiss now.*

But it didn't feel sophisticated or cool or even good. It was odd—a little gross, really. And suddenly, June was struck with something else: For the rest of her life, no matter how many kisses she had, no matter who those kisses were with or what they meant, this was the one that came before all of them, out in the dark with a guy whose name she didn't even know. He would always be her first.

Striped Shirt reached up and put his hand on her boob. His hand felt small, in a creepy way, kind of like a child's. She thought maybe she wanted him to stop, wanted to undo this. But she wasn't sure how.

A moment later Delia and the boys were back, climbing up the rocks, dripping and shivering. June and Striped Shirt pulled apart.

Shirtless said, "Whoa, hey now," and started backing away when he saw them.

But Delia just stood there, wringing out her hair. June felt like she might cry.

"Come over here, D," is what one of the guys said. "I think our boy and your imaginary friend could use some privacy."

"How was the water?" June asked. She tried to make her question sound casual, but what she was hoping beyond anything was that Delia would somehow figure out all that June wasn't saying. And fix it.

Delia raised her pinky up to her mouth and ran it back and forth across her bottom lip. She was staring straight at June.

June scratched her ear. Their code.

A second later Delia glanced down at her phone, then said loudly in a voice only June would know was fake, "We have to go now. Sorry, Junester, my mom just realized we're not at home. She's totally going to kill me."

June scrambled to her feet.

"That sucks," said Shirtless.

"Parents, man," said one of the others.

"So I'll see you back here sometime?" Striped Shirt asked June. And June nodded, not meaning it, not even looking at him.

Silently they walked away. Delia held June's hand the whole way home. She never brought it up again.

Chapter 6

When I get home, the apartment is dark, but I can hear the TV blaring through my mother's bedroom door. It's after nine and she's not at work tonight, which means she's drunk, and what is there really to say about that. I've long since gotten used to things being the way they are; in general I just try not to think about it. But as I climb up the narrow stairs, for one weak second I let myself imagine what it would be like if I could knock on her door and tell her what happened. I imagine her wrapping me up like Ryan's mom did. I imagine her telling me everything is going to be okay. I feel a wave of something then, longing, maybe. I shake it away. My mother wouldn't do it. And even if she did, I wouldn't believe her.

I go into my room, kneel down, and start pulling things from my drawers. In this moment I am calm again, a strange, faraway kind of calm, like I'm not really here at all.

Ryan tried to convince me to stay the night. "My parents won't mind," he said. "Considering everything . . ." His voice was soft and sweet, and even though I could hardly feel anything, I knew that if all of this hadn't happened, it would have made me happy that he wanted me to. And a part of me wished so much that I could say yes, that I could sit there on his family's couch where everything is safe and warm and good. When his dad got home he'd make bad puns and turn on the news. He'd kiss Ryan's mother on the lips, and Ryan would jokingly roll his eyes. Then Marissa would make popcorn with tons of this butter spray she loves, and we'd all sit together. I'd let their normalness swirl around me and envelop me. I'd pretend like none of this had happened.

"I should go home," I told Ryan, "to be alone for a while, I think." And he seemed to understand, or at least he thought he did. He walked me out to my car and stood there watching as I drove away. *Alone.* I felt bad for lying to him. But what choice did I have?

Now, here in my room, I get undressed. I pull out a pair of thick black wool tights. I put the tights on and my jeans back over them. I slip on my dark gray leather boots and lace them up. I am trying so hard not to think about anything, not to think about where I am going and why.

I rifle through my drawers until I find what I'm looking for. The sweater—so soft, dark green with delicate gold threads. This was Delia's. I haven't worn it in a very long time. She gave it to me back when things were still good with us. "It makes me look diseased," Delia had said, throwing it at me. "Please save me." Delia was always so, so generous, acted like it was nothing. Acted like you were doing her a favor accepting whatever she gave you.

It is the nicest sweater I own by far. I put it on, my jacket over it, and a black scarf as big as a blanket, because it's January and I know it will be cold down by the water.

I park in the little alcove at the side of the road and get out. It's been years since I've been here, but I know the route by heart. There's a car right in front of the hole in the fence around the reservoir, and I shake my head. You're supposed to park far away. This is trespassing. No one is supposed to know that anyone is out here.

I squeeze through the hole and walk down the narrow dirt path. My stomach turns over and over. I hear quiet murmurs, and as I get closer the murmurs turn to words.

"You can't start a fire, man. It's too cold."

"Fuck off, I was a Boy Scout. I have skills."

"Oh yeah?" A few people laugh. "They give out patches for rolling a jay?"

I can see them now, a small group huddled in a circle around the bonfire spot. Someone is bent down, flicking a lighter over a pile of twigs. They smolder weakly, thin ribbons of smoke curl up.

My eyes start to adjust, and by the light of the big bright

moon I can make out thick coats, army jackets, hats, gloves. Their breath is cotton in the icy air.

I walk up behind them, my heart beating fast. I don't belong here, here among her friends. "Hey," I say. A couple of people half turn.

I work my way into the circle between a tall wiry guy and a tall girl with short dark hair and lips so red I can see them in the moonlight.

Someone takes out a bottle of vodka, the cheap kind that comes in a big plastic jug. "To Delia," one of the guys says. "A girl who could really fucking drink."

"To Delia," the others say back. And then there's a splashing sound as someone tips the bottle over the ground. And I feel a deep wave of sadness—this is it, this is her good-bye, a few people standing out on a cold January night, pouring shit booze onto frozen earth. They pass the bottle, taking long gulps. Who were they to her? How well did they know her? How much do they care?

When the bottle gets to me, I hold it far from my face so I won't have to smell it. I don't know how to begin, but I know it might be my only chance for answers. So I just blurt it out.

"Was she in some kind of trouble?" My voice sounds strange and hollow.

A guy turns toward me. "What are you talking about?"

"Was Delia in trouble?" I say.

"Who even are you?"

"I'm June," I say. "A friend." And I feel like a liar.

There is a silence.

"Delia wasn't *in* trouble," the guy says. "She *was* trouble." He sounds pleased with himself, like he thinks this is a very clever line. I hate him, whoever he is.

Someone lets out a laugh. I keep going. "But something must have been really wrong," I say. "For her to . . ."

"Well, obviously," another guy says. "People who are fine don't generally off themselves."

"It's not like she would have said what it was though."

"If you knew her at all, you'd know that." Someone reaches out and takes the bottle from my hands. "Delia didn't tell anyone personal stuff about her life."

But she did, I want to shout. *She always told* me.

"Listen," another voice says. This one is female, kinder than the others, slightly southern sounding. Only, before she can say any more, a bright light is slicing through the trees, lighting up our faces one by one. Two car doors slam and the beams from two flashlights shine out into the night.

"Shit," someone says. "Cops."

"Tigtuff?" one of the guys asks.

Tigtuff?

There's another voice then, gravelly and low. "Not on me, thank fuck."

And all at once there's frantic motion, everyone running in every direction. Adrenaline zips through my veins, but I force myself to stand right there. Here's something I know that none of them seem to, that Delia never understood either: if you run, they will chase you; if you stay and fight, you might lose. Sometimes, when there's danger, the answer is to curl into yourself and wait. I take tiny silent steps down toward the reservoir. I climb up over the big rock and crouch down.

It's so peaceful there, the commotion behind me, the moon reflecting off the water, shimmering silver.

I turn toward the road. The cop car's doors are open now, the light pours out from within. I see the silhouette of a cop holding a bottle up in the air. Someone was stupid enough to bring it up with them.

I stay where I am for a long time, as names are taken and tickets handed out. One person is led into the back of the police car, and everyone else is either driven or drives themselves away.

And then I am alone again. And I am afraid. And this time I don't even know why. I start back up toward the road. My toe snags a root and I lurch forward, but I catch myself just in time. My heart is hammering, and I'm not sure if it's the near fall or something else. I keep going, quietly, carefully. I can hear my breath and the wind and the beating of my heart.

Then, footsteps.

Someone else is out here. A square of blue light sweeps by.

I want to turn and run, but I know if I do, this person will hear me. I force myself to breathe. Whoever it is must be here for the memorial, same as I am. But still I reach into my pocket and wrap my fist around my keys so the sharp ends stick out between my knuckles. The light goes by again. It stops on me.

"Hello?" a voice calls out. It's low and male. The footsteps are getting nearer. "Please," the voice says. "Wait."

He's close. He holds his phone up to his face so he glows. Big jaw, thin mouth, short nose. I realize I know who he is.

I saw him with Delia a few months ago, out in the parking lot at school. I remember watching them, curious about her and this guy who wasn't her type. He was a wrestler, not tall, but wide and sturdy-looking, like a bulldog. Wholesome, somehow, too. Delia had jumped up on him from behind, wrapped her arms around his shoulders and her legs around his waist. And he ran around the parking lot, fast like she didn't weigh anything at all.

"I'm Jeremiah," he says. "I recognize you."

"We go to school together," I say, because sometimes when I meet people from North Orchard outside of school, I have to tell them this.

Jeremiah shakes his head. "Not from there. From a picture she kept in her room. You both have these hats on. She talked about you. You're June."

I know exactly what photograph he means, because I have a copy too. Mine is in the back of my closet, and I haven't looked at it in a very long time.

"I'm sorry, you're too late. For the memorial, I mean," I say.

"People were here before." I try to slow my still pounding heart. "Other ones. But the police came."

"I know. I was watching."

"You didn't come down."

"I wasn't here to drink with those people." He pauses. "I came looking for answers."

There is something in his voice then; it hits me in the center of my chest. "Me too," I say. "I'm trying to find out why she did it. Why she . . ."

The wind whistles. I pull my coat tighter.

"She didn't kill herself, June." Jeremiah leans forward. "Delia was murdered."

A pulse of white-hot energy rushes through me. I stare at his face, half lit under that big yellow moon. "What are you even talking about?"

"She hung around with a lot of messed-up people. She wasn't afraid of anyone or anything. Even when she maybe should have been. She wouldn't have killed herself, and if it looks like she did . . ." He pauses. "Then it's because someone made it look that way."

I reach out for something to grab on to. There's nothing but air.

"So we have to figure out who did this to her," he finishes. "Because no one else is going to."

I say, "If someone . . . I mean . . . We need to go to the police."

"I already went. And they wouldn't listen. They pretended to humor me, then gave me some pamphlets on grief and sent me on my way." Jeremiah leans forward again. "We have to figure this out ourselves."

His words are sinking in.

"You're the only other person who cares enough to ask the right questions."

I can barely breathe.

"She wouldn't have done this to herself, what they're saying she did," he says.

"But what *are* they saying?"

Jeremiah is quiet for a long time. "Come with me," he says finally. "There's something I need to show you."

Chapter 7

I follow Jeremiah back to the road. *What the hell am I doing?*

I feel like I'm in a dream. I think, *This guy is crazy with grief. I shouldn't even be following him.*

We get in our cars.

We make our way on the narrow twisty roads. Up Beacon, down McKenna, onto leafy Red Bridge. It seems like we're heading right for Delia's house, but instead of pulling up in front, Jeremiah makes a sharp right and pulls into the cul-de-sac that connects to the woods behind it. He parks. I pull in behind him.

For a moment I sit there in the silent dark, the only light the yellow circle from someone's front porch. I press my hand to my chest. I haven't been anywhere near Delia's house in over a year, but I used to come here nearly every day. This was more my home than my actual house was.

I open the door and step out. Jeremiah is waiting for me.

I will the memories to stay away. I can't handle them now.

"It's down through the woods," he says quietly.

He holds up his phone again, flips on the blue light. He steps up onto the grass between houses and disappears among the trees. I follow.

We're surrounded by darkness. The leaves crunch beneath our feet. I'm breathing heavy. In, out, in. *And that's when I smell it*: this strange scent I cannot understand. It's weak at first, but as we reach the edge of the trees, it hits me like a punch in the face. There's burnt wood and leaves, scorched rubber, melted plastic, gasoline. I pull my scarf up over my mouth and nose. But it doesn't matter—the stench is so strong.

"What the hell is that?" I say.

We are standing at the edge of Delia's backyard now. Jeremiah points his phone toward the remains of a structure out in the grass. I can't tell what it is.

"How they say she did it," he says.

"How she . . ." I stop. Then I remember: this is where Delia's stepfather's shed is supposed to be. *He uses it to drink and jerk off,* Delia had said. And what I'm looking at now is what's left of it—half of a wall, a metal frame, and a pile of burnt things.

Jeremiah turns toward me. "*This* is how they're saying Delia killed herself. That she burned herself to death in there."

I breathe in. I can taste it. My legs start to shake.

"There was firewood inside, she doused it in lighter fluid, herself too, and, *whoosh,* lit it up. So they say."

I can feel the heat crawling up from my stomach. Images flash through my mind—Delia trapped, the fire all around. She's scared, screaming.

And it's real now. I can't breathe. Delia, who was so tough, who would say anything, do anything, go anywhere, wasn't brave about everything. Memories come—Delia shrinking away from a tiny bonfire on the night she first confessed it. Delia flipping out because a guy was playing around with a lighter too close to her. I remember the look in her eye when she told me about her awful nightmares of nothing but flames. *If I have one while you're here,* she had said, squeezing my hands tight, *you must promise, promise you will come and wake me up.*

Delia was scared of just one thing. This was it.

"There's no way she did this," I say. And I know in that moment that what I'm saying is true.

Jeremiah nods. He turns toward me, out there in the dark.

"So now you understand," he says, "why I need your help."

We're up by my car now, Jeremiah and I. And I'm this close to losing it entirely.

"Maybe we can go back to the police," I say. "Maybe we can tell them . . ." I am desperate, grasping for anything.

"They've already seen this place. There's no point in going to them until we can tell them something they don't already know."

"I haven't . . . I hadn't spent time with her in so long, I don't know anything about . . . Where would we even start?"

Jeremiah turns away. "I might have an idea." He raises his gloved hand and puts his finger on the window. "I did something a few weeks ago that I'm not very proud of." He traces a circle in the condensation on the glass. "She got a lot of phone calls when we were together, but she didn't always pick them up. I guess maybe I was a little jealous. She wasn't always the easiest person to have as a girlfriend, you know." The words are tumbling out of his mouth, faster now. "Usually she'd bring her phone with her when she went to the bathroom, but this one time a couple weeks ago she forgot, I guess. The phone was ringing, it had been ringing all afternoon. So I don't know, I didn't even really mean to, but then . . . I answered it. It was a guy, and he said, 'There's no point in trying to avoid me. I know your friends, I know where you hang out. I'll find you.' He was all crazy mad sounding. I asked who he was, what he wanted, but he hung up. I checked, and the name on the phone was Tigger. When Delia came back from the bathroom, I didn't say anything. I knew she'd get pissed at me for snooping if I did, and I didn't want her to be mad at me. I'm such an idiot. I should have said something. I should have . . ." Jeremiah pauses then. He rubs the circle off the glass with his fist and looks up. "If we need somewhere to start, I think he's it."

I am silent. But all of a sudden I realize something:

Tigger. Tig.

My breath catches in my throat.

Tigtuff?

Not on me, thank fuck.

The pieces are clattering together, bits of memory arranging themselves into a shape.

"What?" Jeremiah says. He is staring at me, jaw set, head tipped to the side. "What is it?"

Down by the water they weren't talking about "tigtuff" but "*Tig's stuff.*"

I open my mouth to tell him, and I'm stopped by a thought. Can I trust him? This guy who I've never spoken to before, who spent tonight hiding out in the dark, watching, who answered Delia's phone and never told her about it?

"Nothing," I say. I press my lips together. But what's Tig's stuff? It's the sort of stuff guys like the ones down by the water might bring out for a night of getting fucked up. It's the sort of stuff one would very much want to hide from the cops.

And as I understand this, I understand something else: just what that makes Tig . . .

Chapter 8

Before the sun rose, I was already there, sitting in my car in the parking lot of Bryson High. I haven't been to sleep. For five hours I drove, thinking about Delia. It was like over Christmas when I was alone, only this time I was kept company by images I couldn't escape. Every time I blinked, there was the shed, charred and crumbling. Every time I took a breath, there was that stench. I turned the radio up loud and forced myself to sing along. Scream along. It's what I had to do to keep the tears from coming.

Now I sit huddled in my coat and scarf, watching as the sky turns from black to gray to clear, cold blue. At 7:20 I get out and walk toward the school, waiting for the students to arrive. If this were a regular day, I'd be nervous knowing I'm about to have to talk to so many people I don't know, to ask them for something. But as it turns out, there are many worse things to be scared of.

Finally, they begin to trickle in—two tall girls in fuzzy boots and pea coats, a small guy with an enormous backpack, three huge dudes in football jackets.

I'm not sure who I'm looking for, exactly, and I could barely see them last night, but Delia's type of person is never that hard to spot.

There's a girl in all black with short dark hair. I walk up to her. "Did you know Delia Cole?" I say.

"Who?" the girl tips her head to the side, confused. She smiles slightly. I ask again. She shakes her head.

I ask a guy with a skateboard and two girls wrapped together in one very long scarf, a kid with a Mohawk and a dozen more people after that. They all say no. But someone who knows her is here somewhere and I'm not giving up until I find them.

Three guys are walking toward me now. Two are tall and lanky, one is shorter and sturdier; they're dressed in black and green and gray. I feel a tingling in my gut.

I make a half circle and come up behind them. They don't notice me. They're talking. I listen.

". . . appear in court," says one of them.

"I can't believe you're even here today."

"My mother bailed me out at two in the morning. Then

stood over my bed at six and told me to get up for school."

"Daaamn."

"Yup." The first one snorts. "Thanks so much for backing me up."

"Well, you're the one who *brought the vodka up to them.* What did you think they were going to do, make you a martini?"

These are the guys from last night.

I walk faster, fall in with their steps. "Hey."

They turn toward me. One of them smiles slightly, looks me quickly up and down, the way guys do. I can feel my hair blowing around my face. I've never thought I looked like very much—average height, kind of curvy, eye-shaped eyes, nose-shaped nose, dark blond hair that falls right below my chin.

Delia always insisted I was hotter than I realized. "Everyone else who looks at you sees something you don't" is what she used to tell me. But she was the type of person who would say that anyway, would actually *think* it anyway, because she loved you. Only, maybe these guys are seeing something now—I can tell by the way they're looking at me, smiling slightly. They're glad I'm there until I say, "You're Delia's friends." And then all of their expressions change.

They start walking a little faster. I keep their pace.

"I saw you last night," I say.

"Oh?" says the tallest one. He stops then and looks right at me. "What's up?"

He has dark hair gathered into a topknot, smooth cheekbones, a strong jaw, and full lips. Up close I get a sour whiff of last night's alcohol seeping through skin. I remember them down there, drinking, laughing.

"Tigger?" I say, in case he's one of them.

They're all silent for a moment. "What's that?" Topknot asks.

I pause. "I'm looking for Tigger."

"Bouncing, bouncing, bouncing, bouncing?" Topknot says slowly. "Fun fun funfunfun?"

"Check Pooh's corner," says one of the others, grinning. This one is scruffy-faced, with a black wool hat pulled down low. He smiles.

I grit my teeth and force myself to smile back.

"I'm looking for Tigger the person," I say. "I thought you might know him."

Scruffy and Topknot glance at each other.

"Nope, don't think so," Scruffy says. But he's lying. His voice is gravelly and low. I recognize it. He's the one who said Delia was trouble.

I feel my palms begin to sweat. I have an idea. "I need a hookup," I say. "Delia was always the one who went to him, for both of us. And I don't know where else to go now. I need a little . . ." I pause. "Help."

They stare at me, wary, all of them.

I reach into my pocket. There's a folded twenty I keep in there for emergencies. I pull it out and thrust it forward. "For your trouble," I say.

Top Knot and Scruffy exchange another look, and I know this was the wrong move. Now they're even warier. "Sorry, can't help you," Scruffy says. "Have a good day." Scruffy and Top Knot turn and keep walking.

But the shorter one, he hesitates. He is broader than the other two, and his face looks softer, younger. Maybe he can hear in my voice how desperate I am. Maybe he really needs the money. He looks back at his friends, who have realized he isn't with them and have stopped a few feet away. They're watching him. He reaches out and takes the bill.

"Listen," he says softly. He dips his hand into his black canvas messenger bag and pulls out a chewed-up pencil and little green notebook. There's a tiny sticker on the cover, a fluffy chick with a parasol. He opens the notebook and starts to write. "There's a party tonight at his house. If you need something, you can get it then." He looks me in the eye. "But you probably shouldn't mention Delia."

I force myself to breathe slowly, to try to keep my voice from shaking. "Why's that?"

"They weren't always on the best terms."

"Oh, really," I say. "Delia never mentioned . . ."

The guy shrugs. "I don't really know the deal. I think she

might have stolen something from him, not too long ago? All I'm saying is if you drop her name, he might try to jack up the price. He can be a dick like that."

"Thanks for the tip."

"Don't tell Tig I told you that. Or about the party either, actually."

"No problem," I say. And then, "I don't even know who you are."

He bites his lip as he hands me the folded-up notebook paper. There on the back of his wrist, where a watch would be, is something I've seen before, something I remember from a night with Delia a long time ago—an infinity sign inked in black. I remember when this tattoo was fresh, and I first saw it by a bonfire. I remember how scared I was then, that fear a very different fear than what I'm feeling now. Warmth spreads across my cheeks. When I look up, he is staring.

"No," Infinity says. He looks me straight in the eye and smiles ever so slightly. Does he remember? "I guess you don't."

I unfold the paper. There's the address—Pinegrove Industrial Park, Building 7. And there's my folded-up twenty.

"It's in Macktin, down by the water," he says.

"Thanks," I say.

Infinity nods. "Good luck." He turns to walk away, then stops and turns back. "Be careful. Tig . . . isn't always the nicest guy."

"I can handle it," I say. And I shrug, more confident than I feel.

He gives me a half wave and goes back to his friends. I start the long cold trek back to my car.

What the hell had Delia gotten herself into?

Chapter 9

2 years, 4 months, 17 days earlier

Delia and June lay on their backs on the grass, fingers intertwined between them, staring up at the big blank sky.

"Imagine floating off into that," Delia said. Her voice sounded dreamy and wistful, the way it did when she was fucked up, which she currently was.

"If I ever get the chance to go to space," Delia went on, "I'm definitely going."

June laughed. But she closed her eyes. She didn't even want to look at it.

"I'm serious. I'd do it in a second. Everything down here is meaningless . . ."

June wasn't high like Delia. She was sober as usual. She hated the idea of so much emptiness, above them, around them, everywhere.

". . . but nothing bad has happened out there yet." Delia

finished. "It's all brand-new." Delia inhaled deeply like she was sucking in the sky. "And if I go, you're coming with me."

Without even meaning to, June inhaled also. She felt Delia's feelings curling into her body with her breath.

And when June opened her eyes again, she saw only soft velvet blackness, endless possibilities. It was beautiful.

Chapter 10

It's nighttime again and I'm alone, driving down the dusty streets in Macktin, where I've never been before. It's a strange and uninhabited place full of sprawling industrial buildings, mostly deserted.

I pull into a parking lot. The building next to it looks like a prison. The fear I've been trying to squelch starts bubbling up again. I can take care of myself, but I'm not an idiot. Maybe this isn't really the place, and Infinity was messing with me. Maybe I should have asked Ryan to come too. Or even told him where I was going.

Except I couldn't. I get out of the car and remind myself that telling him would have just made him worry. Earlier this afternoon I brought up the idea that someone might have done something to Delia. Ryan shook his head, worry lines between his eyes. "The whole thing is really, really sad, but that doesn't mean there's a mystery here," he said. He put his hand on my cheek, so softly, talking to me like I was someone he had to be careful with. He'd never acted like that before, and it made me feel embarrassed. To him I am tough. He likes that. I like it too. "She was a very messed-up girl who did a lot of messed-up things," he went on. "It's why you stopped being friends with her in the first place. You said so yourself."

He was right; I *had*. Maybe I even halfway thought it at the time. But it wasn't the whole truth.

I didn't press it after that. And really, it's better that I'm alone for the exact reason that I'm wondering if it's smart to be: I'm unintimidating. Not a threat. People tell me things sometimes without really meaning to.

Maybe someone will tonight.

I'm up at the door now. It's propped open with a brick. I let myself inside.

There are bare bulbs dangling from the ceiling, leading the way down a long hallway. At the end is a set of stairs, a piece of paper stuck to the railing, on which is written MAYHEM: THIS A'WAY over a bright pink arrow pointing up. And so I climb and climb until, legs burning, I'm finally on the top floor. There's another door there. I can feel my pulse in my ears, my temples, my throat.

I open the door and look out into an enormous open loft.

It's eerily beautiful. I've never been anywhere like this.

There are only thirty or so people here, but the place could hold hundreds. Dozens of tiny white lights dangle from the ceiling, and dozens of white pillar candles sit in clusters on the concrete floor. The music is an otherworldly rumbling that rattles the inside of my chest. The air smells like plaster and wax.

In one corner of the loft there's a modern kitchen, all white lacquer and chrome. There are rows of glass bottles piled up on the white kitchen island and a handful of people standing around pouring themselves drinks.

I start to make my way toward them, but I feel a hand clamp down on my shoulder. I turn. There's a man in a suit holding on to me. He has a big round head and a space between his two front teeth.

"What's the password?" he says. His voice is a growl.

Password?

"I . . . ," I start. I think fast. "My friends are already in here." I point toward two girls walking past. They're a few years older than me, wearing short sheer dresses, high shoes. I'm still in jeans and Delia's sweater. "I think they forgot to . . ."

The guy shakes his head. "No one gets in without a password. I'm going to have to ask you to leave, then."

But I can't leave yet. And the idea of someone trying to get me to go makes me brave. *You're the sweetest little honey pie,* Delia said once, *until someone tells you that you can't do something.*

I clear my throat. "Be careful what you say, now. Tig's expecting me, and if you stop me I doubt he'll . . ."

The guy puts his hands on his hips and sets his jaw. And then, suddenly . . . he bursts out laughing, like this is the funniest joke he's ever heard in his life. "Ah, I'm only messing with you, dolly." He looks me right in the eye. His pupils are enormous. "It's the suit, right? Makes me look like I get to make the rules." He winks and steps aside. "Have a big ol' blast!"

I feel a flood of relief, because I'm in. And then right behind that, ice-cold fear, because I'm *in.* I grit my teeth. It's time to do this.

I make my way forward. I'm the youngest person here. Everyone looks like they're in costume—colored fishnets on their arms, top hats, jewel-toned tuxedos, tiny glittering dresses. Delia would have loved this place. Maybe she did.

I look out at the rest of the room. It's all raw open space. There are three enormous white sculptures off to the side—a ten-foot-tall head, a dancer with no arms, two bodies entwined. At the back of the room is an entire wall of windows, looking out over dark buildings and beyond that a cold white moon that looks carved too.

"For me?" a voice says.

I turn. There are two girls standing next to me: one tall and thin with a huge glittery choker, the other shorter, her eyes lined in green. Choker hands Eyeliner a small white pill. Eyeliner raises her perfectly arched eyebrows.

"Yup," Choker says. "His very finest."

They place the pills on the tips of their tongues and swallow them dry.

I stare at them, like I want what they have. "Hey, do you know where I can find Tig?"

Eyeliner gives me a puzzled look, then points toward the back corner of the room. A doorway. "Where else would he be?"

I force myself to inhale slowly, to exhale slowly. I pass a couple swaying against each other. I pass three girls laughing.

This is it.

I look through the doorway now; it leads to another room, much smaller than the first. In the center of the room is an enormous old-fashioned sleigh bed, covered in pillows. And on the bed is a guy sitting cross-legged, head shaved smooth.

Tig.

A girl with long bleached-white hair climbs on Tig's lap and presses her lips to his. I step back. He looks up. He pulls away from the kiss.

"Come on in," he says. His voice is high and breathy. He points at me and curls his finger. I walk forward.

Tig's face is thin, lit from below by the small stained-glass lamp on the nightstand. He could be any age at all.

He leans back, stroking the girl's hair like she's a cat. His shirt is half unbuttoned, revealing a hard, pale chest. "And how may I help you, pretty girl?"

"I was hoping you could hook me up," I say. I press my

tongue to the roof of my mouth. Fear rises up from my stomach.

Tig tips his head to the side. "What are you looking for?"

"Something . . . fun," I say.

Tig twists his mouth to the side. "I don't know you. Who are you here with?"

"No one."

Tig licks his lips and smiles, but his smile doesn't reach his eyes. "So what the hell are you doing in my house?"

Another wave of fear washes over me. But I hold his gaze.

"I'm here because . . ." *Because I want to know if you killed my friend.* "Because I heard there was a party."

"Like fuck, you did." He shakes his head. "Tell me or get out."

A jolt of electricity shoots up my spine. I think of Infinity and my promise, I think of my dead best friend and how no one can hurt her anymore. I think of the fact that someone did. I clench my fists. "Delia sent me."

Tig raises one eyebrow ever so slightly. "Ah-ha, a message from the underworld, then." He whispers to the girl on his lap. She pulls herself up off the bed, smooths her small white skirt, and heads for the door. When the girl is gone, his smile fades. "Save your bullshit," he says. "What do you want?"

Maybe Delia's ghost really is here, because Delia wouldn't have been scared of this guy for a second, and suddenly neither am I.

"I want to know what she stole from you," I say. But, really, I just want to get him talking.

"So she told you about that, did she?" He clenches his jaw.

"She told me a lot of things."

"Well, then you know a hell of a lot more than me." Something in the room shifts.

"What did she take from you? And what did you do to try to get it back?"

"Well, well," Tig says. "Are you here to avenge your poor dead friend?" He purses his lips into a frowny little pout. "How sweet."

Something inside me bursts. I open my mouth, and then it's like I can't stop. "I know where you live, and I know what you do. And if you did something to Delia . . ."

"Are you really threatening me?" His eyes don't look right. I realize then that he's on something—lots of things, probably. "That would be an extremely silly thing to do."

I want to turn and run. I exhale through my nose. "I'm not making a threat," I say. "I'm stating some facts."

"Well, then I'll state some facts too. You shouldn't be poking other peoples' beehives. But you have balls, and I like that in a girl." He pauses. "So I'll do you a favor and tell you a little thing about your friend: She was up to some fucked-up stuff that even I wanted no part of, and that is really saying something. But I didn't *do* anything to her, if that's what you're here to find out. She told me she needed it for protection—that was her excuse."

It. "Who did she need protection from?"

Tig shrugs and his lips spread into a slow smile. "Based on what happened, I'd say herself."

He pulls himself up off the bed then, tall and sinewy. He opens the drawer of the nightstand, takes out a pill bottle. He walks toward me, falling, catching himself, falling again. He grabs my wrist. His hand is strong and too hot. He forces something into mine, then lets me go.

"What's this?" Sitting on my palm is a small white pill.

"A goodie bag," he says. "Because it's time for you to leave my party."

He stands there, hands on narrow hips. And I realize there is nothing left I can do. He's not going to tell me anything else.

My body still buzzing, I walk back out into the main room. Someone is watching me—a girl with short dark hair. For a second I think she looks familiar. She reaches up and waves.

"Go on then," Tig says. He is standing behind me. "I'm not going to ask you so nicely next time."

I drop the pill onto the concrete floor as I walk and crush it under the sole of my boots. I feel angry, sharp-edged, sick scared. I don't know what to make of what has just happened. I don't know what to think or what to believe.

I stop in the doorway and look back at the party one last time. The music is different now. People are dancing with their arms in the air. A girl in a long gold dress is crouched down on the floor where I left the pill, snorting up the dust.

I start down the stairs, taking them two at a time. The crowd climbing up grows thicker the closer I get to the bottom, my eyes are starting to cloud, the faces blending together. Up above, someone cranks the music.

I came here looking for answers, but now I am filled with questions. There's one thing I do know though: if Delia thought she needed protection, it means this wasn't a surprise.

It means whatever happened, she saw it coming.

Chapter 11

5 years, 3 months, 8 days earlier

Later, Delia would explain to June that finding a best friend is like finding a true love: when you meet yours, you just know. But the third week of sixth grade when the cool new girl, Delia, invited June for a sleepover, June was a nervous, happy kind of shocked. And she wondered if maybe Delia had made a mistake, thought June was someone else when she invited her. Or maybe it was because Delia hadn't had a chance to make cooler friends yet.

June was painfully, desperately lonely. She spent her weekends by herself, reading and cleaning up after her mother. June liked this new girl with her big turquoise earrings and enormous smile. She liked how this girl didn't seem to give a shit about absolutely anything. So even though June had never had a one-on-one sleepover before and the idea made her very nervous, she said yes.

The night of the sleepover Delia's stepfather was working

late, so her mother let them order pizza and cans of Coke and eat in Delia's room. "My stepfather's diabetic," Delia said, slurping on the soda. "So the only soda we ever have is *diet*, which is *poison*. My own mother is trying to poison me." Delia didn't sit while they ate; instead she walked around the room pointing things out like a museum tour guide—there was a tiny painting of a winter scene that Delia had found at a thrift store, there was the prescription pill bottle nicked from her mom (Delia kept breath mints in there now), there was a cherry stem that she'd knotted using only her tongue (it was the only time she'd ever successfully done it, so she'd saved the evidence). June had never seen a room like this, one filled with so much interesting stuff. It was like she expected to have friends over to show things to.

Shortly after ten Delia's stepfather came home and started yelling at her mother behind their closed bedroom door, yelling in an unhinged, out-of-control sort of way. That's when Delia said it was time to sneak out.

She climbed out her window and then dropped down into the grass. June was scared, but she followed. They walked up and down the block a couple of times. They left dandelions in peoples' mailboxes. They peeked into the window of Delia's cute high-school-aged neighbor. They saw him changing out of his clothes, and he got all the way down to his boxers before he shut the curtains. "Damn it!" Delia said. And then she grinned. "I have an idea." And then—and even at the time, June couldn't really believe it was happening—Delia reached around back and unhooked her bra through her shirt, then pulled her arms into her shirt, wriggled around, and suddenly her bra was off and in her hand right there on the street. June stared at it in the light streaming from the windows of the houses. It was black, with an underwire. A real bra, because Delia had real actual boobs. She convinced June to do the same, and taught her how to get it off without taking her shirt off. June was embarrassed that hers was barely a bra at all, more like a shiny little undershirt. But Delia didn't seem to notice or care. "Now what?" June said. She felt breathless and giggly.

"Now we mark our territory," Delia said. She grabbed June's hand and then snuck around the front of the house, opened up the boy's family's red-barn mailbox, and tossed both bras inside.

"There," Delia said. "And now we have a secret."

June nodded, like she understood. But she didn't until Delia went on. "Having secrets together makes you real friends," she said. "Secrets tie you together." And June felt suddenly giddy at the idea that Delia would *want* to be tied to her.

Then they snuck back in through Delia's porch. And even though it wasn't cool at all, June told Delia this was probably the first thing she'd done that she wasn't supposed to. Maybe ever in her life. Delia just smiled. "Guess you haven't been hanging out with me enough," she said. "We'll have to change that."

They tiptoed back upstairs, and Delia made a show of

locking her bedroom door behind them. Then she leaned over and lowered her voice to a whisper. "My stepfather is an asshole. So I always keep it locked, in case."

June felt fear prickling her belly. "In case what?"

"In case he tries something."

"Has he?"

Delia shrugged and shook her head. "But if he ever does . . ." Delia reached into her desk drawer and pulled out a switchblade. She held it up. "I'm ready for him." June opened her mouth in a little shocked O. Then Delia pressed the silver button on the base and a plastic comb popped out. Before June could feel the full effects of her embarrassment, Delia started laughing. It was round and rolling and joyful, her laugh. It didn't feel like she was laughing at June was the thing, it felt like she was inviting June to join in on the joke.

"You should have seen your face," Delia said. She shook her head. "You were so shocked, it was amazing." She put her arm around June. "My stepfather really is a shit, though. My family in general is complete bullshit, actually. What's yours like?"

"I only have a mom," June said. "She's pretty bullshit too."

And then for some reason—maybe because June liked the sound of Delia's laugh, or maybe because she couldn't even remember a time when she'd been honest, really truly honest with anyone, or maybe just because it was late at night and that's the hardest time to hold things in—June began to talk. She talked about how her mom was out most nights, even when she wasn't working; how she came home early in the morning, knocking into things and stinking of alcohol. She talked about her father, who she'd only met twice. She talked about the time her mom fell and sprained her wrist after tripping over June's school bag and blamed June, and June felt really guilty, but also didn't totally know what to think because of what she smelled on her mom's breath.

June talked and talked, felt the words pouring from her mouth as though she was a faucet and had forgotten how to turn herself off. And when she was finally done, she was struck with a wave of horrible embarrassment. She had ruined her new friendship when it had barely just begun.

"I'm sorry," June barely managed to mumble. Her cheeks burned with shame and disgust at herself, at how needy and weak she suddenly felt.

But as she looked up, she saw that Delia was staring at her, her head tipped to the side. She didn't look bored or freaked out or like she thought June was a weirdo. She just smiled in this way that made her seem very wise. "Crazy that we have such messed-up families, and yet somehow we both turned out so awesome, right?"

June felt something lifting inside of her. *We.* "Right," she said. She forced a laugh and then she meant it.

They brushed their teeth after that and put on pajamas. Delia got them three glasses of water ("I need two, in case I dream about a fire," Delia said), and they lay side-by-side in Delia's enormous queen-size bed. Delia combed June's hair with the switchblade comb—Delia insisted on doing it, because her own curls were too thick and would break the teeth off, and she hadn't yet used it on anyone—and June felt almost drugged with happiness and relief. Now that this girl was her friend, everything might just be okay. She wouldn't be so lonely anymore. She wouldn't be alone. This girl was going to change everything.

Chapter 12

The pit in my stomach is enormous; it could swallow up my room, the house, the whole entire world.

I *abandoned Delia, and now she is dead.*

A gut punch of sadness hits me, so intense I can barely breathe. I open my closet. I reach in toward the back and feel for the picture. I pull it out and sink down onto my bed.

The frame is glittery pink with two enamel teddy bears on top, holding a heart between them. Delia gave it to me the summer after sixth grade. It was a joke but also not a joke. The photo is of the two of us peeking out from under these ridiculous floppy sun hats that Delia had bought for us. There I am—blond hair, forgettable face—and next to me is Delia, her dark curly hair taking up half the picture, olive skin, big strong nose, fierce chin. Her huge mouth opened in the world's biggest smile. Delia always insisted she was kind of crazy-looking.

"Not pretty," she would say. "Sexy." But she was half wrong, because when she smiled like that, she was the most beautiful person you had ever seen.

When we stopped being friends, I kept telling myself it was only for now, a temporary thing. One day it would all go back to normal. I was always so sure of that.

Finally, finally the tears begin to fall. We will never have the chance to make up. I will never have the chance to apologize. I will never have the chance to tell her anything ever again. She is really truly gone.

I put the frame on my lap and take the phone out of my pocket. I call voice mail so I can hear her voice, hear the last words she'll ever say to me.

"Hey, J, it's me, your old pal . . ."

I had so many chances to fix things between us. So many chances that I didn't take. Whatever was going on in her life, if I had been there, *I would have kept her safe.*

"Hey, D," I whisper over her voice. I need to say these words, even though she can't hear me. "I know we haven't talked in a while, and that a bunch of crap happened, but I really miss you." My chest is so tight, my heart might burst.

"There's something I need to tell you," she finishes inside the phone.

The tears are still coming, an impossible amount of them. I keep talking. "And I'm so, so sorry about everything that happened, I should have . . ."

And then I stop, because here is the weirdest thing: The message is over, but somehow it isn't—there are still sounds coming through my phone. There's a scuffling, and then Delia again. Only, this time, she isn't talking to my voice mail, but to someone in the background. "I'm going to tell," Delia says. There is a teasing lilt to her voice, but underneath there's something darker. "I'm going to tell what you did."

I press my ear to the speaker. There's another voice, male, shouting. I can't make out the words, but I can hear the tone: anger. Fierce and frightening. I hold my breath, and my body fills with ice. And then the message clicks off.

Adrenaline courses through my veins. I'm not crying anymore. What I think I just heard . . . this is not possible. I cannot have heard it.

I start the message again, and again there is Delia's voice. The scuffling. Delia: *I'm going to tell. I'm going to tell what you did.* And then the voice in the background, that male voice, that anger.

The blood is pounding in my ears. There is no mistake. That person in the background, I know who it is.

It's Ryan.

My hands are shaking. I can barely breathe. I check the time. It's after one a.m. Ryan will be sleeping.

The phone rings four times and goes to voice mail. I hang up and call again. It rings and rings.

Finally, he answers.

"Mmm'lo?" I imagine his face pressed against his pillow, one bare leg kicked out from under the comforter, because that's the way he always sleeps. I imagine him with Delia, yelling the day before she died.

"I need to talk to you." My voice sounds strange, barely like me at all.

"Are you okay? What time is it?" I imagine him sitting up in bed now, scratching his chest. I imagine his slow, sleepy heart starting to pound. "Did something happen?"

Yes, I think. *Something very, very bad.* But what I say is, "Can you meet me?" Because I know I need to do this face-to-face.

He hesitates for only a fraction of a second. I imagine him thinking how late it is, how early he needs to get up for swim practice. "Of course," he says, like I knew he would. Because a thing I know about Ryan is that he always does what's expected of him. Then again, maybe I'm wrong about that.

"Should I come over?"

"No," I say. "I'll come to you."

Chapter 13

Fifteen minutes later I'm pulling up to his house, my entire body buzzing. All the windows are dark, but the big bright front door light is switched on, and there's Ryan, standing out on the walkway, rubbing his hands together.

I step onto the grass, ice crystals crunch beneath my feet. I can just barely make out his face. "Baby," he says, all warm breath in the cold air. *Baby* is not even something he calls me. "Are you okay? What's going on? Tell me."

He starts to pull me toward him and for a second I almost let him. I am ashamed at how desperately I want to be held, to feel a body against mine, letting me know that everything, or even anything, is okay.

I step back and hold my hands up.

"You were with Delia," I say. This is the first time I've actually said her name to him in a year.

"What do you mean?" He is whispering. "Did you have a bad dream or something?"

I shake my head. "You were with her in real life on New Year's Eve." I can barely even get the words out.

"You're scaring me, Junie. Because I don't have any idea what you're talking about. . . ."

I take out my phone, dial voice mail, and hold it out on speaker. "Listen."

Message received . . . There's Delia. *Hey, J, it's me, your old pal* . . . I watch the numbers on the timer tick by. At nine seconds, she stops talking to me. I can feel Ryan staring at me. I don't look up. "What's this . . . ?" Ryan starts.

I say, "It's coming."

At second forty-two, the voices start again. Delia: *I'm going to tell* . . . Then the shouting. Only when the message finally finishes and I shut off my phone do I look up.

"I don't understand what that is," Ryan says quietly.

"That was a voice mail she left me the day before she died," I say. "And that's you in the background." My voice is cold. Hard. He's never heard me sound like this before.

I wonder how he is going to begin to explain this. I'm scared to hear what he will say next. I'm scared not to hear it too.

But he stands there, completely silent. Finally, he lets out a long, heavy sigh that puffs white in the air. "Please tell me you're not serious," he says. He's using that gentle, concerned tone again.

"I'm very serious," I say.

"The random yelling in the background that you can barely make out? That's supposed to be *me*?" He doesn't sound angry, just hurt and so honestly confused that I'm starting to feel confused too.

Back at home I was so certain. And that certainty filled my belly with fire. But out here in the cold night . . .

"It's not me," Ryan says. "Have you slept at all since yesterday morning? Have you been eating? I get being really insanely upset. Believe me, I do . . ." He pauses and looks up, like he's waiting for me to think about what he's saying.

And the truth is, I haven't slept much. I've hardly eaten anything. But how can I eat when Delia is dead? How can I sleep when whoever did this to her is out there?

"We were still in Vermont then," Ryan says. "I wasn't even back from vacation yet." He almost sounds sorry to say this, sorry to have to make me face how completely wrong I am suddenly realizing I am.

Because with all that adrenaline coursing through my veins, I forgot all about the vacation he just got back from. And the time line of everything—the entire rest of the world, really, and how it works and what makes sense. I hold the phone to my ear again, play the message again. And this time the shouts sound like . . . nothing. No one I know. That person could be anyone.

"Oh God," I say. My voice is so quiet, I can barely hear myself. I feel so ridiculously ashamed now, for rushing over here in the middle of the night. For getting Ryan up out of his cozy bed and his family's nice house, for accusing him of who even knows what. I'm ashamed for dragging him further into this darkness. "I'm so sorry."

"This is a big, enormous, crazy, shocking thing that happened," Ryan says. "You have nothing to apologize for. But admitting that she . . . that what really happened happened doesn't make this somehow your fault." He holds my shoulders. "This isn't your fault or anyone else's. She was a very messed-up girl who made a terrible mistake and killed herself, and if she fought with some guy before she did it, that doesn't change anything. So please, you have to promise me you'll stop this, before you drive yourself crazy."

I stare at him, at his beautiful face out here in the dark.

I want to say yes, and I understand why he would think that. But Ryan didn't know her like I did. I can only begin to imagine how all this must look to him. He is so calm and reasonable, and that is what I like—maybe, I realize now, even love—about him. He doesn't have access to a certain part of the world that maybe I do, to a certain kind of darkness that I have been trying so hard to shed.

"Promise me?" he says.

I force the tears back into my face, where they sit, burning.

I desperately do not, *do not* want to cry in front of him. Around him I am someone else—myself, only better, but in a different way than with Delia. The version of me he sees is always strong, always unafraid, at least on the outside. Except for that one weird thing in the beginning, our relationship has not been about drama. There is coiled-up fear inside me, though. I'm always worried this will end. But I keep that buried deep, so the surface is left bright and clean and pure. It's not like this is news to me, but standing out there under the black sky, I fully get how much I need this not to change. I loved Delia, love her still. But I can't drag Ryan into this any further than I already have. He doesn't belong in this. I won't bring him here.

"Okay," I say. "I'll stop." And now, in this moment, I'm glad for the dark so he can't see that I'm lying.

He hugs me again, and asks me if I want to come in. "I'll sneak you into my room," he says. "You can stay the whole night."

But I tell him no, I tell him thank you and that I hope he has a good swim practice tomorrow morning and that I'll see him tomorrow evening.

"Are you sure?" he says. "You're okay?"

I nod. "I'm really tired," I say. "I think I need to sleep." And he nods back, like I'm finally making sense.

I get in my car and I drive myself home, where I play that message over and over.

So it's not Ryan on the voice mail. But Delia knew something someone didn't want her to know, that's for damn sure. And she threatened to tell. So whose secret was it? And what were they willing to do to make her keep it?

Chapter 14

Morning. Saturday. Slanty winter sunlight comes through my window. I can hear my mother banging around downstairs. I barely remember getting into bed, but sometime late last night after listening to that message a dozen more times, I fell into a heavy, dreamless sleep. I sit up, heart poundingly awake now. Well, Ryan was right about one thing: I sure as hell needed this. I don't feel better, but I feel sharp, quick; the cloud has lifted. I am, if it's possible, even more determined. This is a cold steel arrow to follow. It will help me ignore everything else.

I swing my legs out of bed, grab my towel, and walk down the hall to the bathroom. I turn on the shower and stand, shivering, waiting for the water to heat up. I haven't showered since Wednesday night and it is a relief to be clean.

Back in my room I get quickly dressed—dark jeans, gray boots, black T-shirt. And Delia's sweater again. I think about calling Ryan to apologize again for last night, or maybe, even better, to say hi and pretend everything is normal. But I'm not even sure I have that in me. When I look at my phone, I realize it's after eleven and he'll have finished swim practice and be out for waffles with his teammates. So instead, I call Jeremiah, glad I took his number two nights ago even though I wasn't sure I wanted it. I need to see if he's found out anything new, and I think I might even tell him about Tig and what I found out at his party. I get his voice mail. "This is Jeremiah Fiske. I'm not able to come to the phone right now. Please leave me a message and I'll return your call as soon as I can." He sounds so formal, like he's expecting a call about a job at a bank.

"Hey," I say. "It's June. De . . . Call me back."

But then something occurs to me and I call him again, get his voice mail again. I close my eyes, really concentrate on his voice this time.

I try to imagine him angry.

I hang up, then listen to Delia's message again, fast-forwarding through the first part because right now I can't bear hearing her talk to me, asking me for something so simple and small that I would not, did not give her. I stop, instead, at second forty-two. The shouting. But it's impossible to tell who the other person is.

So now what?

I make my way downstairs. My mother looks up when I come into the kitchen. It smells like burnt coffee in here and she is scraping scrambled eggs into the sink. She always does this, like she forgets that we have a garbage can, and don't have a garbage disposal. And that scrambled eggs are not a liquid. I used to bother telling her. I don't anymore.

She works the night shift at a nursing home, which means she only got back a couple hours ago. She hasn't been to sleep. And there's something on her mind that she's going to want to talk about. I know that from the way she's moving and the expression on half her face when she turns partway around to look at me. I'm some kind of weird expert at reading my mother, like she's a radio signal and I can always pick up the frequency, even when I don't want to.

"You slept late," she says. Her tone isn't accusatory the way it sometimes is. She sometimes feels bad for not being around much, so she tries to make up for it by occasionally getting mad at things she thinks parents are supposed to. But not this morning.

I shrug.

There is bread on the counter, so I put two slices in the toaster and take out the peanut butter. There's an apple in the fruit bowl and I start eating it. I realize now how hungry I am.

"That girl who went to your school who died . . ." She is prompting me.

I try to keep my face blank.

She continues. "Someone at work was talking about her, one of the night nurses. Said it was a girl from her nephew's school, which is your school." She reaches out for the coffee pot. "Delia. You knew her." She pours the dregs into her mug, adds too much sugar, stirs, licks the spoon. "You used to bring her over here sometimes." She leans against the sink and raises the mug to her lips. She's trying to get me to look at her. I pop the toast early. I spread the peanut butter on thick.

And she is still watching me, waiting for an answer. "I did," I say. And then I take a big bite so my mouth is glued shut.

She nods, half-pleased with herself, as though remembering the name of the only best friend her daughter ever had is some impressive feat to be proud about. Then her face drops. "Sucks," she says then, "that that happened."

She is staring now, and I accidentally look her in the eye. It feels too personal. I quickly look away. I know she is really trying here, that is the thing. Under different circumstances, I suppose I could probably get pretty sad thinking about how this is the very best she can do. But I do not have room for this now.

"Yeah," I say. "It does."

After that we are both silent. My mother stirs her already stirred coffee, clanking her spoon against the side of the mug.

My phone buzzes with a text, and I know we are both relieved. I figure it will be Ryan, or maybe Jeremiah, even. But it's Krista:

You weren't in homeroom yesterday. You okay?

It's weird, because we're not the kind of friends who check

up on each other. I mean we're barely even friends at all. Before I can respond, another text comes in:

Wanna meet up?

I look up at my mom. She glances at me, then her eyes flick over to the cabinets. She's wondering whether I'll say something if she does what I know she wants to do. I look at the text again, and I'm surprised to realize the answer. I guess I need to talk to someone. And right now I don't have a lot of options.

Krista is sitting cross-legged on the trunk of her car when I get to the Birdies parking lot. She's wearing a big puffy jacket, no gloves. Her nose is red in the cold.

It's weird to see her outside of school, because except for the party, I never have. She spots me and waves me over. When I get to her, she doesn't say hello, just slides so there's room next to her on the trunk. Then she takes a breath and starts talking fast as though she was planning out what she was going to say before I arrived. "I was always kind of jealous of you guys. I guess that might seem weird to say now, considering. I'm not trying to complain about Rader or whatever. He's great, obviously, but our thing is not like what you guys had. You always seemed, like . . . so perfectly in tune with each other, like, connected in some cosmic way. Back before, when you were together."

"Wait, what?" I say. It takes me a second to realize what she even means. It's been so long since anyone thought this, though people used to all the time. Krista thinks Delia and I were a couple, in love.

I shake my head. "It wasn't like that. We were friends." And I'm careful not to use the word "just," because I remember what Delia always said. "Friends aren't *just*, dating is just. Friends are the very highest thing."

"No shit?" says Krista. "But you were always . . . all over each other."

I shrug.

Delia and I *were* always kind of touchy. But it wasn't sexual, even though sometimes people, guys especially, wanted to see it like that. I remember once, at a party, she'd been playing with my hair, braiding it and unbraiding it, twirling it through her fingers. A guy was staring at us, practically panting, like he was watching porn. "It's soothing, like knitting," she said to him. My hair was longer then. She took my braid and wrapped it around her neck. "Look, I made a scarf. . . ."

"Kinky," the guy said. And Delia snorted and rolled her eyes, and then ignored him even though he tried to get her attention for the rest of the night. She hadn't been trying to impress him. She did it to make me laugh.

Now I turn to Krista. "Seriously," I say. "That's just how we were."

Krista nods. She looks like she's suddenly realized something. "Well, then I guess that Buzzy thing was a serious long shot."

"Who?" I say.

"You know . . . Buzzy, the girl from the party who asked for your number. The one I was trying to set you up with. I guess I can tell you that now, since, y'know, it's not like I'm going to make it uncomfortable for you guys." Krista lets out an awkward laugh and rubs her nose. "Too bad, though. Buzzy's the best."

And then we just sit there in silence. Coming here was a bad idea, I think. I was looking for comfort when there is no comfort to be found. There wasn't any for Delia, and I don't deserve any either. I start to get up off the trunk.

"Buzzy is how I found out what really happened, actually," Krista says slowly.

And then I stop. My pulse speeds up. "Buzzy knew Delia?"

Krista shakes her head. "No, but this girl Buzzy dated for, like, a minute, who I was hoping you'd help her get over, that girl was Delia's new best friend or something. She feels really sad for her ex now, Buzzy does. Like, wants to be there for her, a shoulder to cry on and all that even though the girl doesn't seem into it. That's what Rader was telling me, anyway. I don't know . . ."

Krista keeps talking, but I'm not listening to her anymore. Two words flash fire inside my brain. *Best friend.* Somehow it had never occurred to me that Delia had one. Other than me, I mean. Especially not after what I saw down by the water.

". . . suicide is a horrible bitch," Krista is saying. "That's why

I texted you. Because you didn't come to school, and then last night Buzzy said what happened with Delia. My dad had a cousin who did it, killed himself, I mean. He was really messed up about it for a long time. So listen, if there's anything I can do, then . . ."

And what I am thinking is this: Delia's best friend was the one person she really talked to. Her best friend was her heart, her secret keeper, her everything. Whatever there is to know, Delia's best friend is the one who is going to know it.

"Krista," I say slowly. "I think maybe there is. . . ."

Chapter 15

Even sobbing, Ashling is beautiful.

Underneath the red blotches her skin is porcelain smooth, and, though swollen, her eyes are clear and blue. And here I am, watching the pain pouring out in the form of snot, tears, and muffled wailing. My gut clenches, and I try to keep from floating off the way I always do when things are too much. I hand Ashling tissue after tissue, while Krista leans in and pats her arm. "Oh, honey," Krista says.

Finally, the ocean leaving her face slows to a stream, then a trickle. Ashling smiles at me, mouth shut tight, perfect lips quivering. She reaches out and squeezes my hands. "I'm so glad Buzzy gave you my number. It's nice to get to talk to someone else who loved her." She shakes her head. "No, screw that. Loves. Present tense."

Ashling finishes mopping the tears. There is a feeling

peeking through the numbness now, a tickling deep in my stomach. Mostly, it's relief that Delia had someone in her life up until the end, a best friend who really truly cared. But under that, way down at the bottom, is the tiniest pinpoint of something else, and I don't want to admit even to myself what it is—it's jealousy. Which is disgusting, I realize. But there's no time for *any* of this now, because I'm here for a purpose: I need to find out what Ashling knows. And to do that, I need her to know the truth.

But how do you even tell someone something like that?

You blurt it out. "Do you think it's possible . . . that Delia didn't . . . really kill herself?"

Ashling opens her big eyes wide. She looks like a doll.

"You mean like her spirit is still out here?" Ashling says. Her voice is low, slightly Southern sounding. She nods and smiles a bit. "I feel it too."

"No," I start. "I mean, what I'm trying to say is . . . that maybe someone else did. Kill her. Who wasn't her."

There. The words are out. I can't take them back now. I brace myself.

Out of the corner of my eye I see Krista lean forward, like, *holy shit*. Ashling is clenching her jaw.

"I'm sorry," I say. "I didn't want to say it like that, but I'm not sure how else to do it."

"Why would you think that?" She sounds disgusted.

And so I tell her everything, from that first moment at the

memorial when I met Jeremiah and then saw the burned-down shed, to the voice mail she meant to leave me and the voice mail she didn't but left anyway, and my visit to Tig, and Delia's need for protection. I tell her everything up until this very moment with the three of us sitting here together in this coffee shop, where Ashling is slowly shaking her head, and Krista is staring at the two of us like she's watching the very best episode of her very favorite TV show.

"Delia was no one's victim," Ashling says. Her voice is soft. "She lived life by her own terms, and she died by them too." Ashling's eyes fill up again, but underneath the sadness there is something else. She seems angry. "And how dare you say otherwise."

It would never have occurred to me that someone would *want* to believe their best friend had killed herself, that somehow that would be preferable to the alternative. But if she cares about Delia as much as she obviously does, I can't stop here. I have to keep going.

"I know it's so completely beyond insane to even imagine that someone could have . . ." I'm trying to make my voice calm, to modulate my tone so she'll listen. I know the look that's in her eyes now, I've seen it before on my mom—that wild animal look. And you have to be careful to keep them from biting you or bolting. "Did you see her or talk to her the day she died? Did she maybe mention anyone who was . . ."

"I talked to her for, like, three seconds. But she didn't say anything about anything. She was coming off a bunch of drugs from the night before. She picked up to say she felt like shit and she was going to go back to sleep. And that's literally all."

"Okay," I say. "But it's just that Jeremiah said—"

Ashling snorts and cuts in again. "You're actually going to believe that idiot about anything?" She shakes her head. "He was totally out of his depth with Delia. He never had any idea what was going on." She sets her jaw and shakes her head again. "He didn't even know his girlfriend was cheating on him is how much of an idiot he was. So if you want to take his word for anything about anything? Well, that's on you, girl. It has nothing to do with me, or *my* best friend, or what *happened*. She was miserable. She was using drugs. Her life at home was even shittier than usual. If you were her friend, you would have already known that, and you wouldn't be questioning any of this. What *happened* to her is, she made a choice. And it was hers to make."

Ashling stands. She looks like she's going to cry again, but then instead narrows her eyes and grits her teeth.

And then before I can say anything else, she turns and starts toward the door.

"Wait!" I call out. My entire body is tingling. I get up and chase after her. "You said Delia was cheating on Jeremiah."

Ashling blinks. "So . . ."

"Who was she cheating with?"

Ashling raises an eyebrow and smiles slightly. "That was her own business," she says. Then she shrugs, pushes through the door, and she's gone.

And I am left standing there as the thoughts swirl in my head, arranging themselves into shapes. And then arranging themselves again.

I feel Krista's hand on my shoulder.

"Do you really think she was murdered?" she says very quietly.

But I don't turn. I'm barely even aware of her. I'm thinking of Jeremiah standing alone in the dark, his big hulking body and Boy Scout face. I'm thinking about how Delia was cheating, and Ashling said Jeremiah didn't know. But what if she's wrong? What if he somehow found out?

Chapter 16

Ryan's hair is damp from the shower, and the chemical tang of chlorine still clings to his skin. I can smell him from his bed, where I sit, cross-legged, watching his naked back. It's hours later. After Ashling left, I left Krista. I needed to be alone. I spent the rest of the day just driving and thinking, running everything over and over in my head.

And now here I am, trying to pretend like everything is normal, like anything is.

"You sure you're up for going?" Ryan asks. He opens his closet and takes out a shirt—green with PANTS printed on the front. His favorite. He slips it on over his head. And then, just like I knew he would, he takes out a green button-up shirt to wear over it. A couple of days ago, before any of this happened, I would have felt oddly satisfied to notice this. There's a sweet comfort in knowing these kinds of things about a person.

He turns back as he does up the buttons.

"It's only that usually . . ." He trails off. "Hanny's parties have never really seemed like your thing." He is putting it mildly, being polite.

Max Hannigan is part of the popular sports crowd, which is one of the ones Ryan is a part of. He's tall and rich, with a big giant jaw. Delia once said, "He looks like a date rapist, but one who'd only stop raping you because his dick wouldn't stay hard." She said things like that, and I'd laugh in spite of myself. I still think of that sometimes when I see him.

He has an enormous house with a pool, and his parents are always going out of town and either are oblivious or do not care that whenever they go away, he has fifty people over to drain their liquor cabinet. We've met dozens of times outside of school, but every time we meet, he acts like he's never seen me before in his life.

Ryan comes over to the bed. He leans down and kisses me lightly on the lips.

And I feel a stab of guilt. Because the truth, which I can't tell him, is that I only want to go to this party because of Jeremiah. And his text from a half hour ago.

Found something. Need to show u tonight, is what he wrote.

It's not like I'm so scared of Jeremiah now. Since this morning, nothing has even changed, really . . . but I have this feeling in my gut that it's better not to meet him alone. So for now, I'll trust that.

"It'll be good to get my mind off things . . . ," I tell Ryan.

When he leaves his room and goes to the bathroom to put the tiny touch of gel into his hair that he thinks I don't know he uses, I take out my phone and write back.

Hanny is having a party, meet there at 9?

Jeremiah is part of that big group of guys too. A second later he writes back: See u then.

I look up at Ryan, back in the room now. "So we're going, then?" he says. It scares me how easy it is to break a promise.

"Yeah," I say. "Sounds fun."

Hanny's parties are not fun. I know I'm only seeing the very surface when I look at these people. Everyone has their shit, but when I walk into Max Hannigan's big living room full of people laughing in unison, their big white smiles glowing under Max's parents' customizable mood lighting, it's easy to imagine that no one here has ever been lonely or sad or scared for a single second of their entire lives.

I feel myself starting to sweat under Delia's sweater. Ryan leans in and whispers into my ear. "We can blow this pop-stand whenever. You know that, right?"

And I turn to him and nod.

He takes my hand and leads me forward into the crowd. "Fisker," a guy calls out. Fisker is what some of Ryan's friends call him. Up ahead is a guy they call Rolly. Rolly gives Ryan a bro hug.

"Hi, June, nice to see you as always," Rolly says. Rolly talks to me like you'd talk to someone's mom.

"Hi." I can't do the small talk thing, not even at the best of times and certainly not now. "I'm going to find the bathroom," I tell Ryan. "Don't wait for me, I'll find you after." And we lock eyes, only for a second, before I slip away.

I spot him almost immediately—Jeremiah, standing near the door, hands in his pockets, scanning the room. When our eyes lock, my stomach twists and I don't even know why.

Jeremiah motions for me to follow him outside. I look for Ryan. He's in the kitchen where someone is handing him a beer. I head toward Jeremiah, feeling a couple girls watching me. They turn to whisper as I pass. I think I hear "Delia," I think I hear "suicide."

Outside now, the sounds from the party are muffled through the big thick windows. The night is barely getting started. Two girls I recognize from school run across the lawn, tumbling over each other. The air is fresh and cold, a few tiny snowflakes drift down.

Jeremiah pulls something out of his pocket and holds it up: a phone.

The wallpaper is a photo of a hand—chipped lemon-yellow polish on a stuck up middle finger, three thin strips of leather wrapped around the wrist. This is Delia's hand. And this is Delia's phone. In front of the hand is a number pad, ENTER PASSCODE written at the top.

I'm staring at his face, suspicion coiled in a tight ball in my belly.

"Where did you get that?"

"I went back to her house this afternoon," he says. "And this was right there in the woods like someone had thrown it. There must be something in here that'll help us. We'd know who she was talking to, who she was texting. But I can't get it open."

I take the phone. I've held it a million times before—reading texts out loud, writing back as her, or sometimes just listening to her stepfather yelling when she couldn't deal.

"I brought it to one of those shady phone repair places in the city," Jeremiah continues. "The guy said he could wipe it clean if I wanted to use it, but that was it. He couldn't unlock it." He's looking at me now, curious and intense. "Anyway, so I was wondering. Do *you* know the passcode? I know best friends tell each other that sort of thing sometimes. . . ."

White flakes fall faster, like we're shooting up through space now.

"No," I say. "I'm sorry." I keep my gaze steady. "Like I said, we hadn't been best friends in a long time."

He nods, and I watch as he slips it back into the right side pocket of his gray and red ski coat.

He rubs his hands together. "Freaking cold out here." Jeremiah looks around. "So what about you? Anything? Any news?"

I shake my head.

There's laughing; a guy and a girl are making their way up the driveway.

"Okay then," Jeremiah says.

The girl sticks out her butt and shakes her hips.

I try to keep my face calm. I can see the top of the phone peeking out of Jeremiah's pocket.

The girl tumbles forward with a shriek. The guy wraps his arm around her to keep her from falling.

"Come inside?" I say.

Jeremiah shakes his big square Boy Scout head. "I'm not in the mood for a party."

I look down at Jeremiah's pocket again.

"We should have a toast," I say. "For Delia." He hesitates. "A real one, from people who care." I'm thinking about the memorial by the water. I know he is too.

"Okay," he says.

Back inside, the music is loud. People stand in clumps of twos and threes. It'll be a couple hours before things get sloppy and ridiculous. I see Ryan in the living room, so I lead Jeremiah to the kitchen. I feel eyes on us.

I think I hear someone say, "girl who died." I think I hear someone say, "fire."

The kitchen table is covered in party stuff. I grab two red plastic cups from a stack, and a bottle of vodka. I spot a little jar of maraschino cherries stuck in with the tiny plastic mermaids. So I take those, too.

To our right, three guys are chugging beers. I pour Jeremiah a shot. He reaches for a two-liter Coke and fills up the rest of his cup. His big hand crushes the bottle.

I fill my own cup with vodka, pouring till I reach the top.

"Hold up, there, cowgirl," says a guy next to me. He's wearing a lime-green polo, collar popped. "Save some for the rest of us. On a mission, huh?" He's smiling.

"Something like that," I say.

Jeremiah is watching me. I fish a cherry from the jar, then I pass the jar to Jeremiah, who does the same.

"No mixer?" he says.

"I like to be efficient," I say.

And then I raise my drink. "To Delia."

"To Delia," he says, "who deserves a hell of a lot better than what she got." We clink our plastic cups. I bring mine to my mouth. The smell is nauseating. The vodka wets my lips. I try not to breathe. I keep my lips clamped together and my mouth empty, and swallow nothing, twice. I fake flinch.

Then I pop the cherry into my mouth.

Jeremiah is still watching, and so I let my eyelids droop just a little, let the corners of my mouth turn up, the slow smile of alcohol hitting me quick.

Jeremiah looks off into the distance. I pour half my vodka

into a cup of brown liquid with a bloated pretzel bobbing in it.

"Do you believe in heaven?" Jeremiah says.

Behind me someone lets out a laugh.

"I'm not sure," I say. Only, what I'm really not sure about is whether I want to tell him the real answer, which is no. I don't and I can't. I'm jealous of anyone who does.

"I do," Jeremiah says. There is desperation in his voice. Maybe he believes this, or maybe he just wishes he did. "And I think Delia is there."

I nod. I take another fake swallow, and then dump more of my vodka into the cup on the table.

"I've been praying a lot, y'know? For her. I know she wasn't religious, and that maybe that means if there is a heaven, she won't be in it . . ."

A girl in a pink tank top reaches around him and grabs a bag of chips off the table. Her elbow brushes his pocket where the phone is. "Oopsy," she says. "Skyoooz me."

"But I don't think that's true. I think, maybe, because of what happened, she'll get to be there anyway. So I've been praying for her, that where she is now is better than where she was before. . . ." His jaw is set and his eyes are dark and shining. He takes another sip of his drink, the cup crunching in his big hand. "And that whoever did this to her gets what they deserve." There's something simmering in him, a fierce anger, leaking out into the air between us.

Another burst of laughter comes from behind me. Jeremiah looks up.

I raise my drink one more time. "To justice," I say. I am swaying a little bit now, bending my knees, letting my weight carry me forward and side to side. And I fake swallow, dribble vodka down my chin.

But Jeremiah doesn't toast this time. He is watching someone behind me. The guy in the green polo is across the room now, talking to friends—a tiny blond girl, a tall skinny guy. Polo holds up the vodka bottle. He mimes drinking, then says, voice jovial and drunk-loud, "And then she jumped. And she screwed some fish at the bottom of the reservoir and then drowned. That's what I heard, anyway. . . ." He is smiling.

Jeremiah slams down his cup and in one swift motion swoops across the room, grabs Polo by the collar, and pulls him in close. Polo struggles against him, but Jeremiah is too strong.

People are turning to watch, excited. I slip through the crowd. "Let him go," I say. "This won't help anything . . ." But Jeremiah pulls Polo in even closer, holds his collar tighter. Polo's face is bright red. He's wheezing now, his shirt choking him. *"Let him go,"* I say again.

For a moment Jeremiah just holds him there, their noses touching. "That's not what happened," he whispers finally. He drops Polo, who stumbles back, eyes wide. Jeremiah pushes through the crowd and out the front door.

"Psycho," Polo says quietly after him.

I catch up with Jeremiah on the front steps.

"I don't . . . ," he starts to say. "I just . . ." There are big fat tears rolling right down his cheeks now. "This should not have happened like this."

My heart squeezes. I don't like what I'm about to do, but I know I have to. And this is my chance. "You're right," I say.

I lean toward him and put my arm around him as though I'm drunk now, warm and loose, limbs flopping. "It deff-nitly should never have happened." I am slurring my words, acting as trashed as I'd be if I'd drunk all I pretended to. I let my legs wobble, collapse forward against Jeremiah's warm bulk. He feels solid and strong, like nothing could ever topple him. He catches me.

And I slip my hand into his pocket.

Chapter 17

I'm upstairs in a bedroom, Max's parents', I think—it smells like fabric softener and old man cologne. I shut the door behind me and double-check that it's locked. Only then do I take out Delia's phone, her yellow painted finger's final fuck you on the screen. I key in the code 5-8-0-0-8.

It was the code she used for everything, because upside down, it spells out BOOBS.

And just like that, the phone unlocks.

I scroll through her recent texts. There's one from her mom on the first. Happy New Year! On our way back. See you soon, sweetie! And my heart catches in my throat, at the hopeful earnestness of this message, the tone of which does not even remotely match their actual relationship. But her mom was always like that, trying to pretend things were different than they were when she was in the mood for it, as though by lying to both of them, she'd make a different reality.

There's one from Jeremiah sent the same morning. Things are so boring here with my parents' friends. Wish you were here even though I know you'd hate it. Hope you're feeling better. Tried calling you. Will try again!

The next one is also from him too, received at exactly midnight. Happy New Year!!

I keep scrolling—there are a few other New Year's texts from random names I recognize from back when we were friends, random people she saw sometimes. But then I see something else—a message from earlier that same afternoon. December thirty-first at 3:55 p.m.

hey sexy, ready to start hte new year off with some fireworks. outside your house

The message is from someone saved to her phone as "FUCKER."

Right below is her reply, the last message in the conversation:

Doors unlocked . . .

My heart starts pounding because oh my God, *this* must be the guy Delia was cheating with. But then my heart pounds even harder as I start to realize something. I take out my own phone, go to my missed call log. Delia called me at 3:59, four minutes after she received this text, which means that when Delia called me, FUCKER was inside, which means *he was the one yelling in the background.*

This was the person she was with, whose secret she had threatened to tell. And maybe, just maybe, this was the person who stopped her.

Someone is turning the door handle. "Hey!" a voice calls. "What are you doing? No one's supposed to be in there." Hanny.

"Sorrrrrry!" I call out. I try to keep my voice sloshy, drunk sounding. "Jussa second."

As fast as I can, I save FUCKER's number into my own phone. And then I scroll down, to J, just to see. I'm still in there—J JUNE JUNIE JUNEBUG.

Bang bang bang, the door rattles. "Open the door! If you're having sex on my parents' bed I will literally kill you."

But I'm in a trance now, and I can't stop myself. Who knows when I will get a chance like this again. I open up her pictures, telling myself I need to do this. Maybe there's a picture of FUCKER in here or some other kind of clue. And I *am* looking for that, but also I want a glimpse of her and her life. I'm greedy for bits of her, whatever I can get.

Only there aren't many photos in here, and they're all from months ago—a hand holding an ice-cream cone, the inside of a pocket, a dog, the guy behind the counter at the 7-Eleven who always checks out teen girls' asses even though he's probably about fifty. But then . . . I stop breathing. Because there's a picture of the two of us. She's holding a chunk of my hair next to her face so it looks like it's growing out of her head, and I'm doing the same with hers. Our eyes are shining bright and beautiful, mouths stained cherry red. I've never seen this picture before. Where was this? When was this?

Suddenly it all comes rushing back. I remember the feeling of the night, the sense that anything could happen. The moment when the flash went off.

BANG BANG BANG.

I slip both phones back into my pocket. I open the door, lean heavily against the door frame. "Sorrrry, I was trying to fine the bathroom-an . . ." I look up at the angry face of Max Hannigan, head square and hard like a block of wood. And next to him is Ryan.

"Junie," he says. "I was looking for you." He leans in and sniffs me. "You're trashed . . ." I've only ever drunk in front of him once before, and it was over a year ago.

"Jeremiah . . . ," I say. "We . . . toasted."

By the time I get back downstairs, Jeremiah is so trashed, I could shove my finger up his nose and I doubt he'd notice. Getting the phone back to him is easy. He is not aware of anything—my hand in his pocket, the couch under him, the fact that he is passing out in the middle of a party. I wonder where his friends are, if he actually has any, because why else, when his girlfriend died three days ago, is he here all alone, with only me to think to take his keys away because there's no way in hell he should be driving. It makes me feel sad for him. But I shake it off. I don't have any sadness left to spare.

I ask Ryan to get me some water. And then I take out my

phone and I call FUCKER. My heart pounds as the phone rings and rings. It goes to the default voice mail greeting, telling me to leave a message. I don't.

Not long later the three of us pile into Ryan's car. He's agreed to drive Jeremiah home. Jeremiah gets in back, leans against the door. Ryan is staring straight ahead.

And all I can think about is FUCKER. What he did, who he is, and how the hell I am going to figure it out.

Chapter 18

5 years, 1 month, 2 days earlier

Delia said it was her diary, so when June unrolled the narrow paper scroll she was immediately confused. *My To Do List* was preprinted in purple at the top. Delia had crossed out "To Do" and written "Did." Below that was just a list of names, a half dozen or so.

"I don't understand," June said.

"Well, it's the only diary I will ever keep. Everything else, you can help me remember." She grinned. "These are the boys I've kissed. I wrote really small because I figure there's going to be a lot of them, and I'm going to keep this list for my whole life." She pointed to the first name, Fraser Holmes. "We were in first grade. He tried to stick his finger up my nose after, the little perv."

June had never kissed anyone, though recently she'd let a cute boy on the bus have a sip from her water bottle and it felt kind of like *something* at the time, his mouth where hers had been and all that. But now, here with Delia, who was her brand-new friend and her very own age and had kissed—June counted quickly—five people, she felt the full weight of how silly that was.

"You've done a lot of kissing," June said. She meant it as a compliment.

Delia laughed. "Well, I'm not sure the first few count. But yeah . . ."

June stared at Delia's lips—shiny with mango gloss. You couldn't usually just look at a mouth and tell whether they got kissed much. But the thing was, with Delia's you kind of could.

Delia shrugged, then went on. "Why is it that so many of the most important things happen with your mouth? Kissing, telling secrets, eating cake. I don't know."

"Aren't you afraid your mom or someone will find the list?"

"Nah. I keep it hidden in a really good place. Which is lucky, because shitbag would kill me if he knew. Like it's any of his business at all *what* I do." Delia tipped her head to the side and bit one of her very-kissed lips. "The messed-up thing is how so many people think your body is their business, especially if you're a girl. It's not really the same with boys. But your body *isn't* their business . . . unless they're your pimp or, like, a plastic surgeon. Or a pimp plastic surgeon. Then it totally is." Delia stuck out her tongue. They'd only been friends for a couple months, but June already knew this was classic Delia—she'd say something real and true, and then something ridiculous in the very next sentence. And the world would suddenly seem bigger and smaller and more serious and less serious. And Junie would feel just how incredibly lucky she was to have found this girl.

"Showing you this list is an important moment in our best-friendness," Delia continued. "It's like when a couple is dating and one gives the other a key to their house and that's how they know it's true love." Delia paused. Then smiled. "Except, of course, we already knew it was . . ."

Chapter 19

Standing there in the sun, the charred wood is the blackest thing I've ever seen. I force myself to look away and watch the house. I'm checking for signs of movement inside, even though I already know there won't be any—it's Sunday morning, and if they're around at all, her mother and stepfather will be at church.

I'm not ready. But if I wait until I am, I'll never do it at all. I give myself a countdown, 3-2-1. I pretend Delia is here with me now, holding my hand and pulling me forward. I run.

I make my way across the backyard, up the back stairs leading to the porch. I open the screen door, heart hammering. There's the row of rocks. I spot the gray one, third from the end. It glitters in the sunshine. I lift it, and the key is right there where it always was, where it has been for years, tarnished and freezing cold between my fingers.

I slide it into the lock. And then . . . there I am, inside Delia's kitchen for the first time in over a year.

I'm struck by the smell, exactly the same as it always was. Like air freshener and new paint, even though the house hasn't been painted for a very long time, and that indeterminate Delia's house smell that's impossible to describe. The kitchen is all tile floors and yellow walls and cabinets made out of some kind of fake wood that is apparently more expensive than real wood. Delia said her stepfather claimed it was all "top of the line." And when Delia imitated him saying it, she used a voice like a 1920s gangster. "Toppa the line, fellas!"

I run up the cream carpeted stairs and down the hall. I'm struck with a million memories at once. *There is no time for this.*

At the end of the hall a cord dangles from the ceiling. I reach up and pull. The attic stairs come down slowly, unfold like bent legs. I climb up into the attic, heart hammering.

I make my way across unfinished floorboards to a bunch of cardboard boxes, and then to an old trunk, black lacquer over peeling cardboard. Delia's box, still here, same as always. I need to know who FUCKER is, and the answer might be here. Right inside.

I open it.

And what I see now in front of me is this: three empty Wolfschmidt vodka bottles, two empty cigarette packs, four metal nitrous canisters stolen from someone's job at a coffee shop. There are condom wrappers and two empty Robitussin bottles. But none of this is what I'm looking for. No. What I'm looking for is a small paper scroll, light blue, worn from years of rolling and unrolling. The name at the top will be Fraser Holmes, and the name at the bottom . . . is what I am hoping to find out.

I rifle through the box, touching each item one by one. There's a salt shaker she stole from the diner for no reason, a handful of loose googly eyes, a teeny tiny plastic bag with tiny red lips on the front, a dozen other random items. Only, no scroll of rolled-up paper. I check three times: it isn't here. But flush against the bottom of the box is something I didn't notice at first: an envelope, address written on the back in Delia's lumpy little-boy handwriting. And the name at the top is mine.

My breath catches in my throat. When did she write this? And why didn't she send it?

I slip the letter into my jacket, close the trunk. I walk back across the attic, down the dark stairs, and push the staircase back up into the ceiling.

I check the time. Delia's mother and stepfather won't be back for at least twenty minutes. I go to her bedroom, the place we spent so many hours together, snuck out of and snuck back into, where we laughed ourselves sick, where we told all our secrets.

I turn the knob. The door swings open, and I freeze. Her room is completely cleaned out. The walls are bare, no sheets or pillows on the bed, the surface of her desk is empty, and the floor is spotless. I open a dresser drawer; there's nothing in it, in any of them. *She's been dead for four days.*

I feel a swell of anger at I'm not even sure who. I wonder

if her stepfather did this, claiming it would be easier on her mother not to have to see Delia's things. As though cleaning out a room means she never existed at all.

Where is all her stuff? I need to see it. The only bits of her that are left.

Down in the garage I find a pile of trashbags stuffed full. I open one. There are Delia's clothes—a purple sweater she always wore drooping off one shoulder, a pair of jeans with huge holes in each butt pocket, a brown leather jacket she loved. I lean down, and the smell of her rises up. I have a sudden intense desire to take all these things, to take them away and keep them safe, in case . . . in case what? In case Delia comes back from the dead? The second bag contains more clothes, and books with fairies and dragons and princesses peeking out from their covers. There's one full of bedding, her pillows, comforter. The last bag is trash—crumpled-up paper towels, tissues, cotton balls streaked with eyeliner. And there at the bottom of the bag is a plastic stick with a clear plastic cap over the top. A pregnancy test.

Holy shit.

Heart thudding, I reach in and flip it over, and there I see two pink stripes. Pregnant.

Was Delia . . . ? Again?

I check my phone. I have five minutes or less before they come home. I close the bags, put them all back where they were, walk through the house, and shut off every light.

Then I go out the back door, lock it behind me, and I'm gone.

Chapter 20

1 year, 3 months, 17 days earlier

If June was anyone else on earth, she wouldn't even have realized anything was wrong. But June was incapable of not noticing the tiniest detail about Delia—she did it without even trying. It's like when Delia was around, the borders of June's skin weren't there. Delia wrapped her up and sunk right in. At its best it felt like the most delicious kind of relief, to have someone in there with her, in her brain and heart, filling them up. Someone to make her less alone. But other times, when things were like this, it felt scary having to share her inside space with someone whose light was so bright but so easily, suddenly, switched off. And lately, Delia's light was flickering.

Last week Delia had come to school high twice. She kept a water bottle full of vodka in her bag and sipped from it often. The other day June mentioned, very gently, that maybe Delia might want to take it easy a little. "I'm not your mother, June,"

Delia said, her voice sharp. "And you're not mine." It was the first time Delia had ever brought up June's mother like that. And June had felt . . . she wasn't sure. Protective wasn't it, exactly. But hurt, somehow, which was of course silly when she really thought about it, because basically everything Delia even knew about June's mother was because June had told her. And besides, Delia was right of course, they *were* different, and the stuff with June's mother was probably why June got so worried about Delia. But June's own mother, messed up as she was, was at least consistent in her messed-up-edness. Delia, on the other hand, you never quite knew what she was going to say or do, especially lately. You never knew whether she was going to be the sparkly, charming person who glowed from the inside, who everyone loved, or more and more lately, a girl with a core of darkness that scared June sometimes, because as much as she thought she knew everything about Delia, June honestly couldn't say how dark it was or how deep it went. There was a giant black hole inside her, she wanted to drag June into it. And June would let her, is the thing. She wouldn't be able to help herself if she wasn't very, very careful. Delia absorbed her. Phagocytosis, June had learned at school, that's what it was called when amoebas did it. It's how they ate. It's how they survived.

But June needed to survive too. For the longest time that meant she needed Delia. Only now, sitting in Delia's kitchen, staring at her friend, June didn't quite know what she needed anymore.

She just knew this: something was going on with Delia. June could feel the light flickering inside her own chest.

Delia crunched down on a sunflower seed, spit out the shells, and ate the tiny seed inside. Then she looked up thoughtfully and said, as though it had only now occurred to her, "If I got pregnant I'd kill myself." Then she crunched another seed, shell and all, chewed it, and swallowed it down. June stopped, a seed halfway to her lips. She paused only for a second before tossing it into her mouth, salt stinging her tongue.

"No you wouldn't," said June. She tried to keep her voice as light as Delia's, even though this conversation was making her heart pound. She'd been planning to make a joke, like, "You'd get fat and *then* you'd kill yourself." But there was something about Delia's tone—June couldn't even bring herself to say it.

Delia looked up and smiled. "Okay, maybe not. I sure as hell would kill that baby though." Delia watched June, one eyebrow raised. June knew Delia was waiting for her to react.

"It wouldn't be a baby yet," June said. "I mean, not at first." She pulled out another seed, cracked it open. "It would be goo." But even as she was saying the words, she knew it was more complicated than that. That she didn't mean anything she was saying nearly as casual as she said it.

"Yeah," Delia said. "I guess you're right." Delia threw another seed into her mouth and split it. Then spit the shells into her palm. She stuck one onto the tip of her finger so it looked like a pointy black-and-white fingernail. And then, without glancing up, she said, "So I had an abortion this morning." She put the other half of the shell on her middle finger and held her hand out. She didn't look up.

"Samesies," June said. "My third this week." She knew Delia was kidding, trying to rile her up the way she used to. June used to fall for this sort of thing all the time. Not now, though.

June scanned Delia's face for the tiny hint of a smirk that would bloom into a naughty grin. Only the thing was, the hint of smirk was not there. June closed her mouth and swallowed, anxiety sliding all the way down into her gut. "Wait, but really? Are you okay?" June was calling Delia's bluff, she thought. She knew it wasn't true. She didn't like this particular game anymore. She wanted to play her part and get it over with.

But, still, Delia didn't smile. "Sure," Delia said. "No big." She shrugged like it was nothing. Which is how June knew she was serious.

June stared at Delia's face, the ground shifted, Delia looked like someone June maybe didn't actually know very well. Then the world lined up again and everything snapped back into place. June's head was filled with a million questions she knew she wouldn't ask.

"Did it hurt?" June said finally.

Delia shrugged. "Not more than the boning that got me there."

June opened her mouth, her heart beating hard. Was Delia saying . . .

Delia looked at June's face, shook her head, and let out a cold laugh. "I wasn't *raped*," Delia said. "Jesus, Junie. It hurt because it wasn't *good*."

"Oh," June said.

"Because I wasn't that into it. So the condom broke."

"Right."

"It was this guy from Sammy's party last week. Boring party, you didn't miss anything. The dude was so awkward with his hands, like he'd just been issued a pair and hadn't read the instruction manual yet. And his breath smelled like . . ." Delia started to perk up then. "Okay, remember that time that weird girl at the diner showed us her infected belly-button piercing and we almost threw up because it smelled so horrible? Well, his breath smelled like he'd been sucking on that chick's belly button. So it's lucky I got an abortion. It would have been a really stinky baby, probably would have stunk me up from the inside with its weird-ass breath."

June tried to smile then, but she couldn't. She felt sick. Delia went back to her sunflower seeds, crunching away. She seemed relieved, like a weight had been lifted. The weight was lifted because June had to carry it now. Delia kept the tiny striped shells and stuck one to each of her fingers with spit. When she had ten, she held up her hands.

Chapter 21

Back in the car, driving away, heart hammering, a letter from my dead best friend on my lap. As soon as I've gone far enough, I pull over.

I tear open the envelope. The letter inside is dated over a year ago, a fact which fills me with disappointment and also, somehow, relief.

Dear Junie,

Oh, hi there. It's me, Delia. Isn't that a weird way to start a letter? Isn't it weird that I'm writing you a letter in the mail? It's just like a text message but longer, more like an e-mail, except that a tree is involved. Heh. This is starting off weird. But I guess that's sort of the point of this whole thing . . . things have gotten kind of weird in the past couple of weeks. And I don't know how to unweird.

I'm sorry things have gotten weird is the first thing I wanted to say. Did you just count and see that I used the word "weird" five times already in this letter (and six if you count that last one and, like, fifteen if you count all the ones I wrote in invisible ink). I love you (you know this). You're my best friend (you know this, too). And if you think I did something, I wish you'd talk to me about it. Because we used to talk about everything. Although I guess lately there's been stuff I haven't told you, either.

So here's something: Ryan isn't right for you. And the reason I'm saying that is not because he's too boring and normal or because his face is made of meat or because I'm worried he's taking you away from me (I mean, all of those things too of course, ha-ha, but it's not just that). Really it's because he is, as it turns out, an asshole. He's been calling me lately. I picked up the first time because I assumed it was you on his phone, but it wasn't. And he wasn't calling about you, either. He's been calling to . . . It feels weird to write in a letter, but let's just say when things got super odd the other night part of that was my fault. But not most of it, most of it was him. Here is a thing that you will not like, but I hope you will believe me because I swear it is true, and I was not too drunk to be a good judge of this (we drank the same amount, but, girl, you have the tolerance of a fruit fly and I have the tolerance of the big burly hairy dude the fruit fly landed on): while you were out of the room when we were playing that game, he tried to go on without you. And I'd been planning to tell you

this. I thought we'd have a chance to discuss everything after that night but we haven't really talked since then, not in the way we always do. And maybe some part of me is hurt that you just immediately assumed I was to blame. When I wasn't.

I'm not sure if I'll have the balls to send this letter or not. I guess if you're reading it, you'll know what I did. And if you're not reading it, then I guess I'm writing this to myself. Hello, D, you're looking pretty sexy today, hotness.

But really, Junie, you have to believe me. I would never, ever, ever lie to you.

Yours always and forever,

D

I let the letter fall into my lap. My heart hammers. I don't know what to think, what to make of this. I just know I need answers, and that of the two people in the world who ever had them, only one is still alive to give them to me. . . .

I'm watching Ryan's face as his eyes move across the page. I keep having to remind myself to breathe.

"I'm not sure what I'm supposed to be looking for here."

He leans back against the wall next to his bed, crosses his legs at the ankle.

He knows I'm staring. I can tell he's trying to keep his face calm, but I can see it in his eyes the moment he gets to his name. "What the heck even is this?" he says. *Heck.* When he usually says hell. "You don't . . . actually believe any of this, do you?" He looks up then.

The world is spinning too fast, and I am going to fly right off. I might be sick. My head nods.

"But how can you? She was messed up in the head! When did she send it?"

"She didn't," I say.

"Then how do you have it?"

But I don't answer. There is no way in hell I'm going to tell him. No way in heck, either.

He keeps going. "From the very beginning I knew that girl was messed up, and I tried to be her friend for your sake, but I never liked her from the start. And she tricked you into thinking you had some sort of special relationship beyond regular friendship. But did you even know how crazy she was? Do you know *she* hit on *me* that night? And after?" His words are coming out in a frantic rush now, like he's scared to stop talking. "This letter is a fantasy. What she wished would happen, I guess. She hit on me so many times I can't even count them. I never told you, because I didn't want to hurt you and you already didn't seem to be seeing very much of her anymore, so I thought there would be no point. Like, who the heck wants to know their friend, even a former friend, could do something like that? But it's true." He softens his voice. "Come on, you know I wouldn't do this . . ."

"I'm not sure what I know," I say.

And then he gets this expression on his face, an expression of such pure hurt. I wonder, for a moment, if I'm making a terrible mistake.

He stands up. "I can't believe you don't trust me." He shakes his head. He looks like he is starting to panic. I've never seen him panic before. "I have to go. . . . I . . . I can't be here anymore . . ." He turns then and heads for the door. I follow Ryan out of his room and stop at the top of the stairs. He walks down slowly, as though he's waiting for me to come after him. But I just stand there until I hear the quiet thunk of the back door closing.

The wet meat of my heart is flinging itself against the walls of my rib cage. I don't know what to do now. But I know that I am finally choosing her, choosing Delia the way I should have back then, even though she is not here to choose anymore. I feel the strings that always held us together holding me now. I can feel my insides tied to hers, even though hers are nothing but smoke and ash.

* * *

Ryan's mother is in the kitchen. I wonder how much she's heard. I'm walking toward the door, toward my car. When she sees me, she smiles.

"Oh, good. You can be my taste tester." She motions toward the big blender on the countertop. It's half full of chopped mango. "I'm trying out something new. You know, New Year's Resolution, blah-blah, all that. You can tell me if it's awful." She turns her back to me as she goes to the fridge. She pulls out a container of blueberries, some raspberries, a bag of spinach. "I want you to feel comfortable here, like part of the family." She tosses things into the blender as she talks. "You know, with me, with Ryan's dad. We all think . . . think you are wonderful." She turns back and smiles again. She presses a button on the base of the blender. And then says, over the whirr, without turning, "I couldn't help hearing your fight."

I look at the door. I want to run.

The blender stops. "I mean, not the words, but that you were fighting. I wasn't trying to eavesdrop." She pulls glasses from the cabinet, and fills each with smoothie. She pushes one toward me. "I know that having relationships is hard, and sometimes the person you're with might act like a jerk. I mean, goodness, Ryan's father certainly does!" She lets out a little laugh. "And I am sure I do too. But I know how much Ryan cares about you—I guess that's what I wanted to say. Ryan would kill me for meddling but . . ." She lowers her voice. "I know how serious he must be about you, so I hope he tells you that sometimes. He wouldn't come home early for just anyone."

"Sorry?"

"Oh, you don't need to apologize. We missed him, but of course we understood. And we've had sixteen New Years with the kid, so what's one without, right? "

"Wait," I say. "I . . ."

"Please don't be mad at him for saying anything. He didn't tell us any details. All he said was that the two of you had some things you needed to discuss, and he wanted to do it before the new year began. Honestly, that's it." She pauses. "Maybe next year all of us will be together."

"Ryan came back . . ."

"And that's the thing, he wouldn't do that for someone who wasn't very special to him!" She nods, as though I'm finally getting the point. "To things working out," she says. My hand is shaking as our glasses clink together.

Ryan came back from vacation early. He told his parents it was to see me. But he didn't.

So what the hell was he doing?

"You know, Ryan's father and I got together when we were only in high school. Sounds crazy, but it's true!"

I nod weakly. "I'm sorry, I'm suddenly not feeling very well. Do you mind if I go to Ryan's room?" And I don't even wait for an answer.

Back upstairs, I take my phone out of my pocket. I scroll to "FUCKER" and hit talk. The ringing starts on my end, but my heart is so loud in my ears I can barely hear it.

It rings once, twice . . .

For a few seconds Ryan's room is silent. And what I am terrified might happen hasn't happened yet. Then I hear the muffled buzz of a phone on vibrate.

And I tear his room apart.

It's not in the bed, not the nightstand, not the desk . . . the ringing stops, voice mail. I dial again. I search the top drawers of his dresser, full of sweaters, T-shirts, underwear. I make my way down. I'm closer now. Dial again. *Bzz. Bzz. Bzz.* I yank open the bottom drawer. I shove my hand into a pile of jeans, and all the way at the back I hit hard plastic. I pull out a little old-school flip phone, black. My own number flashes on the screen.

I open the phone and scroll to the call-log: There are the missed calls from me, and then nothing but calls to her, texts to her. And two calls received and answered: from Delia on December 29, and one more the day before she died.

I hear another buzz. But this time it's coming from my own phone. I look down. Texts from Ryan, two in a row: I'm sorry for blowing up. I was upset htat you don't trust me . . . but I know how much you've been going through. Want to meet at the diner? I could go for some pancakes . . .

I put his phone back into his drawer. And then I am

running down the stairs. I am running toward the front door. "June? Are you okay?" I can hear Ryan's mom calling out behind me. I keep going. Down the front steps. Hands shaking, I unlock the car, throw myself into it, and start to drive.

And then, finally, I let out a silent scream, as what's deep in my brain, the thoughts I'm scared of even having, start working their way forward.

Chapter 22

1 year, 2 months, 6 days earlier

"Say cheeeese," Ryan said.

"Not so fast, fucko," said Delia. She leaped up and made a grab for his phone. Ryan held it behind his back. The two of them tussled, and June watched from the couch, her entire body filled with warmth.

"What are you smiling about, smiler?" Ryan said.

June touched her mouth, which was all curled up on the sides, and realized he must be talking to her. She hadn't even known she was smiling! She guessed it must be because of how well all of this was going, because of how happy that made her. (Also, possibly a little tiny bit because of the alcohol.)

They'd made the plan weeks ago once they found out Ryan's parents would be out of town. It was supposed to be four of them: June and Ryan, who Delia had never really hung out with before, and Delia with her new boyfriend, who June had never even met. His name was Sloan and he was the drummer in a band that Delia liked. Delia had met him after one of his shows. The first thing he ever said to her was, "If there are an infinite number of parallel universes, then in at least one of them we're already fucking."

"I was into it," Delia had told June. "Obviously. I mean, that's a hot line right there. Turns out he stole it from a much smarter friend." But Delia said he was so sexy it didn't even matter. "Being interesting is not what he's here for."

June had seen many pictures of him, including a picture of his dick, because Delia would do things like that, show you a bunch of normal pictures with a penis thrown in like it was nothing. "And there's Sloan's dog, and there's his roommate whose beard has fleas, I think, and there's a naked Sloan peen." She was so good at being completely deadpan about it, as though she didn't even know that what she was doing was out of the ordinary at all. So yeah, June had hoped she would forget about seeing Sloan's crotch by the time she met him, because, y'know . . . But then, well, it turned out she never *would* meet him, because an hour and a half ago instead of arriving with Sloan, Delia showed up with a half-filled jug of cheap vodka, a jar of maraschino cherries, and a story about how she'd dumped that snoozy loser on the car ride over (but not before, because he was giving her a ride). "More vodka for us," Delia had said with a wink, and then toasted the air and took a long chug right there on the front steps.

But as June had watched Delia, standing alone, pouring vodka into herself, June had gotten a feeling of deep dread down in her gut. The feeling like something *bad* was going to happen that night.

Lately, when it was her and June alone together, and Delia was drinking—which she was doing an awful lot now—Delia got dark. They'd always looked at the world as us-against-them, but while it used to be in a because-no-one-else-quite-*gets*-it sort of way, now it was *because-everyone-else-and-the-rest-of-the-world-is-shit.* Alcohol was the fuel that powered the Delia rocket down-down-down to the pitch-blackness. June didn't *want* to see everything like that, but Delia's feelings wrapped around her and slid under her skin until they were indistinguishable from her own.

When they originally planned the night, June had hoped, assumed even, that with Sloan there, Delia would be her sparkling, fun, charismatic self. Being around guys she was currently having sex with or might one day want to have sex with usually kept her on her best behavior. But without him, who knew what would happen? What would it be like, just the three of them?

At first the answer to that question was: *very awkward.* Ryan was being uncharacteristically quiet, and Delia was talking a lot, the way she sometimes did when she'd been drinking. June was glad that Delia hadn't immediately sunk into a pit of blackness, but Delia kept bringing up private jokes between her and June, things they hadn't even talked about in years. It was like she wanted to make sure that Ryan knew how close she and June were, that if there was going to be a third wheel, she wouldn't be it. Then Delia started saying how boring Sloan was, but how she was going to miss *certain things* about him, and then she looked at June meaningfully and winked. "June knows what I mean," Delia had said. And June felt embarrassed, since it was obvious what Delia was talking about, and she hoped Ryan wouldn't then assume she'd told Delia very, very private things about *him*, which actually wasn't true. Though if it had been a few months ago, she would have told Delia everything. But because things had been changing, she hadn't. She was, in that moment, oddly grateful for that.

So things started out very awkward. But then what happened on that crisp clear night in early October was that June, who never drank at all, decided she would, just this once, because, dear Lord, was this hard. And because Delia was already half drunk, and Ryan had started too.

"Hit me, barkeep," June had said then. And if Delia was surprised—which she must have been, how could she not have been?—she didn't show it in front of Ryan.

The first shot burned and made her cough, and Delia gave her some of the syrup that came in the jar of maraschino cherries to chase the shot with, which didn't make it much better. But right away June felt a warming in her belly and up the back of her neck. And the second shot wasn't nearly as bad. And a few minutes later things didn't feel quite so awkward anymore; that impending *doom* feeling had vanished. After the next shot she wondered why she'd ever been concerned at all—about Delia and her darkness and the weirdness that had worked its way into their friendship, about Ryan and whether he'd leave her, about her mother, school, life. About anything, really.

And now, watching Delia playfully try to steal the phone from Ryan, watching Ryan smiling at her, June felt a rush of pure joyful pleasure and realized that actually, it was much better this way with just the three of them. And that everything that was happening right then was better than anything else that had ever happened. This was maybe the happiest moment of her life so far. Which, come to think of it, was sort of ridiculous.

June giggled.

"She's laughing at how her best friend is so much slicker than her boyfriend," Delia said to Ryan. And then Delia yanked the phone out of his hands, threw it on the couch, and sat on it.

"Something like that," June said. And she smiled even wider at her two favorite people on this entire planet. June leaned back, and Delia started pouring more vodka into the mugs they were using as shot glasses.

"I don't know if I . . . ," June started to say. She felt perfect right now; she didn't want to ruin it. Actually, maybe her head was already spinning a little.

"Shh, shh, shh," Delia said. "Listen to your father." She pointed at WORLD'S BEST DAD printed on her mug. Then handed VERMONTER! to June.

June drank her shot. It didn't even taste like anything at all.

Ryan was standing up at the end of the couch, sipping from the beer that had somehow appeared in his hand. And for a second June wondered if maybe he felt left out, and she thought about going over to give him a hug or to tell him to come and sit with them. June started to stand up. Delia grabbed her arm and pulled her back down.

"Okay, NOW take a picture," Delia said. June looked up at Ryan. He wasn't the sort of person who could be commanded. She'd heard how annoyed he got when his younger sister Marissa tried to tell him what to do. But right then Ryan only smiled and nodded. Delia tossed him her phone, then pressed herself right up against June. She grabbed a chunk of June's long blond hair, pulling it across her own forehead and behind her own ear. "How do I look as a blonde?" she said. She was using this funny accent she only ever did when they were alone. In the accent, "blonde" sounded like "blow-nd." Delia's cheek was warm against hers and her elbow was digging into June's chest, but June could barely feel it.

June took a fistful of Delia's curls and held them behind her own ear. Trying on each other's hair was something they'd been doing for years.

"CLICK," Ryan said loudly. And he snapped the picture. Then he put the phone back on the table.

"You girls are like kids playing hair salon," Ryan said. And June realized she and Delia were still squashed together. They were so touchy, her and Delia. It was nice, to be like that with a friend, to cuddle up together when watching a movie, or walk with your arms around each other. "You don't get hugged ever at home," Delia had said a few years before. "And whenever I get hugged, it's creepy. But there's a chemical that has a name that I can't remember, and it explains why hugging is so good to do with someone you love."

June had forgotten that Ryan had never seen her and Delia together before, really. She felt, for a second, the tiniest bit embarrassed, or like maybe he would feel awkward about the whole thing because he was the one who was supposed to be her boyfriend.

But when she looked up at Ryan, he was grinning. She thought about how sexy his grin was. He didn't usually grin, he smiled. He was sweet and acted like the boyfriends—the nice ones—on TV shows and in movies, which was not unwelcome and always made her think how different he was than other boys who'd liked her, how different she felt around him. But this, this grin, it was not something she'd seen before. Maybe his face looked this way because he was drunk. Or maybe because she was.

Things went on like that for a while, the drinking, laughing, every moment melting into the next one. At some point Delia sat straight up, stretched her arms up over her head, and said, as though it had just occurred to her, "Hey, I know a better game we could play."

Later June would think about this, the casualness with which Delia had suggested this. She'd wonder how drunk Delia had been and if she'd known what might happen next. June might go back and forth forever, but she wouldn't figure it out. You could never be sure, that was a thing June had learned. You could just never be sure about anything.

"So how do we do it?" Ryan said.

"Well," said Delia. "First we all sit down, and then everyone has to get a pillow. And then . . . Do you have some cards and also some dice?"

Ryan nodded and went into the drawer under the TV where his family kept games, because they were the type of family who had a drawer for that.

"Great," Delia said. "Now, everyone"—June thought it was funny that Delia kept saying "everyone" like there were many more of them—"needs to have somewhere between four and six cards, which is to say five cards, since that's the only number in the middle. Unless you want to tear the cards up. Do you?" She turned toward June and held up her hand, then whispered loudly, as a joke, so that Ryan could hear, "I'm making this up as I go along. Help me out, babycakes."

"Oh wait," June said, trying to sound serious and sober, which was actually really hard right about then. "Delia, you forgot the part about the shoes."

"The shoes?" Delia said. "Oh right, how silly of me."

"Ryan," June said, "you sit down on the couch and take off your shoes and then . . ." And she couldn't think of anything funny to say, because her brain was moving so slowly, with the alcohol that was in it, so instead she said, "And take a shot!" She pointed at him. "You there! Sir! Take! A! Shot!" She was yelling now for no reason. Did she even *want* him to take a shot? He was looking at her, seemed amused, maybe. And then he did it. And afterward he winked at her, which he'd never done before. She didn't even know he *could* wink. He was good at it!

And . . . the game started to evolve. Later June would try very hard to figure out which one of them had made it go in the particular direction it went.

They decided it was a drinking game, kind of like truth or dare and spin the bottle and strip poker all combined, with some other stuff from other games in there too. None of them were entirely clear on the rules. Or if there even were any.

They tossed cards into the center of the table and everyone had to drink, and then Ryan danced like a stripper and took off his shirt while Delia laughed hysterically.

"You're right," Delia said loudly. She wiped laugh-tears off her cheeks. "He isn't boring."

Ryan pretended to look offended. "You were right," he said to June about Delia. "She's not a *complete* freak."

"Oh yes she is." Delia waggled her eyebrows.

"Okay," said Ryan. "But only in a good way."

And the game went on. They drank more. Delia spit a shot directly into June's mouth, and Ryan talked dirty to a pineapple, and June tried to take off her bra without taking off her shirt and somehow ended up falling off the couch.

And then they were kind of playing Twister! They were kind of dancing! They were in a pile on the floor! And it was so weird and so fun! But the moment she saw Ryan and Delia's lips meet, which was really part of the game somehow, she was pretty sure, June knew this whole thing was a terrible mistake. Even numbed by all the alcohol, she immediately felt hot panic rushing around inside her.

And suddenly she was very sick.

She stood up, shaky on jelly legs. She had to get out of there. She was not feeling well at all—this was possibly the worst she'd ever felt in her life. "I am going to go to the bathroom," she said. But her voice barely worked and maybe no one heard her.

She didn't want to throw up here on the floor. She started walking away without turning back, so she wouldn't have to see them. Her face was on fire and she was sweating but so cold. The walls kept moving and she gripped on to them, and then the whole room tilted like a carnival ride. She somehow made it to the bathroom. The lights were bright, and when she accidentally looked in the mirror, she saw some kind of monster with messy hair, puffy face, and red cherry syrup on her chin like a goatee. She did not want to look in the mirror anymore then, so instead she turned off the light and sat on the floor and leaned her cheek against the cool porcelain of the base of the sink. She waited for the throw-up to get ready to come out of her mouth, but it didn't. She thought, *I wonder if being able to drink a lot and not throw up is generic,* and then she was sort of impressed with herself that she could think of the word "generic" then. Only a few seconds later she realized that wasn't the word she meant, but she wasn't able to think of what word she did mean. And then she thought about her mother, and she thought about Ryan and Delia in the living room, and then she started to cry.

But when she stopped crying, she was still there in the bathroom. Where were they? Why was she alone? And who knows, but she might have fallen asleep, because the next thing she knew, Ryan was flipping on the lights and holding a glass of water and rubbing her back and saying, "Hey, Junie, are you okay?" And for a second June forgot what had happened that led up to all of this. Except, oh yes, there was Ryan, rubbing her back. And there was Delia, her best friend.

They'd been gone a long time, hadn't they? And she'd been here alone, hadn't she?

"Hey, Dee Dee," June started to say. She had wanted to ask her something, needed to ask her something very important, but right then she couldn't remember what. "Dee Dee?" June said again. June tried to look Delia in the eye, but Delia wouldn't meet her gaze.

Chapter 23

I have no idea where I'm going, but I know I need to get away from here. I drive fast, steering wheel gripped tight. What the hell is happening?

I go over everything, trying to wrap my brain around what I know: A little over a year ago Delia wrote me that letter but never mailed it. Ryan has a secret phone that he only ever used to talk to her. And he sent her a message from outside her house the day before she died, and it wasn't the kind of message you send to a friend. He was there when Delia called me, yelling in the background. And the next day she was dead, a positive pregnancy test in her trash. My head connects the dots, forming a shape in my brain, and when I look at it, I feel like I might throw up.

My phone is in the cup holder, buzzing. Ryan's name flashes on the screen.

I pull into the parking lot of a park. The sky is white and gray.

A father and little boy are walking a big dog. Powdered-sugar flakes of snow drift down from the sky. My body is on fire.

The phone rings only once before he picks up.

"Jeremiah," I say. My voice comes out strained and tight.

"June? Are you okay?"

I imagine his big square face, pale bloodshot eyes. I can barely get the words out. "Was Delia pregnant?"

"What? No, God, definitely not. Why are you asking me that?"

"But how do you know she wasn't? How can you be so sure?"

"Because we . . . I mean . . ." He lowers his voice. "We only slept together, like, twice ever, and we were totally safe both times." He pauses. "I guess I'd always thought I'd wait until I got married or something, so I felt guilty about it because, I don't know. So unless she was cheating on me . . ." His voice catches. "But I know she wouldn't have done that . . ."

"I found a pregnancy test," I say. "At her house." I stop, heart pounding. "In the garbage outside, I mean. It was positive."

He is silent then, for a long time. I hear his breath, heavy on the other end of the line.

So I go on, I tell him about Ryan's secret phone with calls to Delia's number.

"Wait, you mean Fisker?" Jeremiah says. "He used to . . ." He pauses then. "I don't understand. Isn't he your boyfriend?"

Out on the cold gray playground, the little boy has climbed up into a swing. His father is behind him, pushing.

"He was," I tell Jeremiah. "I don't think so anymore . . ."

And hearing myself say those words, I realize yes, this is done. After all this time, after so much thinking and worrying, clinging so tightly. Just like that, there is nothing to hold on to.

When Jeremiah finally speaks again, his voice is a whisper. "I have to go," he says. And then he hangs up. I sit there, staring at the boy and his father. The boy is laughing now, flying through the air.

A moment later the phone rings again, but this time it's a number I don't recognize. I pick up.

"Hey there." It's a girl's voice, low with a Southern twang.

Ashling.

"Listen, before you say anything else, I'm sorry," she says. "That's what I called to tell you. I'm sorry for being . . . how I was being before. I was just trying to protect Delia, or whatever, which is stupid. This isn't easy for either of us. I wanted to call and say that." She takes a breath. "So now I have." She pauses then. "I also wanted to make sure you're not still thinking any of that crazy stuff you were saying the other day about Delia . . . I mean about what happened to her."

And I know she won't want to hear this, but I also know I have no choice but to tell her. "Yes, and it's more complicated than I thought. I know who she was cheating with . . ."

"Really . . . ," says Ashling. There's something in her tone, something I can't place. "Who?"

"My boyfriend."

"Damn."

"And I think . . ." I can hardly bear to say it, but I have to now. "I think she might have been pregnant. And I think he might have . . . maybe it was his. And what if he found out? What if she threatened him and he got angry . . ."

"Okay, June, hold up. Seriously. It's not what you think."

I don't say anything.

"Where are you?" she asks.

I tell her.

"Wait right there. I have something for you."

The letter in front of me was written by Delia, that part is clear. It's the words that I can't wrap my head around. I read them again, again, again.

My dearest Ash,

So I guess by now you know what happened. I turned myself into your name. HA-HA! Please don't be mad and please don't feel sad.

I just don't want to do this anymore. This being any of it. We all have to die sometime, right? I've decided my time is now.

I love you so much.

D

"I got it in the mail this morning," Ashling says to me. "Dated the day she died."

"A suicide note," I say.

Ashling nods.

"She wouldn't have . . . She was . . ." My voice cracks. *"She was scared of fire."* But as I hear myself, I suddenly realize how absurd my logic is, has been all along—her fear of fire doesn't prove she couldn't have done it like this. If anything, it's exactly why she would have.

"Look, if some part of you wants to believe she didn't kill herself so that you don't have to feel guilty thinking that you could have stopped her . . . don't go down that path, okay? This has nothing to do with you. Don't feel bad that you didn't pick up the phone. If you'd known what she was planning, of course you would have. But it wouldn't have mattered. She was going to do what she was going to do. Delia always did. . . ."

And I shake my head, I have no words left. I know things could have been different. Dear Lord, I wish they were.

Ashling gives me a hug. "Be well, June," she says. And then she leaves. And I just sit there, crying now. The tears are falling down my face so fast. I imagine them filling up the entire car, drop by drop until I drown in them.

It's only later when I'm finally driving home that I realize something: Ashling said if I'd known what was going to happen, I would have picked up the phone. But I never told Ashling that Delia had called me and I hadn't answered. And Ashling said she'd only had a three-second phone call with Delia and that's it. So then . . . how did Ashling know?

Chapter 24

By the time I pull into my driveway, the sun is down and the trees are black paper cutouts against a dark gray sky. But all I can see is Delia's face. And all I can think about is what her last moments must have been like, pouring the gasoline, lighting the match.

I get out of the car and slam the door behind me.

There's shouting, "JUNE! Please listen!" It's Ryan. Waiting for me outside. I hear footsteps, fast, faster. My heart pounds. He is running toward me from the road. I run too. Something is very wrong.

I reach the door, keys clenched in my fist, frozen fingers fumbling. My hand is shaking. Ryan is twenty feet away. Ten. Five. Finally, the key slides in.

"JUNE!"

I slam the door behind me, twist the deadbolt.

Ryan's cries are muffled through the door. I press my ear against the wood.

I hear what sounds like "crazy" and I hear what sounds like "Jeremiah." And then five words, perfectly clear: *"I think he did it."*

My entire body is tingling. I flip on the outside light and look through the peephole. Ryan's face is covered with something thick and dark. It takes me a beat to realize what this is—blood. It is streaked across his chin and cheeks. His nose is oozing it. His eyes are desperate and wild.

He takes out his phone. A second later mine rings. "Please!" he shouts through the door. I don't pick up. Thumbs fly across the keyboard. A text comes through.

Please listen. i came here to warn you.

And a second later another . . .

Jeremiah came to see me

Ping. Ping. Ping.

he said I got Delia pregnant he was completely insane

he said it was because of me that her baby is dead

was she pregnant? if she was and her baby is dead

it's because of him. he killed her

she wasn't pregnant from me there is no chance

june I'm not lying. he is crazy

he was so jealous and yelling

something is not right with him

I can feel Ryan's panic leaking through the door. How

quickly things can change. How quickly the unimaginable can become real.

Why would I believe you about anything? I write back.

You've already lied.

You were with her. I already know this.

Ping. Ping. Ping.

For a moment, he just stares at the screen. His shoulders heave.

Okay okay yes I was at her house.

I already know this. But still the words feel like a punch.

when i was on vacation

she called me and said she wasn't going to be around later

That is the phrase she used

but told me if I came back early we could . . .

i came back early to meet her over break but when i got to her house it wasnt like i thought it would be

she seemed high or was acting very weird at least

And suddenly, just like that, I understand something he doesn't and never will: *She was screwing with him. And she was doing it for me.*

That was the secret. She was going to tell me what he did, but only if I picked up the phone or called her back. Only if I deserved to know . . .

I'm crying now, and I'm not sure who I'm even crying for. For Delia? For myself? For both of us? I thought I knew her so well, and that she'd never have killed herself. But what the hell do I even know about anything?

I chose Ryan, I chose wrong.

Ryan wipes his face, smearing blood across his cheek.

then we heard the announcement

I thought that she killed herself, that she was crazy

now I don't know anymore

Only, for all my doubts, there is one thing I'm sure of: Ryan didn't hurt her. He is a liar and an ass, and so weak. But he didn't do this. And I do not want him here anymore.

Leave.

"Listen!" Ryan's muffled voice is coming through the door. "Please! I don't think Jeremiah is safe to be around. He's hiding something, I know it!"

Leave

now

just go. There's nothing you can say that I'll listen to. Leave before I call the police.

He stares at the door for a long time, hesitates, rubs his face, takes a breath. Then, finally, he starts to walk away.

Now I am alone with my thoughts, and I realize something: All along I've been trying to solve a mystery, but it was the wrong mystery. The bigger one, the real one is this: How the hell am I going to go on without her?

A few minutes later Ryan sends me one more message.

what do you think happened to Jeremiah's hand?

Chapter 25

1 year, 2 months, 6 days earlier

June was still in bed when she saw Delia's name flashing on her phone. It was 4:36 p.m. on Sunday. And if it were any other Sunday up until recently, June would be with Delia by now. They had a Sunday tradition, had for years: Cake Church is what they called it.

Every Sunday, while Delia's mother and stepfather were out at regular church, June would go over to Delia's house, and Delia would bake something ridiculous. Delia's love of baking was totally unlike her, which of course made it extra totally like her. "I'm nothing if not completely inconsistent," Delia would say. She would make the most decadent and beautiful things for June—a towering birthday cake on her 264/365 birthday, or fat chocolate cupcakes with thick layers of butter-cream frosting, which Delia insisted on calling "frosted muffins" to make them sound like a breakfast food, and once a cake with June's own face piped on in icing. June and Delia would cuddle up in Delia's room, eating whatever treat she'd baked, or sometimes just eating the batter of whatever treat she'd decided not to bake after all, until they were both giddily buzzed from sugar. They'd watch stupid movies, or read or talk, it didn't matter. The ritual made June feel almost like she was a part of one of those families who had a regular Sunday dinner. There was something so *wholesome* about it, and some weird part of June, who hadn't even realized she *cared* about wholesomeness, really liked that.

But the past couple months had been different. And it wasn't only because June had started seeing Ryan and Delia had started seeing Sloan. It was that Delia was getting messed up a lot more, and by Sunday she'd be too hungover or strung out to get out of bed, let alone bake some crazy rainbow confection made with seven different colors of impossibly bright sheet cake. June would still go over there sometimes, though. Delia would call June in the late afternoon. "Come over, come over, come over," Delia would say. And when she was in a good mood, which wasn't often lately but still did sometimes happen, she'd add, "You're the only one who loves me enough to saaaave meeee." And June would bring sacks of greasy french fries and trashy magazines and try to pretend that everything was normal.

Except they weren't normal, was the thing—a space had been opening up between them where previously there was no space at all. And it made June both sad and strangely relieved, though she couldn't quite say why.

But that particular Sunday in October, while the phone flashed with Delia's name, June was the hungover one. June was the one who was still in bed. And June was the one who needed saving. Only, she wasn't sure who there even was to save her. She just knew that it couldn't be Delia anymore. Not after last night.

June had woken up in Ryan's bed. He was next to her on the floor. "Listen . . . ," he started, the moment she opened her eyes. Had he been watching her? Waiting for her to wake up? His words tumbled together. "I hope you know that nothing . . . I mean, we were really drunk and I wouldn't normally have . . ." He could barely get a sentence out, and her head was pounding too hard to make sense of anything anyway. "Last night was . . ."

June so, so wanted him to stop talking. She couldn't begin to think about what had happened and what hadn't. Her memory was hazy, coming back in flashes.

"Last night was crazy," June had finished for him. And she didn't want to say anything else right then. The panic was already rising up into her throat. Ryan invited her to stay, offered to cook them both breakfast. But June had told him she needed to go home. "My mother will be wondering where I am," she said. They both knew that wasn't true.

So June left. And as she drove, very slowly so she wouldn't

puke right there in the car, the thoughts tried to worm their way into her brain, very unpleasant thoughts about her best friend and her boyfriend. *What the actual fuck?*

June had never felt jealous of Delia before—not once, not even for a second. She knew that some best friends were competitive with each other, but she had always assumed that those friendships were less pure than her and Delia's, less *real* somehow. Because the thing was, when Delia was being extra hilarious and charming and sparkly and people noticed, June just felt *proud.* And when someone wanted Delia—and so many people did, and Delia ate that shit *up*—June thought, if anything, it was a testament to their good taste. The only way she'd ever have been able to imagine being jealous in relation to Delia was if *Delia* seemed to love someone else more, and that was impossible.

At least that's what she'd always thought, no, *known*, deep down in the center of herself.

But in the car she felt something hot and sick in her, completely brand-new—she was jealous. And not only that, but *angry* at the way Delia had acted, sparkling like that in front of Ryan on *purpose*. Of course it was on purpose. Delia was way too smart for *anything* to be an accident.

Ryan was supposed to be entirely off limits. He was hers, wasn't he? She'd never thought of him like that before, but she couldn't help it now. She hated herself for it, but, no, screw it, it was . . . was it wrong to feel that way? Didn't *most* girls feel that way about their boyfriends? Maybe it was normal. And even if it wasn't, she didn't know how to make herself feel something else.

June stopped on the way home and got a toasted everything bagel with cheese, because that's what Delia sometimes wanted when she was hungover, but June could barely eat a quarter of it before she was dry heaving into the toilet. And then she'd gotten back into bed, adrenaline pumping. She felt like she was dying, or wanted to die. *This is a hangover*, she told herself. But she couldn't convince herself that it wasn't something far worse.

Finally, curled under the covers, she let herself go over the events of the night again, what she could piece together. She remembered being nervous, she remembered deciding, *fuck it*—even though she was usually so careful, so *not* fuck it about *anything*. She remembered taking her first shot. And then her second and third and more. Almost everything else was fuzzy after that, and mostly what she could recall were flashes of things—a very stupid game, Delia and Ryan, lip to lip, the view from Ryan's bathroom floor, cheese puffs, water, Delia's face, Delia not looking her in the eye.

But there was one moment that stuck out more than the kiss even. Delia had been teaching her a drinking trick. "Just open up the back of your throat," Delia had said, "anything will slide right down. No gagging, once you really learn how to do it." And then, June remembered this part with strange clarity: Delia had smiled slyly at Ryan. "Think I mastered that one," she'd said. And had she winked? She had.

How had Ryan reacted? Did he laugh? Smile back? June tried to picture it, but she could not remember. The only clear thing was Delia's face, luminous, eyes glowing the way they did when she was all lit up and looking at something she wanted for her very own.

This moment played over and over in her head. June couldn't stop it.

She lay in bed. She picked up a book, but reading would be impossible, and she tried to put on music, but the sound gave her a headache, so instead she just lay there, trying to think of nothing at all.

That's what she was doing when the phone started ringing. And that's when, for the first time in their entire friendship, June saw Delia's name flashing on her phone and she didn't reach for it.

June told herself she'd call Delia back later, she didn't feel well, that was all. But she knew then that something significant was changing, had changed, and that—and maybe more importantly—Delia would know it too. Because it was like Delia was inside her head sometimes. And June couldn't imagine anything happening in her own head without Delia immediately figuring it out. But maybe that was the other thing. Maybe she no longer owed Delia access to every part of herself . . . With that thought, June felt a weight lifting, a great weight that had been tied to her for so long. The phone rang and rang, and June watched it until it stopped and the screen went dark. And all of a sudden, just like that, she was free.

Chapter 26

I cry myself to sleep, wake puffy eyed, and drag myself to school.

There is no mystery, no clues to uncover, there's nothing to do but miss her.

The first text from Jeremiah comes when I'm in homeroom, before the announcements start. I've just finished telling Krista everything that happened, and she's staring at me, eyes wide and round. I look down at my phone.

"Who's that?" Krista says. "Ryan? Jeremiah?"

Sorry I had to beat up your boyfriend. Did it for Delia.

"What did he say?" Krista edges forward in her seat. I wish she didn't sound quite so interested. I'm too exhausted to bother resisting, so I show her.

"Wait, he's not still . . . ," she starts to say.

I shake my head. I write back: he's not my boyfriend anymore

I feel a squeezing in my chest. I try to remind myself that the Ryan I thought I loved doesn't actually exist. I didn't know him, not the real him. But that is not much comfort at all.

I get another message a few seconds later: good.

Are you okay? I type back. Can you meet after school?

I need to see him, to tell him what Ashling showed me. He deserves to know.

"That dude is weird." Krista is still staring. She has a little smile on her face. "Do you think there's any chance that Ryan is right, though? That maybe he did do something?"

"No," I say. "I told you what happened."

Krista shrugs. "Okay, but let's say for a second he *did* though, right? Do you think it would be that he's crazy and was in some weird altered state so he doesn't even totally know that he did it, and that's why he asked for your help? Maybe he has a split personality. Or was really high. Or was in so much denial . . . I don't know. I'm trying to think about what the reasons would be if this was a movie or whatever . . ."

I hate how excited Krista looks now. I turn my back to her and stare down at my phone.

The announcements start and end. I wait for another message, but it doesn't come. I wonder if Jeremiah knows how little I've trusted him. I feel a stab of guilt about that, but then again, didn't I have good reasons to be a little suspicious?

I can feel Krista's questions sinking into my skull and spreading like a fungus. I've been working so hard to figure all of this out, it's like my brain doesn't remember how to stop. *Why* was Jeremiah looking for Delia's murderer if he was the one who did it? Well, maybe that's not really what he was doing after all. Maybe all along he was trying to answer a different question—not who killed her, but who was she cheating with. And he was using me to help him do it.

I shake my head. This is my brain wanting to keep figuring; this is my brain afraid to rest in the grief that I know is coming. Jeremiah didn't do anything. Even though Ryan said . . .

This is crazy. Why would I trust Ryan at all? Why would I listen to him ever again?

Just as I'm walking out of homeroom, Jeremiah finally texts back.

can't

All day my brain won't stop. Jeremiah. Ryan. Jeremiah. Ashling. I don't know who to trust. Maybe I don't trust any of them. I don't even trust myself.

Lunchtime I get a text from Ryan. For a split second my body has the old reaction—a lifting, a fizzle of joy. It drains away.

I stayed home from school today have you thought about what I said??? Have you seen jeremiah? should we call the police?

It seems so insane that he could still think there's a "we" to make decisions, but also that up until only a few days ago, there was.

No. I write. Definitely not.

Before last period I spot Jeremiah down at the end of the hall. I watch him, moving slowly, all alone, pain radiating off of him like a stench. I can smell it from here. And just like that, the doubt is gone.

I call out to him, but he doesn't turn. A moment later he disappears into a classroom.

I send him a text. I need to talk to you.

No answer.

Five minutes before the final bell I slip out of class. I walk to the parking lot. I remember his car—the big green station wagon with a UMass bumper sticker. I find it and stand there and wait. I hear the bell ringing in the distance, and then a few seconds later the sound of hundreds of students leaving school.

I turn and look into the window of his car. There's a tube of Bacitracin on the passenger seat, a bottle of Advil, bandages, gauze. I remember Ryan's words. *What do you think happened to Jeremiah's hand?*

I try to picture his hands. Surely I've seen them before, haven't I? But maybe one was always hidden, in gloves or behind his back, in his pocket . . . This is crazy. I know what happened to Delia, I have the answer now. It is time to stop investigating, to stop churning, to stop resisting, to really feel this.

I close my eyes, open them, and when I look up, there he is, lumbering toward his car, left hand tucked in his coat pocket.

I feel a tingling in my gut.

I know this is ridiculous, I know it is, but still I step back so he won't see me. I slip between cars until I reach my own, three rows away. I get in and watch him through the window. People are all around him, but his face registers no expression, like he's sleepwalking or in a trance.

When he starts his car up, I start mine too. And when he eases out of the parking lot, I follow.

He makes his way down Oak Avenue and up Two Bridge Place. He glances in the rearview mirror a couple of times, but I don't think he sees me. . . .

He pulls into the parking lot of a CVS, gets out, and walks inside. I park a few spaces over. I wonder if I should move farther away in case he comes out and spots my car, but just then a big white van pulls up and parks between us. Good.

I follow him in, straight back to the pharmacy. The store is mostly empty. I pause in front of the deodorants. I hear him talking to the pharmacist, a gray-haired woman with a smooth young face.

"It hurts a lot," he is saying. "I thought it would have stopped by now. But it hasn't, and I don't know what to do."

"Has the skin blistered?"

"Yes."

"Let me have a look . . ."

For a moment there is silence and then she lets out a quiet gasp.

"You really need to see a doctor about this," she says. "When did this happen?"

"A few days ago."

Jeremiah's back is to me. I creep closer. And then, I see it: Jeremiah's hand. His flesh is raw, red, wet-looking, dotted with blisters oozing puss. I raise my fingers to my lips, feel my stomach curdling. *This is a burn.*

"How did this happen?" the pharmacist asks.

Jeremiah pauses only for a second. "It was an accident," he says.

My heart is hammering so hard I cannot breathe.

She shakes her head. "This is much too severe to treat on your own."

"Okay, but until then," Jeremiah says, "what can I use in the meantime?"

The pharmacist starts leading him toward the first-aid aisle. I turn my back as they go by.

They stop a few feet from me. I make my way quickly toward the door as the thoughts click into place:

Jeremiah was jealous when Delia got phone calls.

Jeremiah answered Delia's phone.

Jeremiah "found" Delia's phone and wanted to unlock it.

Jeremiah almost beat up that guy at the party.

Jeremiah did beat up Ryan.

Jeremiah was alone in the woods watching everyone.

Delia died in a fire.

And Jeremiah has a burned hand.

This is too big, too much for me now. I can't breathe. My heart is drumming hard and fast.

Out the door, I'm halfway to my car when my phone rings. I hit ignore. It rings again. I look down. Ashling.

Footsteps. Jeremiah walks right past me. *Shit.* He stops for a moment, just stands there like he's considering something. He's between me and my car now. Did he see me?

I turn and I run, around the side of the building, out toward the Dumpsters in back. I lean against the wall panting. My phone rings a third time. Ashling again. I pick up.

"Where are you?" she says. "I came to look for you at school. I wanted to make sure you were okay."

"Listen," I say. "Jeremiah . . . His hand is burned. . . ."

Ashling's answer is drowned out by the sound of a car pulling up behind me.

"Hello?" I say. "Ashling?" She doesn't answer. "Did you hear me?"

I step back, then suddenly I feel a pair of strong arms wrapping around my waist. I try to turn, but something is shoved over my head, and everything goes dark.

I start to scream.

Hot adrenaline surges in my spine. I reach for my face—there's cloth, so thick I can barely feel my fingers through it. My arms are wrenched behind my back, my wrists bound together.

I keep screaming, but the sound is muffled by the fabric against my mouth and nose.

I feel myself lifted off the ground. I kick my legs. The toe of my boot connects with something hard, and my knee sinks into flesh. I hear a sharp intake of breath, but no words. I'm placed facedown on a cold flat surface. The floor of a van, maybe. My ankles are held together, hard, tied tight. I am still screaming, throat raw, eyes tearing with the effort. *What the fuck is happening?*

Part of the bag is lifted from my head, and I feel warm breath against my cheek. And a voice, so quiet, I can barely hear it over the beating of my heart: "If you want to find out what happened to Delia, don't struggle."

Chapter 27

We are moving now, speeding fast, blasting dance music drowns out the sound of my screaming. I feel cold metal against the bare skin of my back where my jacket and shirt have ridden up. Through the fabric over my face I can make out only flickering light.

"JEREMIAH?" I shout. Could it be? "RYAN? TIG?"

I wrench my arms, kick my legs, strain my wrists and ankles against the bindings, but they're far too tight.

Whoever killed Delia, they're taking me somewhere so they can kill me, too.

With this thought my heart explodes, but I force myself to lie still. I take a slow breath, and then another one. Now is not the time to struggle. I must be quiet, curl into myself. Save every bit of strength I have. Eventually the van will stop, and they'll come back here and I'll be ready for them. Whoever did this to her, they're not bringing me down without a fight.

A few minutes later the van comes to a halt. I lurch forward and then back. The music shuts off. I hear quiet voices. And then the slam of two car doors.

The back of the van is opened. Whatever is over my face is lifted off. There's a blast of cool air, and I'm blinking at two masked figures in the late afternoon sun. They're both tall, dressed in all black. One leans in toward me and unties my legs. The other unties my arms. I look around, take in all I can: We're at the edge of a patch of woods. I have no idea where we are. We could be anywhere.

They take me by the arms and lead me forward. I clench my jaw, grit my teeth. I'm waiting for my moment. There are two of them, and I know I can't take them both. But I can run. And I'm fucking fast.

I breathe in. Dead leaves crunch under my feet. I don't bother asking any questions. I feel the muscles tensing in my legs. I'm ready to go. Ready to start, and then . . .

. . . standing there, right in front of me, is Delia.

My heart stops, starts again, stops. She's staring right at me. Her eyes are bright.

"Oh my God," I whisper. I feel a flood of happiness, relief, then pure ice-cold fear. I have no idea what is going on.

"Hey, J," Delia says softly.

The wind is blowing against my cheek, I am flying through space, hurtling toward earth.

"Oh my God," I say again. Am I insane? Is she a ghost? Am I dreaming?

My eyes feel full, my cheeks suddenly wet.

For a moment she just stares at me. Then she holds out her arms and I tumble forward, sink against her. My entire body is shaking. She wraps me up. I feel my heart open wide.

"You're always jumping to the wrong conclusions," Delia says in my ear. Sounds escape through my lips, bubbled up from inside. I don't know if I'm crying or laughing now.

"Hey," she says, so quiet. "Shhh, Junie, it's okay." She sounds like she used to, she sounds like my best friend.

I close my eyes. But a moment later she lets me go. She pulls back and she looks away. The sun is going down. Soon I won't be able to see her at all.

"So clearly you can see that no one killed me." Her tone is different now. "You can go back to your life."

Your life. Everything outside of this moment feels like something I made up. Only this is real.

"What about you?" I say.

I look at the two masked figures, still watching us. I want to ask her if she's okay, only they're too close, they'll hear us.

But suddenly I know what to do. I put my pinky to my mouth and run my fingertip across my bottom lip. This is our code—has been for years—we used to do it at parties when one of us was trapped talking to some random guy. *Do you need to be rescued?* I feel a frizzle of connection when our eyes meet. She remembers.

But she doesn't answer the way she's supposed to, with an ear scratch or a bitten lip. She says out loud, "No, I do not." And then, "I already have been."

Her answer offers no relief. Sometimes the people who most need saving don't have any idea.

She shakes her head, like she's reading my mind. Then she reaches out and takes my hands. "Seriously, go home, Junie," she says. "Forget about me."

The idea that I ever could is completely insane. But maybe no more so than the fact that for a while, I really did try to. "What's going on? I need to know that you're okay."

It suddenly feels like no time has passed, like the last year never even happened.

Delia tips her head to the side, and her expression changes, hardens. "You were fine not knowing for a very long time. Why do you care so much all of a sudden?"

"I wasn't fine not knowing. I was . . ." But I don't have an answer for her, not a good one. "I'm so sorry." I look up at her. Our eyes meet. I feel her understanding everything. The way she always did. I forgot what it was like to be this connected. "Whatever trouble you're in, let me help you. Please."

"You sure?" She is trying to hide the hope in her voice.

"Once you get involved, once you know what happened, you won't be able to un-know it, and"—she stares at me then—"you won't be able to go back. . . ."

"I'm sure," I say.

Delia's lips spread into a smile, radiant and beautiful. She turns to the two people still standing behind her. "She's coming with us," she says. "You guys can take the masks off now." The shorter one removes it first and I look at her face—even features, wide eyes, a pixie cut. Beautiful.

"Ashling?"

"Hey, lady," she says.

"Wait," I say. "You . . ." *Knew all along, were lying, helped her do this, are still her best friend . . .*

Ashling inhales slowly. "Of course," she says. Then slips her arm through Delia's, pulls her close, and kisses her on the lips. The kiss is much more than friendly. But before I can even process this, I feel a hand on my shoulder.

I turn. The sun is sinking fast, but I can still make out the lines of his face—dark eyebrows, strong nose, wide mouth. He's around my age, or maybe a couple years older. "Sorry about before." His voice is soft and low. "I told Ash we could just ask you to get in the van, but she insisted . . ." I look up at Ashling, who shrugs. I turn back to the guy.

"It's . . ." I don't know what to say. I'm staring at him. The air is freezing, but my body feels warm. "Fine," I say.

He leans in close—for a split second it feels like he's leaning in to kiss me, but instead he whispers into my ear, so quietly that I'm the only one who can even hear him. "Are you sure you know what you're getting yourself into?"

He is watching me closely. My heart is pounding, pounding.

"I know I'm not leaving her again, ever, no matter what." For the first time in a long time, I feel completely certain and clear. "That's enough."

He steps back. I can't see his face anymore. "Well, let's go then," he says.

He starts walking back toward the van, Ashling and Delia are already there. I hesitate for only a second, then I turn and follow.

Chapter 28

Delia

Fire is hungry. It is a ravenous beast, devours everything in its path. It got inside me, somehow, and it is choking me. Most of the time I can barely breathe.

I don't remember the last time my insides weren't vibrating hot and sick. Ashling, the rest of them, they don't quench it. But now the fire in my gut is shrinking. If I open my mouth, flames won't leap from my lips. She is here, she is here, she is here. It is a surprise, but also I knew it all along. Deep down, I must have. I know that I did.

Lighting that match felt good. Going to that party. Meeting them, making this plan. It felt in-fucking-credible. But this is different.

I want to spin around laughing, fall over, stand up, do it again. I am a newborn fucking baby now, I'm so fresh and happy. I know that is only part of what is happening; there are layers. This is just one of them. I can't be the kid, because I'm the damn adult here, so I have to keep my face calm and still. I feel Ashling staring at me, wondering what I'm thinking. So I do what I sometimes do when I feel like she's trying to climb into my brain and I need to stop her—I turn and I kiss her on the mouth. Her lips are soft and she smells good. She always smells good, that's the thing about this girl. Even when we haven't showered for two days, alcohol climbing through her pores, teeth unbrushed. She tries to slip her tongue into my mouth, but I don't want her to. Not now, at least.

I turn back to see what June's doing, to make sure June's still coming. She is hesitating, I can feel it. No one else would notice, but I *know* her, that's how I know what it means.

I close my eyes for one moment, fire-bellied entire body vibrating. I can't bear this.

Please, fucking God, let her come with us, let her come with me. After all this. Please.

I open my eyes. She is walking toward us, toward the van now. And my heart slows down, starts pounding, slows down all over again. The fire fizzles, lets off tendrils of soft gray smoke.

It has begun.

Chapter 29

June

It is strange how fast everything can change, and then how quickly it can feel like it's always been that way. I have always been here, in the front seat of this van, Delia pressed up against me. I have always been confused and scared, but also so impossibly happy in a way that there are not even words for. This is all completely insane, but if anyone was going to do this, whatever *this* even *is*, it would be Delia. The rules do not apply to her, the human-made ones, the science-made ones.

She turns toward me. "We need to stop and pick something up," Delia says, "on the way." Her hand is warm on my arm. "Is that okay, Junie?"

I want to ask, "Stop where? On the way to where?" But I just nod, because it doesn't matter. I'd go anywhere with her. I know that soon my head will be filled with an infinite number of other questions. For right now all I feel is the buzz of happiness, and the sense of being firmly held, tethered, my empty spaces all filled up.

We aren't driving for very long before I recognize where we are. The buildings are squat and industrial, flat fields full of nothing. We're in Macktin, down by the water. We're heading for Tig's.

We pull up at the edge of the lot. The guy hops out without a word. Now it's just the three of us. Delia turns toward me.

"I'd introduce you to my girlfriend, but I guess you've already met." Her tone is light, as though we've bumped into each other on any regular day.

"Right . . . ," I start.

My girlfriend. Delia has never had a girlfriend before, or at least didn't when I knew her. And she'd never expressed any interest in any girl ever, not even as a friend, except for me. I wonder when things changed, or if she knew all along. Or if there's just something about this girl in particular.

Delia is watching me, a tiny smirk on her lips, like she knows what I'm thinking.

"Don't be mad at her, okay? We didn't know if we could trust you. We needed to make sure you'd be able to . . . keep this secret. And the other ones."

My stomach tightens. *We.*

"I get it," I say. Only, of course I don't get anything. But suddenly I realize something. I turn to Ashling. "When you said Jeremiah was an idiot because he didn't realize who else Delia was with . . ." I don't finish; I don't need to. The person she was referring to was herself.

Ashling looks up me and tips her head.

"So, what did you think of all of it, anyway? My acting, I mean. Be honest. Believable? Over the top?"

"You're really good at crying," I say.

Ashling grins. "It's my specialty."

And then we just sit there. There is silence. Awkward. I take a breath. "So, how did you guys meet?" Asking a normal question in such a bizarre situation feels ridiculous.

"At a party," says Delia.

Ashling points toward Tig's building. "One of his. I know you maybe didn't have the best time there, but I swear they're usually pretty fun."

An image flashes in my mind—Tig's house, the tall girl with the short dark hair, waving at me like she knew me.

"That was you," I say slowly. And then suddenly I remember something else: when I was asking questions down at the reservoir, a girl started to answer me in a soft southern accent . . . "And at her memorial . . ."

"Yup." She nods. "Making sure everything went smoothly for my girl here, and that no one got any"—she pauses—"wrong ideas."

"Does Tig know?" I picture his blank dead eyes, remember his simmering energy.

Delia shakes her head. "Hell no. That guy cannot be trusted for a fucking second."

"And yet you fucked him," Ashling says. She's trying to make a joke, but she sounds jealous.

"So I was close enough to get what I needed," says Delia. They've had this conversation before.

I look at Delia. What did she need from him? Something he sells? Whatever she stole from him? And what *was* it?

Ashling leans in and kisses Delia again. I see her slide her tongue in between Delia's lips. I can't look away. But it isn't because Ashling is a girl, that's not what's remarkable about it. It's that Ashling loves Delia really and truly. You can tell from the way she is cradling Delia's head, the way she is smiling behind the kiss. The love is radiating off of her. But Delia . . . I'm not sure she loves Ashling back.

The door opens. They pull apart.

The guy gets back into the car with a brown paper lunch bag in his hand. He tosses it into Delia's lap without a word.

"Home?" says Ashling.

"Home," says Delia. And Ashling starts to drive.

The house up ahead is small and modern, glowing warm orange through the big plate-glass windows. Behind it is a flat expanse of earth and a huge gray sky. Ashling turns off the car.

My legs are shaking when I get out. We go inside.

It is beautiful here—fresh and new, like a picture you'd see in a design magazine. From the doorway I'm looking directly into the living room and the kitchen. There are light wood walls, a big L-shaped sofa. The back wall is almost all glass, looking out onto grass and trees and a river.

I wonder whose house this is.

They are in motion now, all of them, moving like people who each know their role, their place. Like a family. The guy takes our coats to the closet. Delia goes to the cabinet and gets mugs. "Ev," Ashling shouts through the doorway into the next room, "we're back!"

A moment later a guy comes bounding in. "She's here," he says. He crosses his arms and looks me up and down. I stare back. He is small—a few inches shorter than I am. He has dark hair, black jeans, and a bright red shirt with a bunch of black zeroes and ones printed on the front. Binary. He has short arms and big hands, like a puppy not done growing yet. There's a leather bracelet wrapped around one of his wrists. "I'm Evan," he says. He sticks out his hand, awkward but sweet. I take it. His grip is firm and warm. "I already know all about you."

I wonder what he knows, exactly. But I guess they must be good things, mostly, because when our eyes meet, his smile splits his face in half.

And then we all just stand there, and no one says anything at all. And I know it must be because of me. If I weren't here, what would they be talking about? What would they be doing?

How does Delia know them? Did they help her do whatever it is she did? I have one million questions, but when I look at Delia, standing off to the side, her face, her smile, the fact that she is on this planet feels like answer enough for now.

She comes over and takes my hand. "We have some catching up to do, I think," she says. I can feel all of them, the tall guy, Evan, especially Ashling, watching as she leads me out of the room.

We're in a bedroom now, all whitewashed wood with an enormous platform bed low to the floor, covered in rumpled bedding, soft peach. The room smells like Delia, but someone else, too. Ashling, I guess. There are two water glasses on one side of the bed, a can of Diet Coke on the other. There are jeans and a bra tossed onto the dresser, a pair of gray sneakers next to the door.

I look up. Delia is watching me take it all in.

"So here I am," Delia says. "Looking pretty good for a dead girl, huh?" She grins.

I try to smile back. This all feels so fragile, my being here, the fact that I've been let in at all. I do not want to mess it up, but the questions are bubbling up again.

Delia is still staring at my face. "Go ahead," she says, "ask. You can."

I stare back at her. My mouth opens. A single word floats out: "Why?"

Delia nods, then takes a deep breath. "I couldn't go on living like that," she says simply.

"Like what?" I am ashamed not to know. If I'd been there for her at all, I already would.

"My stepfather," she says. My stomach tightens. She always called him other things when she referred to him: William, Willy, Shitbag, Pecker Head. "He . . . wasn't very nice to my mother. You remember how it was. But it got worse. There were bruises." Delia grits her teeth. "Things I heard at night. I hated him for doing it to her, and I hated her for letting him." She shakes her head. "She's pregnant, you know."

I raise my hand to my lips. I remember sleeping over, the sounds of them fighting. I remember picking up that stick, the two pink lines. "I thought it was you," I say.

"What was?" Delia's voice is slow, confused.

And before I can stop myself, I am telling her. I can't hold back now. I don't remember how to. "I . . . snuck into your house looking for answers. I found the test in the garbage. I thought you were pregnant."

She is smiling ever so slightly. "Did anyone see you?"

I shake my head.

"Good," she says. "I love you for doing that for me." And then she looks down. "But the truth isn't in that house. It never was." She pauses. "I want to make the pregnancy her excuse, like the hormones made her unable to think clearly, like it's their fault she didn't believe me. Only, I don't think that's it."

"Believe you about what?"

She smiles then, wryly. "Remember a million years ago when I used to say I wish he'd rape me so my mother would leave him?" The smile melts away. "I may have slightly overestimated my mother."

Blood pounds in my eyes. I think I'm going to be sick. "Oh my God."

She closes her eyes, and then words tumble out in a rush. "He came into my room to 'talk' before Christmas. I thought he was going to give me crap for staying out so late all the time, for worrying my mother." I feel my stomach in my throat. I am outside of my body now. "He sat down on my bed. He leaned in so close I could smell him. His breath was disgusting, like he drank all the whisky in the world and threw up from it, and then drank it down again. I could see the pores in his nose, tiny hairs growing out of each of them, that's how close he was. He started saying that he felt bad that the two of us had never really gotten close, but that now with the new baby coming, we were going to be a real family. The craziest part is that at first I actually . . ." She clenches her jaw. "At first I thought he was being kind of weirdly *nice*. Even though his breath was making me sick and I didn't want him on my bed, I thought maybe he was coming to try to sort out stuff between us, maybe, suddenly somehow for the first time ever. I don't even know. But then I started getting a weird feeling in my stomach, like something bad was going to happen. And turns out I was right. . . ."

"No." I hear the word come out of my mouth in a whisper, a little puff of air that does nothing, means nothing. I am as useful here as a puff of air, that's how little I can help her now.

"Before I even knew what was happening, he was on top of me. He was so heavy. I tried to push him off and I couldn't. I couldn't breathe. I could feel his dick, J." She inhales deeply. Steadies herself. "It was pressing into the side of my leg through his pants. He was breathing heavy in my face, whispering something." She closes her eyes as she talks, her hands clenched into fists. "He was so heavy, and he started unbuttoning his shirt and pulled my sleep shirt half up. He kept saying, *I just want to feel your skin, that's it, that's all.* And I was trying and trying to push him off, that fat piece of shit . . ." Her face is red. I reach out and grab her hand. She holds mine, squeezes it so tight.

"But I got away. I got a mouth full of his chest and I bit down *hard*. I can still remember how it tasted, salty like meat. And how it felt, like biting into leather." She shakes her head. "He *groaned* when I bit him, Junie. He groaned like he liked it. But I didn't let go, I held on like a pit bull. *I bit until I tasted fucking blood.*" She is staring straight at me, her eyes shining. "And that's when he backed off. He stood up and staggered backward and looked at me, and then, I will never forget this for the rest of my damn life, he *smiled* like he was *flirting* with me, like he thought he was being *charming*. 'You like it rough?' he said. 'Me too. More next time.' *Next time* is what he said. And then he left my room."

I've lost the ability to form sentences, to form speech. There's something hot in my belly, boiling up, about to spill over.

"At first it didn't even seem real. I was numb, felt nothing at all, but I looked down at my hand and my hand was shaking."

"Where was your mom?" I finally say. My voice is a whisper.

"She was sleeping. Ever since she got pregnant, she sleeps all the time. I didn't want to wake her up—I didn't think she'd believe me anyway. I don't know. I didn't know what to do . . . so I got up and I left. I drove and drove alone all night. I slept in my car."

"D, no," I say. I want to go back in time and find her, take her out of her car and bring her somewhere safe, keep her with me. To go into her house and fucking kill William.

"I came back in the morning . . . I didn't know what I was going to say or what I was going to do. I thought about leaving forever, but I didn't have money and I wasn't sure where I was going to get any. I thought maybe I'd talk to my mom, so I went back, and get this, the whole house smelled like omelets. Because, hell, you really do learn something new every day, J. And that day I learned that the would-be-rapist shitbag can fluff the fuck out of some eggs." Delia looks at me and shakes her head. "My mom was sitting at the table, all *proud* like she'd won the goddamn lottery, because her asshole husband, who literally never once made breakfast for her in the entire time we've lived together, had thrown some eggs in a pan. She's grinning all big and crazy when I come into the house. 'Look, honey, William is making breakfast, isn't that nice?' Her tone is the most pathetic thing you've ever heard. It's like this is the best thing that has happened to her in her entire fucking life. 'You love omelets,' she says, and she sounds all hopeful. Like I'm some little kid and she's going to remind me what I love and then we're all going to sit down to a family breakfast. I'd been planning to come in right then and tell her what her shit-bag husband tried to do to me, but when I saw her sitting there, I couldn't bring myself to do it. I thought, 'Okay, let her eat and have this one moment of thinking everything is okay before I tell her that nothing is.'" Delia looks up at me. "It's weird to know you are about to tell someone something that's going to change everything. I hated it, having that kind of power. I can feel William watching me. He is completely silent, but I can feel his eyes, and I feel like they're touching me, and I remember the feeling of his dick pressing through his pants and it makes me want to vomit. I don't know how my mom sat through that breakfast so oblivious, as though it was any regular day." She breathes deeply. I have no idea how to process this, how I or anyone ever could.

Delia looks down. For a long time she is silent, and when

she looks back up at me there are tears in her eyes. "After breakfast William went upstairs. I thought for a second what an idiot he was for leaving me alone with her. So I sat down with my mom and I told her everything that had happened the night before. And when I was done, there was this moment where I actually thought she believed me. I thought I saw it in her eyes that she believed me. And maybe she did at first. I mean, she's my mother . . ." Delia's voice cracks, her eyes about to overflow. "She's supposed to believe me, right? But either she didn't, or she wouldn't let herself. Her face changed, and she looked confused and then mad and then confused again and said, 'Delia, why would you *liiiie* like that?'" Delia stretches out the word, making her voice breathy and high. "She said he'd told her what I'd *really* been up to, about the drugs, she said. He told her I was on drugs and had been acting crazy and he tried to keep me from leaving the night before, from driving. She said I couldn't act that way anymore, or they were going to have to think seriously about *sending me away*. That's what she said, like they were going to ship me off to some juvie boot camp." Delia shakes her head slowly. "I went upstairs after that. William was in the hallway. He *smiled* and told me he heard I was making up stories. And I better not do it again, or I wouldn't like what would happen, and then he paused and looked at me and said, 'Actually, maybe you will.' And that was it—I knew then that I had to get out."

I am staring at her as it all sinks in. I am in a fog, in shock maybe. I don't know what to say, how to feel now, anything. I pull her toward me and she grabs on. I feel the warmth of her through her thin shirt. She rests her cheek on my shoulder. "Oh my God," I say. "I am so, I am . . . I wish . . ." I stop. I want to tell her that I wish that that night, instead of driving alone in the dark, she'd called me. I want to tell her that when she didn't know where else to go I would have been there, I would have come and gotten her and taken her away. But it feels so beside the point, so selfish somehow to even mention this.

Only, when we pull apart and I look up at her and our eyes meet, I realize she is reading my mind. "I thought about calling you," she says. "That was the very first thing that I thought to do, but then I wasn't sure if . . ." She stops.

She doesn't even need to finish—her words hit me like a fist in the gut. "I'm so sorry," I say. I am useless. I am nothing. "What about the police?"

Delia shakes her head. "Where's the evidence? And who do you think they'd believe? The well-respected surgeon or his messed-up stepdaughter? Later he said if I told anyone, he'd set me up, get me arrested for drugs somehow. He could arrange it, I know he could. He knows everyone in this town."

"Wasn't there anyone who could help you? What about your other friends or Jeremiah or . . ." I am desperate now, trying to change the unchangeable past. She had no one. She should have had me.

Delia shakes her head again. "Jeremiah was sweet and stupid. And my friends were . . . you saw the kind of people they are. They thought I was fun to party with. They liked how much I could drink and that I was fun and crazy. They didn't care about me." She looks at me. "You're the only one who ever really did."

And I am ashamed, so ashamed. At what I've done. At how I left her.

"What about them?" I say. I motion to the next room, where I can hear the quiet chatter of voices.

"Well, them too now."

"Do they know?"

"Of course. They're how I'm here."

"They helped you do it . . ."

"They arranged everything."

"Have they done this before?"

She is silent. She shrugs, but she's smiling ever so slightly. I know what this means: they have.

I close my eyes. I want to tell her how sorry I am, how horrified I am, how I can't believe all of this was happening while I was there, not knowing, at Ryan's house watching him eat expensive burritos. I want to tell her how I will never forgive myself for not being there when I should have been. But the words are stuck against the lump in my throat. And instead what I say is this: "I can't believe he'll get away with this now."

“Oh, don’t worry,” Delia says. And I recognize something in her expression then, and I feel a lifting inside me. The dark scared space is filling up with light. I’ve seen Delia make this face a million times, when life seemed bleak and gray. This is the expression she makes when she has a plan. “He won’t.”

Chapter 30

Delia

On the screen in front of us Dastorio has reached the castle kingdom and is about to enchant the princess with the acid-laced lollipop. This movie is basically as stupid as it sounds, but I've watched it twice a day, every day since I died. I don't know why. We have laptops, the Internet. It is weird to engage with the real world now, with the world outside the one I've created. Maybe I don't want to. And no one can make me.

Now I'm not paying attention to the movie anyway. Bits of information from this room are flinging themselves toward me—smells, sights, sounds: there's the TV flashing, there's the whoosh of the wind blowing through the trees outside, snapping branches, the smell of bodies, someone warm and familiar who wasn't here before but now is.

We are on the couch, sitting in a row. Ashling is running

her fingertips up the inside of my arm from my wrist to my elbow. We're playing that game you play as kids when you close your eyes and try to stop the other person as close to your elbow crease as you can. "Stop," I whisper, when she's right there on the thin skin. She presses down against my vein, against my blood, her nails digging in. And then, like usual, she doesn't stop. Because not stopping, that's the game too.

I remember all those games, no point except you want human contact feverishly, desperately. You're craving it without even knowing what you're craving. You haven't been fucked yet, you don't know the taste of it, you just want someone, anyone, to touch you. It's so hard to ask for what you need. It is so goddamn embarrassing to need the things we do. But with Ashling it has been so easy. She offers, offers, offers, and I take, take, take. There is no end to how much she'll give and how much I can consume. If I wanted to bite pieces of her, chew them, swallow them down, she'd let me.

Sometimes in bed, stroking her skin, I'm filled with this ferocious feeling that I don't understand. Like anger, but not quite, more hungry than hot. I want to mark her, sink my teeth into her soft perfect skin and ruin it. I've almost done it before in the flesh at the side of her waist. I managed to stop myself before I drew blood, but just barely.

She liked it. She wants me to be a wild animal, to tear her apart. She doesn't know how easy it would be for me to do that. She tried to hold me afterward, wrapped her thin arms around me and pulled me to her chest. I think she thought that was about what happened with my stepfather. But I know she's wrong about that.

Now, on the couch, pretending to care about the movie, I look over at Ashling and she smiles, this gooey, dreamy look in her eyes. I can feel June watching us. I wonder: Does she know how little this stunning creature next to me matters? How little anything else does?

Evan turns toward June. "Have you seen any of his other films?" He's pointing to the screen. June shakes her head. "They're good," he says. "You might like them." I can hear the need in his voice. He's getting a crush on her. It's pathetic but sweet. I feel a flicker of jealousy, but it's only instinct.

I lean back and unfocus my eyes, let time pass.

The movie is almost over. June is uncomfortable—I can feel her discomfort inside my own body. She wonders what happens now, what happens next, who these people are. Questions float inside her sweet head. I need her not to be scared. To believe that this is okay. I need to be secure for her, even though I am terrified.

Whatever looks sturdy is actually made of the thinnest of glass. Whatever feels solid could, at any moment, crackle, crackle, fall down to nothing. It's so hard to live believing that, but it's *true*. It's so much better to lie to yourself, but I can't. I *know* how quickly things can go away, how hard it can be to make them come back. You have to clench your jaw so tight you can barely stand it, grind sand between gritted teeth in a fire-hot mouth, then wait till it melts, spit out glass. Build it all again.

Fucking breathe, Delia.

I have to remember that I am in control. I have to stop being afraid. I am going to have to ask her for something soon. That's the next step. But I can't bring this up now, not yet.

The movie ends. Sebastian stands up and gets a box of cookies, which is what he always does. He eats an entire box a day, cramming them down his throat because he has a fierce vacuum of empty space inside of him, like all of us, I guess. Constantly hungry. What does he really want? He feeds himself sugar but instead of growing out, he is growing straight up toward the sky, even though he's tall as a goddamn building already and is eighteen now, at least that's what his ID says. But all of our IDs say different things, and none of them are true. Soon I will have one of my own. For now I have nothing. I am no one. I like this.

Evan makes mugs of hot sweet mint tea, crushing up leaves with spoonful after spoonful of honey. What I want is a drink, the sharp twist of tequila against my tongue, burning its way down. I'm not going to have a drink now. Not now and not in front of her. Ashling and I will have one later, alone in our room. She got this bottle of fancy gin. She dumps it down my throat, a shot at a time. I don't like expensive alcohol. It's too smooth. It's better when it hurts a little. "Next time, get the shit stuff," I told her. And she looked insulted. But it's not like she paid for it.

She took it from behind the bar when we went in somewhere once to use the bathroom. Ashling steals things, things she wants and things she doesn't. The silk scarf tied to a woman's purse, the fancy lipstick from inside, which she throws away before ever even trying it on. Cell phones, earrings. That's what she's hungry for—whatever doesn't really belong to her. Maybe why she likes me so much.

For now, only pure and cozy things are happening. And I know June likes that. But her eyes are darting around the way they do when she is nervous, scanning for signs of danger even if she isn't aware of doing it. She's scared so much of the time, she doesn't even know what not being scared feels like. Seb is looking at her. She has no idea, which is funny—she notices everything else with her big round darting bunny eyes. But the one thing she's never aware of is how often people are watching her. She thinks she's invisible, that she slips under the radar, but she doesn't, never has. At least not to anyone worth being noticed by. She never even realized if I wasn't there to point it out. Ashling and Evan are talking about the movie. It's so loud in my head now, in my heart now. I have to close my eyes, slow down everything inside my body and block out the outside to even really hear them.

June is cupping the mug in her hands, calming down. She smiles, watching them. Evan is trying hard to impress her, saying how much he likes the director's other films, the symbolism and his use of color. Ashling is making fun of him for saying "film" instead of "movie," and Evan is pretending to be irritated. "Movie is an antiquated term. Do you know where it even came from? A *movie*, because the characters are *moving*, like as opposed to a *stillie*, which is a photograph, I guess."

And Ashling says, "Oh, is it *antiquated*, Evie? Is *that* what it is?" She pokes him in the side. And he rolls his eyes like she's being dumb. But I know that he loves when Ashling teases him, loves when any girl does, really. We're all starving for what we're starving for. For Evan, that is any attention from any female at all, but especially Ashling. Here's something: Ten months ago, before I knew them, Ashling fucked Evan, just to be nice. Even though she is gay—most definitely gay. But she's slept with worse guys for far worse reasons. Evan was a virgin, black pit depressed, falling down a hole with no bottom. Back then he was a super nerd, too, inside (where he still is one) as well as outside (where he now passes for something else). She did it as a favor, because she felt so incredibly sorry for him and thought it would help. And it did.

Now he says she's like a big sister to him, which is pretty pervy considering how much he obviously still wants to do her. But he only says that to try to pretend he's not also deeply in love with her, even though we all know he is.

June is watching them and smiling, engaging tentatively, like a little bunny hopping out from under the couch. "C'mon, J," Evan is saying. "Whose side are you on, here?"

And June looks back and forth between Ashling and Evan. "Sorry, pal," she says. "Going to have to go with the lady on this one." June grins. I grin too. I know she only talks like this when she's with me.

Seb is silently observing, like he usually does. But he doesn't have that same passive look on his face. His eyes are sliding over her skin, with *interest*. I've never seen him look at someone like this before. I've seen gorgeous, stunningly beautiful specimens of humanity throw themselves at him, both sexes, all sizes, everywhere he goes, and he is unfazed, just does not give a single fuck. Literally. He never fucks anyone. He also never smiles. And he isn't smiling now. But this is the first time I've seen him look at anyone like this.

I think, *Ah-ha.* I think, *There is something here . . .*

And June keeps on not noticing, like always. Only when I told her did she ever understand at all. I was the one who pointed out Ryan in the very first place, watching us as we walked together to meet some guy whose name I can't even remember who was picking us up to bring us who even knows where. Ryan was staring at us, at her, eyes following her every move. I reached out then, smacked her on the ass. "What was that for?" I cocked my head to the side where Ryan was staring still, mouth open then. "That's what he wants to do," I told her. I thought it would be a joke between the two of us—of course she wouldn't like him. He was no one. A meat mannequin, a human-shaped sculpture made of ground beef. But I heard the breath catch in her throat, which surprised the shit out of me, actually. "Wait, Ryan Fiske you mean?" She was blushing ever so slightly. I thought about that moment for a long time after, because by that point in our friendship I'd thought I knew her so well that she couldn't surprise me. But people, they always can, no matter who they are. And everything that happened after that, between us, that surprised me too.

Thinking about him now—about his smug potato face, blandly handsome even though he doesn't deserve to be handsome at all, about what I did for the very wrong reasons, how he almost destroyed us—I feel my hands curling into fists, as though each of my hands is a drawstring bag and someone is tugging the string, tugging so tight that my nails press into my palms and it hurts. It is hard to stop. I know what to do now, how to fix this, what has to happen.

"Hey, Junie?" I say. She looks up, smiles. "Come to the kitchen with me." And she stands quickly. How easy it is to slip back into this, the two of us against everyone. I can feel Ashling watching, jealous but trying to hide it.

"More secret chats?" Ashling says, trying to sound casual and joking. And I can feel Seb's eyes on June, I can feel it as though her skin were my own. And for the first time, the first time maybe ever, I don't let on that I notice.

Chapter 31

June

"I'm sorry he turned out to be such a shit," Delia says to me in the kitchen. And when she notices the confused look on my face, she laughs one of those big round laughs that always made me feel so proud of whatever I'd done, even if all I'd done was stand there not understanding something.

"Over it already then, huh?" she says. "Poor, forgettable Meatface."

And then I know she's talking about Ryan, even though she hasn't called him that since before everything happened, before he was anything to me while she was still everything. She called him Meatface and the name felt right somehow at the time, before I knew him and what he was actually like, but it stuck and so that's what we called him when the we of us was the primary thing, miles and miles ahead of the we of him and I.

I want to tell myself I've forgotten about him now, because this all matters so much more than he ever did. And it's true that it does. But also, on some level, I've squished all my feelings about him way, way down. Sometimes being able to ignore things I desperately wish weren't true, at least for a while, is maybe a skill I have . . . if you could indeed call that a skill.

"Good riddance, Meat," I say. I force the words out. I'm trying so hard to sound casual like she does. But now that we're talking about him, I feel a snake uncoiling in my chest, choking my heart. Fuck Ryan.

She leans back, looking at me, and puts a warm hand on either side of my face, so gently. "I should have told you earlier what a shit he was."

I think about the Ryan I believed I knew. I think about our relationship. I worried about it, a lot maybe. I told myself it was my own baggage making me worry. And it was comforting to think that; it meant I didn't have to take my own concerns so seriously. But maybe I should have. "Why didn't you tell me? Why didn't . . . ," I start to say.

Then I stop. I shake my head. I know the answer. I chose him. I didn't deserve to know.

"When I knew I was leaving and it was my last chance, I tried," she says.

I nod.

And I feel both ashamed and grateful. Then I think about Ryan and his handsome face. The way I felt when his arms were around me. I am struck by the sudden jarring realization that everything I thought I had with him, maybe none of it was real at all. I look up at Delia. She is staring at me so intensely, her eyes bright and beautiful.

"He doesn't deserve that," she says. She takes her thumbs and gently pulls up the corners of my mouth. "Don't frown for that meatshit."

But something is still gnawing at me. I feel the words slipping out before I can stop them. "That night when things got . . . weird," I say. "At his house, with that game and all that . . ." I shake my head. After everything that happened, how can I even ask this? It all feels like a thousand years ago, like a story about other people who are not us. "Sorry," I say. "Forget it."

"No, it's okay," Delia says. "You want to know what happened when you left the room."

I feel myself nodding. I've thought about it so many times, pictured it so many times, when I didn't want to. Sometimes when I missed her, sometimes when I missed him. I thought about it because I couldn't *not* think about it. I assumed I wouldn't ever know the truth.

There's something in Delia's eyes that I've never seen before. "This is it," she says. "The whole thing." She looks—I'm not even sure what—maybe she looks scared. Her hands are on my cheeks again. I think I can feel her pulse, or maybe that is my own. Her pupils are enormous in the dim kitchen light. And then she is leaning forward, slowly toward me. She is leaning forward to tell me what happened, what Ryan did, what she did back.

And then, Delia's lips are on mine.

This has never happened before. Or has it happened a million times, a billion times, over and over since we met. But no, this is the first. And she holds me there, our lips together, hers so warm and so, so soft. Our hearts are pounding and I can't tell whose is whose, her palms on my face, her lips on mine, her heart inside my chest.

"I was Ryan there," she says, her voice low. "And you were me." And then she leans back. "So you see"—her eyes are still locked on mine—"no big deal." I can't speak, can't move. She smirks then, just slightly. And then her smirk spreads into a smile. She leans forward again and gives me a peck on the cheek. Whispers, "Really no big deal, Junie."

Then she turns and slowly walks back into the living room. And I stand there, legs shaking, heart hammering, and it is a few full minutes before I can breathe, before I can move at all.

Chapter 32

Delia

Nerve endings firing into brain holes firing into space into time. Here. Here. Here. Fire. Fire. Fire. Fire. Fire. I take out my list, add her name to the end, tear it into a thousand pieces. Sometimes I even surprise myself.

Chapter 33

June

For a half second I am nothing, no one, just a hot open mouth and fierce thirst. I am awake, face pressed against a thick pillow.

Everything comes rushing back—who I am and where I am, how I got here. *Who I am here with:* Delia, who was mine and then not and then dead and now alive, alive, alive. And I am on the couch in this place she brought me to. Where so much has happened, things I don't know even how to think about.

I sit up.

I can see into the kitchen from my spot on the couch, lit by a small red lamp. I walk toward it. The house is silent. I search through the cabinets until I find a glass, turn on the faucet, and drink cold water, cup after cup of it until I am no longer thirsty. And now I'm fully awake.

And suddenly starving again, even though I'm not sure how

that's possible. Last night, everything happened. And nothing did. I had so many questions but didn't feel like I could ask any of them.

So we watched movies like it was normal, and we hung out. *Delia and I talked in the kitchen.* And *that* I could not, cannot even begin to process.

Later the friendly guy, Evan, made a giant pot of spaghetti. And I realized again how hungry I was.

So I sat with them at this big thick wood table. I ate like a ravenous beast. I couldn't help it. At one point I looked up and the tall guy, whose name is Sebastian, was staring at me, this blank look on his face, because what I've learned is that his face is pretty much *always* blank. He never smiles at all. And I wondered what was under that nonsmile and felt embarrassed.

Around nine I texted my mom and told her I was going to stay over at Ryan's house, since his is the only place I could possibly imagine telling her I'd be. Lying about staying at a guy's house so I could be with my best friend . . . the irony wasn't lost on me there. Nor about the fact that Delia was the one who told me that I would have to go to school in the morning. "People will notice if you go missing," she said. "They'll start to wonder, they'll look for you . . ."

I said surely not after only a day. It's not like my mom would even care.

But Delia shook her head. "It's not just that. You need to dig up the seeds you planted and kill the roots . . ." She knew that I'd been trying to figure out what happened to her, who might have done something to her. Ashling had been everywhere I'd been and some places I hadn't. "People are suspicious now," Delia said. "But they can't be."

So I promised I would fix it.

And now, here I am, standing in the kitchen in the middle of the night, hungry and awake. I go to the refrigerator, start to open it, then freeze because on the counter next to it is that bag they picked up from Tig's.

I think of all the questions I didn't ask, couldn't ask.

Who are these people? What are they doing here? Where does their money come from? When they were all awake with me, when Delia was awake, it was easier to squish all the questions down. But now that I am alone, the blinding joy has faded into the background; I *need* answers.

And maybe this bag contains some. . . . I find myself reaching out, grasping it, lifting it. I know I should stop—from now on anything I find out about her should be because she wants me to know it, because she tells me herself—but I don't stop. The bag is light; the paper crinkles like dry leaves as I unroll it. I peer inside at a pile of tiny plastic bags, dozens and dozens of them, pink cupcakes stamped on the front, yellowish crystals inside. My heart speeds up.

I know what this is.

I remember, near the end when our friendship was changing,

Delia would do this at parties sometimes, chop it up and snort it through two inches of drinking straw, stay awake for hours, wired, clenching her jaw. "It's not even *fun*," she'd say. Later she'd be exhausted, hard edged, miserable. So why do they have this now? And why so much of it?

I stand there, heart pounding, unsure what to do, what to think.

And that's when I hear it—a low guttural sound, like the cry of an animal. At first I wonder if I've imagined it, so strange and soft. But a second later, there it is again—not animal, definitely human. I put the paper bag back where I found it, start walking down the hall toward the source of that sound. And I swear, at first, all I'm thinking is that someone might be hurt, someone might need my help.

It is only when I'm right in front of the bedrooms that I realize what I'm actually hearing. Not pain. Not just pain anyway. And not one person, but two—*Ashling and Delia.*

I feel a stab of loneliness opening up a big sucking hole in the center of my chest. There is a door and I am outside of it. I am alone.

I hear whispering—I can't make out the words.

Then the animal sounds come back, louder now. I feel my face growing hot. I try to move. I can't. I am frozen, melting, then on fire. I close my eyes, feel the blood in my cheeks, and everywhere else.

For a moment it is as though I'm in that room with them. I see mouths together, skin sliding skin, Ashling's hair held in a clenched fist, Delia's darting tongue.

I press my fingers to my lips. Close my eyes. Remember what it felt like.

Stop.

There is silence. The burst of a giggle I don't recognize. Then one that I do. Hard and fast, loud. *Pop-pop-pop*. Wild, reckless, scattering like shrapnel. Voices, muffled. Then the sound of footsteps coming toward the door. The door I am standing right in front of.

I race back down the hall, fling myself onto the couch, and pull the covers around me. Turn. Twist. Close my eyes.

And then Delia comes into the room. I know the soft padding of her bare feet on the floor, like the beating of my heart, which I hope she can't hear.

I try to stay perfectly still. A cabinet opens, there's the clink of a glass, the faucet turning on. I hear gulping, imagine the water sliding down her throat. I hear the refrigerator door opening and shutting. Then footsteps again, getting closer. She is standing right over me. For a moment there is silence. My eyelids twitch.

Delia leans in, her breath smells sharp, like gin, maybe. "You could have just asked," she says, so gently. My face is on fire again. Asked what? To listen in on her and Ashling? She knows I was standing there. And I have no idea how to explain it, how to begin. "And stop fake sleeping." She pokes me in the ribs. I open my eyes. Her nose is inches from my own.

"Whatever you think this is for," she says, "you're wrong."

And I realize that I have no idea what she's talking about. Until I look down and see what she's holding—the bag from Tig's.

"If you're going to snoop, at least fold the bag the same way, Junie."

"I'm sorry," I start to say. "I shouldn't . . ."

She reaches out and puts a finger to my lips. *Shhh.* "People say that everyone gets what they deserve. But the thing is, that isn't *true*. The world isn't fair"—she is so close now—"unless you make it. You need to trust me. I think after everything, I've earned at least that. We're going to right the wrong things. *That's* why we have this. And you can help." She pauses and leans back, looking at me. *"You in, J?"*

I have so many questions. But as they pop into my brain one by one, I realize, one by one, that none of them are important.

Outside is alone, alone, alone, floating in space with nothing to hold on to.

In is here in this house.

You in, J?

Outside is dark and nothing is real. Outside doesn't even exist.

And in is with Delia.

Delia, who is staring at my face, her bottom lip bit. I think she's holding her breath.

You in, J?

She asks as if it's even a choice.

I feel my head moving almost beyond my control. Up. Down. Up. Down. Whatever comes, whatever happens, after this moment, whatever it is.

I'm in.

Chapter 34

Delia

Dear fucking Lord is the sun beautiful this morning, these bright hot beams of it coming through the sheer curtains here. It's been waking me up every day since I arrived; it shines in at that weird winter slant, directly into my eyes. I felt angry at it, at first, like that sunny beast was trying to fuck me right in the face. Now I am solar powered, charged up by the light. *Go go go go go.*

I spring out of bed. I open the window. The air is fresh and clear. "Get up," I whisper into Ashling's ear. "Get up, get up, get up." And then, even though I know she is still asleep and hates waking up alone, I race out into the hall.

June is sitting at the kitchen counter, drinking a cup of juice. She hasn't seen me yet. I stand there and watch her.

She seems nervous, and I know it's because of what she has

to do when she gets to school. It's not even because of later, because I haven't explained later to her yet. No, for now there is just school. There is doing what I told her she needs to do to keep all of us, all of this, safe.

She finishes the juice, looks around. Her eyes meet mine and she smiles. And I swear it's like the whole goddamn sun is beaming right out of it.

I remember what it was like, before, when getting through each day was such an effort, a struggle, a slog. Now they just fucking fly.

Chapter 35

June

Last night feels like a thousand years ago, like something I made up, a dream I had. And now, walking into school this morning, there's a knot in my stomach I cannot even begin to untangle. I've been here for ten minutes and am ready to leave already, to go back home. *Home* means back to Delia now. More than anything I do not want to mess this up.

I reach down and touch the letter in my pocket. It's there, safe and snug, folded and unfolded and refolded to look like I've read it a million times, which I would have if it were real.

The entire world is different now that I know. And as scared as I am, I also have to remind myself not to smile. The scent of Delia's death is still in the air, floating through the hallway, dampening everything. I am so far removed from all of this now. She's dead, but she's alive. And I'm here, but I'm not here too.

No one here matters. I see Laya, two juniors I recognize, Hanny, another friend of Ryan's from the party. One after another, left right left right left right. I look at them and I think, *None of you know.* I look at them and I think, *I do not give one single fuck about any of you.* And then I smile, because I realize that is a Delia thought, channeled right into my brain.

I forgot how this happened, how easy it was to think like her when I was around her. How much fun it was. Is.

I am on a mission now, though, special from Delia. "You need to undo this, Junie," she told me. And then she explained how.

I walk into homeroom. Krista is there waiting for me, her big orange purse on the table. I sit down next to her and try to control my face. I turn slowly.

Krista narrows her eyes and looks at me. "You wore that yesterday," she says. It's true, same jeans, gray T-shirt, green sweater. And I slept in them too. "And you look like shit."

I shrug.

"You're here, though, that's good."

"I got a letter in the mail," I say. "From Delia, written the day she died." I don't need to tell Krista anything. She's so unimportant, but I'm practicing.

"No shit," says Krista. "What does it say?" And she's not even trying to hide the excitement in her voice.

"That she is sorry, that she loves me."

"A suicide note?" asks Krista.

I nod.

"Damn," she says. She shakes her head. "I guess that's it, then." She shrugs. "Do you want to come over later? I mean, to Rader's with me? I promise I won't try to set you up with anyone this time."

I watch Krista run her tongue over her weird yellow teeth, over her too big gums, and it occurs to me that I don't like her. Not even a little. I think of Rader's apartment, I think of the smoke and that sad party. I think about how, if I hadn't found Delia alive, I'd probably say yes to this. I'd say yes to this invite because I'd have no other choice.

"No thanks," I say.

"No thanks?" Krista looks at me. "Why, do you have other plans or something?"

I stand up. Homeroom isn't over yet, but it doesn't matter. I walk toward the door, and when I hear Krista calling my name, I don't bother turning back.

Ryan is the first one out when the homeroom bell rings. He has a fat lip and a black eye, but even busted up, he still looks handsome. And it annoys me that I notice this. When he sees me, he smiles almost shyly. And the idiot actually holds out his arms, like I might let him wrap me up in them. Like I might ever let him touch me again.

"I'm so glad to see you," he says.

A sophomore girl walks by with her friend; they whisper to each other and look back at us. Standing there with him, I feel less strong than before. I want to get this over with.

"She definitely did it herself," I say. "I was wrong."

I hold out the folded letter. And he just looks at it. "It's safe. This one doesn't even mention you." He flinches. He deserves it.

I see his eyes moving across the page quickly. "This is so insane . . . all of this. I mean. I can't . . ."

"Don't say anything. I wouldn't believe you anyway." And I feel the slightest flicker of guilt. Guilt because I know she's still alive—I have her back. And he doesn't, and never will.

"But Jeremiah's hand," Ryan says. "I think it's burned. He was acting so insane and . . . he beat the crap out of me. I think we should . . . I mean, I don't know."

I try to keep my face calm and still.

"Leave him alone." My voice is firm. I am in charge. "Jeremiah has been through hell. You tried to fuck his girlfriend. You've already done enough."

Ryan looks down at the note again. I feel adrenaline buzzing hot and fast through my veins now. "Okay," he says. He is is quiet, defeated. He will do what I tell him.

Fuck guilt, *I like this.*

Ryan twists his lips. "Well, that's that, then, I guess." He hesitates, then hands the letter back to me. But he won't meet my gaze. And it only takes me a split second to realize why: there are tears in his eyes. And I then understand something—he actually cared about her. Maybe even more than he'd admit to himself. Maybe even *loved* her. It seems so obvious now.

"Yup, that's it," I say.

"I . . . ," he starts. Good ol' Meatface.

I shake my head.

"Good-bye," I say.

"Junie . . . Wait . . ." He is begging. I look back at his face one last time.

And as I walk away, it occurs to me that those tears in his eyes? I think some of them are for me.

It takes me almost the full rest of the day to find Jeremiah. I've trained my eyes to search for his giant sloping back, his big square head. I spot him at the end of the hallway, moving slowly. This part is going to be the hardest of all.

"Jeremiah!" I call out.

He looks so, so tired.

"How are you doing?" I say. I feel a pinching in my heart. He doesn't answer, just shakes his head. It's hard to imagine I ever suspected him of anything other than loving someone for whom he was no match, a girl he could never really have. I see him so clearly now, in that kind of pain that makes the entire world feel unreal. The pain I was in until just yesterday, before it shifted to amazement, to pure joy, to shining possibility. I have a flash of wishing that I could tell him the truth, that I could relieve him the way I've been relieved. But, of course, that's impossible.

I take the letter out of my pocket. I need to get this over

with. "It's a suicide note," I say. "She sent this to me before she died. I just got it."

I hold it out. He takes the paper with his right hand, keeps the burned one in his pocket. I can't watch his face as he reads.

When he is done, he folds the letter back up and holds it out to me. I don't even glance at the page. I've already memorized Delia's words, the words Ashling wrote for her. "I do her handwriting better than she does now," Ashling said with a grin. "I can do anyone's."

I'm sorry it needed to be this way, Junie. Please don't feel guilty, there's nothing anyone could have done. I love you and I was lucky to know you, and that is what I'll take with me. Please find Jeremiah and tell him I love him and I know how much he loved me. And please tell him good-bye.

Jeremiah is staring at me. I take the letter. All around us, students are walking to class.

"I was definitely wrong," he says. His voice is thick and scratchy, like he hasn't used it in a while. "About a bunch of things. I've been thinking pretty much nonstop, doing nothing but thinking, thinking, thinking." He is speeding up now. "I can't sleep so I'm up all night thinking. And I'm finally figuring some things out. Like, for example, this: if you were really her friend, you never would have stopped being her friend." He looks me straight in the eye. It's like he's waiting for me to argue, but I don't. He keeps going. "She talked about you like you guys were still so close, you know? For the longest time I couldn't understand why I hadn't met you, why she never wanted to introduce me to this supposed *best friend* of hers. And then I realized it's because you weren't really her friend at all."

I didn't think there was anything he could say that would hurt me, but this does. She forgave me. I have to remember that. And it's for her that I'm doing this.

"I'm trying to be her friend now," I say. I keep my voice soft and low. "And that means honoring her memory and accepting the truth of what happened. And not looking for a mystery where there isn't one."

He looks at me, nodding, For a moment I think we're having an understanding. But then his eyes flash. "So, did you write this letter yourself, or did he help you?" He tips his head to the side.

"What are you talking about?"

"You think I don't know a person can fake another person's handwriting?" Jeremiah shakes his head. "Jesus, June. You're working so hard to cover up for him, huh."

My stomach clenches. "For who?" I say.

"Oh come on. Ryan, obviously."

I feel suddenly sick and groundless.

"I'm not. He didn't do anything." My voice sounds weak. And even though it is the truth, somehow to me now, the words don't sound right.

Jeremiah takes his hand out of his pocket and points to the bandaged burn that he has no idea I know about. "Well, someone did. And I know how much it hurt when they did it."

I should leave it alone, but I can't. "What happened to your hand?"

"I lit it on fire," he says, without a change in tone or expression. "After I found out how she died. I wanted to feel how it felt for her. And guess what? It hurts a whole fucking lot." He smiles, then. He looks unhinged.

And I am suddenly understanding something—all along I was *right* to be wary of him, just not for the reasons I thought. He is riding on the power of his pain, channeling his grief into something dangerous. And it's only getting worse.

Jeremiah is not smiling anymore. "I'm going to find who made her hurt like this. And if it was your boyfriend—sorry, your *ex*"—he pauses—"he'll get what's coming."

And with that, Jeremiah turns and walks away.

"Stop! Ryan didn't *do* anything," I call after him. "Delia did this to herself, it's horrible but it's true . . ." He is far down the hall, he is not looking back. I am dizzy and breathless. Everything is spiraling out of control. And I have absolutely no idea what to do to stop it.

Chapter 36

An hour later school is done, and I am still shaky and sick and no closer to having an answer than I was before. I am walking toward the parking lot, turning it all over and over in my mind. Delia asked me to fix this. She told me what to do, but I couldn't and I didn't. I fucked it up. And I don't know how to unfuck it.

"Aw, c'mon, it can't be that bad?" I look up. Sebastian is standing in the parking lot, ten feet away. "It's not like someone *died* or something, right?" He isn't smiling, because he is never smiling, but his tone is teasing. This is a joke, I guess. "I've been sent to retrieve you." He motions to the car behind him.

"I have a car," I say.

Sebastian shrugs. "She told me to come and get you, so here I am. I don't know why."

She. Delia.

I look at him, at the curves and angles of his face, at his big shoulders, his hands. He doesn't know why he's been sent to retrieve me, but I think that I do. And despite everything, I smile.

Delia is doing what she's always done, starting back when I got my first kiss all those years ago down by the water. She's giving me Sebastian as a present. *I know your type better than you do, J.* I can hear her voice in my head. Only, the thing is, I don't think Sebastian is givable, at least not to me.

"So that's him, then, huh." He is staring at someone behind me now. He motions with his chin.

I turn. Ryan, watching me as he walks by.

"Delia showed you?"

"No, but it's obvious from the way he's looking at us. You give him that black eye?" I can't tell if he's kidding.

I shake my head.

When he sees me looking, Ryan starts to bring his hand up to wave.

I turn away.

"Handsome fellow," Sebastian says, nodding. "The bones in his face are very . . . well arranged."

"HA," I say. "Yeah, I always thought the same thing, hope the punching didn't ruin that."

Sebastian gives me a very serious nod, but then his face splits into an actual smile. It's luminous there for less than a second and then it's gone.

"You think he's jealous?" Sebastian is still watching Ryan, who is still watching us.

I shake my head. "Doubt it."

Sebastian steps forward. "Should we make him?" He has this confusing look on his face, different than I've ever seen before: challenging, mischievous, a little bit mean. And suddenly all at once, so swiftly I don't even realize it's happening until it is, he's wrapping his arm around my waist, pulling me in close. I can feel the muscles of his chest against my chest, the hardness of his stomach against my own. I don't understand what is happening at all. But he is leaning in, as though he's about to kiss me. Closer and closer, our lips are almost touching. *I remember her breath, her lips.* I can feel his breath against my cheek and my heart pounding. "I hate people like that," he says into my mouth. "Liars, people who fuck with people's hearts." He looks over my shoulder, then lets me go. "We should get going."

I step back, stumble, almost fall. But somehow my legs manage to hold me up. "Right," I say. And for a moment I've forgotten everything else—all the rest of life, the crazy things that have happened and may still be happening, how terribly I have fucked things up with Jeremiah and how hard it is going to be to fix it. All I am aware of is the feeling of Sebastian's hands still on me, like where he touched me is on fire now and has acquired a pulse of its own.

"It's unlocked," he says.

In the car now. Sebastian reaches out, clicks the radio on, and flips through channels. Turns it off. He takes a breath. "Sorry your boyfriend turned out to be an ass," he says. "Sucks when someone reveals themselves to be totally different than you thought."

I shrug. "Yeah," I say. "Maybe I didn't actually know him at all, I'm realizing now."

Sebastian pauses. "Did he know you?" There's something in his voice that makes me stop, makes my heart speed up. He isn't asking just to talk, he's really *asking*. Like he actually cares what the answer is.

"No, I guess not. I was . . . never really honest with him about a lot of things." I'm thinking about my life, about my mom, about how I felt about Delia, all of it.

"What did you guys talk about?" Sebastian asks.

I shake my head. "These bunnies, mostly." I turn toward Sebastian, who is raising his eyebrows. "There was this rabbit live stream thing we liked to watch. We made up lives for these two rabbits and . . . at the time it seemed kind of fun, and it *was* fun. But it wasn't in addition to other stuff, it was instead."

"To avoid talking about anything that was really going on?"

"Maybe, I don't know. Whenever real life things came up, family questions and that stuff, I kind of glossed over the hard parts. His life is . . . not like mine is." It's strange to suddenly be talking like this with a stranger.

Sebastian nods like he understands perfectly. "So you chicken-McNuggeted him," he says.

I turn toward him. Bare trees zip by outside the window. "I have no idea what that means."

"I made it up," he says. He is smirking ever so slightly. "It's when you give someone the totally fakey processed version of a thing to make it easier to swallow. So your brother joined a cult and he's not allowed to talk to outsiders? You say, 'My brother and I aren't really in touch right now.' Your drug addict dad didn't pay the rent again and you're getting kicked out of your apartment? 'Yeah, we're thinking of moving somewhere a little more convenient.' A thirty-year-old gang member was trying to rape your twelve-year-old sister and so you killed him and then . . . Well, you get the idea."

I feel myself nodding. I remember what I said to Ryan about my mom. *Yeah, we're not that close, we kind of both do our own thing*. "I told myself I was doing it for both of us, not to sully him with drama or depressing stuff. But maybe it was partly selfish—I got to pretend I was someone different. It felt good to be."

"Getting to pick who you are . . . ," Sebastian says. "It's a lucky thing." He's watching me out of the corner of his eye.

I think about Ryan, about how even when he thought he was being deep, he was mostly saying things he'd heard other places. Everything he knew was from books and movies. His life was too easy. Until Delia "died," we'd never really even had a serious discussion. And the few times I did say anything about my family situation, I got the weird feeling he *liked* that it was dark, felt like it gave him an *edge* to have a girlfriend like that. But he never even knew how to ask the right questions, and I barely told him anything at all.

"Anyway," Sebastian says. He presses his lips together. His tone changes. "So, how did everything go, what you had to do at school, I mean. Talking to everyone." He is speaking slowly, deliberately.

I don't want to answer, but there's no hiding this, it's too important. So I tell him about Jeremiah, his accusation, the crazy look in his eyes, all of it.

"And I don't think he's going to stop," I say. "He's going to keep digging, keep poking around." Everything I've been trying to forget is back.

I turn toward him. Sebastian's face registers no emotion at all. "Don't worry," he says. His voice is calm and even. "There are always . . . glitches."

Always. "You've done this before." My fear has made me brave. "How many times?"

Sebastian takes a breath, then pauses like he's not sure if he's going to speak or not. Opens his mouth. Closes it. Opens it again. "Three."

And I understand what I think he's telling me—Delia isn't the only one of them who died and came back. One for Ashling, one for Evan, one for himself. Three.

"All of you . . . ," I start. They had lives before this one. They had other lives and they left them behind.

"Stop," Sebastian says. And then, more quietly, almost to himself. "It isn't safe."

"I would never tell anyone," I say. "I promise."

But Sebastian just shakes his head. I lean back and watch the trees out the window, head swirling with questions I can't ask. A few minutes later we pull up to the house.

Chapter 37

Delia

Right away I know something is wrong. Even before I can see her, I feel it in my gut, that hot sick canary-in-a-coal-mine feeling deep down where I carry that blackness. I'm watching from the window as they pull up. When she gets out, she moves fast and shaky, like a terrified little animal. At first I think it has to do with Sebastian, tall and lean with his hands in his pockets. I think, *Boy, if you hurt her, I will chop you down like a goddamn tree.* But when she gets close enough, I can smell it, the sour fear radiating off her sweet skin. I realize what she is scared of is *me.*

This makes me sick.

She comes inside, says she needs to tell me something bad, bites her lip, covers her quivering little mouth. And then a story about Jeremiah comes tumbling out. "I messed up," she says. "I couldn't convince him. I am so sorry. I don't know what he'll do now."

And then I just want to laugh. Laugh at Jeremiah, his big dumb face. He is a fucking kitten in a bulldog body. He was nothing but a warm thing to hold on to for a while in the winter. A toy. Hearing about the burned hand, the passionate vow to *right* the *wrongs* that have been *done to me.* I almost feel something for him, *almost*, but not quite. He is benign, sweet, harmless, but *even the harmless can cause harm.* Bumping around dumbly in the dark, knocking things over, making big mistakes. And he upset my Junie.

"It's too bad we can't let him go to town on Ryan, huh?" I say. "Or Ryan go to town on him. Cancel each other out."

June looks at me, her sweet mouth open.

"I'm kidding," I say. And she looks at me like she's not so sure. Smart girl.

Thoughts *pop-pop-pop* fire through my brain. I have a thousand thoughts, a million thoughts, one entire billion thoughts in the time it takes between when I let my face fall and when I open my mouth and say, "Don't worry, Junie. I promise we will figure it out." But *we*? Please, I'm done already. I see that she is starting to relax. She knows I will take care of it. Take care of her. *Good.*

I keep my face calm. But the truth is . . . now I'm the fucking scared one.

Because it's time. I need something. I need it *so badly.* And if she won't do this, nothing that has to happen will. *You in, J?* She said she was. I *know* she is. But I need to be sure.

So I open my mouth and I ask her.

Chapter 38

June

I said yes.

I will always say yes.

From now on, no matter what she asks, YES. That's my answer.

How could it be anything else?

Besides, he deserves it, and worse.

I take a final breath and hold it. Then I push the bell. I hear it ringing through the door, and then it stops. For a moment, there's no sound at all. "William doesn't do surgeries on Tuesdays," Delia said. "And my mom went to stay with her sister for a while. He'll be there. Alone." His car is in the driveway. Maybe he's asleep. Maybe he's not coming.

And then I hear a voice.

"Hold on!"

5 . . . 4 . . . 3 . . . 2 . . . 1 . . . This is happening.

The door swings open, and there's William, big and barrel-chested in a dark red button-down shirt. His lips are thick and dry, colorless. Delia once told me lots of people found him handsome. *His patients are always trying to bang him,* she'd said. *Their cancer probably makes them insane.*

"Yes?" he says. He rubs his watery blue eyes, rubs his big hand over his face. "Can I help you?"

I think about Delia's words, delivered voice shaking. She didn't even sound like herself when she said it. *William deserves to be in jail, but he'll never get in trouble for what he did . . .*

I am filled with hot boiling rage. I want to pick up one of these decorative flower pots on the steps and smash it against his skull over and over until his teeth fall out and his face breaks and there is nothing left of his head but shards of bone.

Instead, what I do is smile, brave and sad.

"Hi, Mr. Grosswell," I say. "I'm June. A friend of Delia's. I mean, I was. I was over here a lot."

I need to calm down. I sound nervous. *I'm the only evidence,* she said. *And I'm gone.*

He blinks, looks confused, as though he has no idea who I am, or who Delia is either. His expression changes slowly, like he is not processing things at the normal rate. "Right," he says. "Yes, of course."

"I'm here because . . ." I pause. "I hadn't really seen Delia in a while, which is why I feel so terrible about everything and . . ." I recited this so many times when we practiced. He needs to believe I don't have any idea what happened, what he tried to do. He needs to believe he's not in any danger. But like Delia, when she thought she was safe inside her own room, inside her own home, *he will be dead fucking wrong.*

"We're putting together a picture montage thing at school," I continue. "And I was wondering . . . if you might have any old photo albums I could look through, maybe borrow some pictures of her for it. Like, from when she was younger."

"I remember you, I think. You used to come over here all the time." He pauses then, closes his eyes. Opens them. "You stopped."

I nod, heart pounding. "We grew apart. I wish I'd been a better friend to her."

Does he look relieved? "You can't blame yourself. She was having a hard time there, at the end especially." He shakes his head. *Because of you.* I think. *Because of you, you piece of shit.* "Please, come in."

I step into the entryway. He shuts the door behind me.

He leads me through the kitchen, into the living room, across the soft beige carpet. "Her mother keeps a couple albums over here." I have to stick my hands in my pockets to keep them from clenching into fists, reaching out, punching him. He opens a big wooden cabinet. Down at the bottom is an album, fake burgundy leather cover peeling. He pulls it out and puts it on the coffee table.

"Her mom has originals of all of them in the computer. I don't think she'd mind you taking some of these. She'd be glad that . . ." He presses his lips together and swallows hard. "She'd be glad to know there's a tribute, I think. For the funeral she wanted it to be just family. And she said she won't be able to stomach having it for a while, so . . ." He stands there for a moment, then he starts toward the door. *No, no, no.* He needs to stay here with me, watch me look at the photos. Give me the chance to do what I came here for.

"Let me know if you need anything," he says. "I'll be . . ." He motions toward the kitchen.

Now what?

I pull the album onto my lap. There's Delia, age seven or eight, with no front teeth, standing on a bike. Delia eating ice cream. Delia holding a turtle. Delia when she was only a few hours old, eyes not even open yet—I've seen this one many times before. "But can you believe how *small* I was?" Delia would always say, sounding so surprised, as though she didn't quite believe this could really be her, as though everyone on earth wasn't once a baby.

I fish out a few photos. Then I walk to the kitchen.

You're our best chance, Junie. He'll remember you. He'll let you in.

There he is at the table, *World Journal of Surgical Oncology* in his left hand, an oversize blue coffee mug in his right.

His Diet Coke. He drinks it by the gallon out of a coffee mug because he thinks that makes it more manly. Put it in there, he won't notice a thing.

I reach into my pocket, slide the tiny bag into my palm. Ashling made me do it dozens of times. She is an expert at making things disappear into her hand and then reappear when she wants them. "You're a magician," I said. "I have practice," she said, then smiled at Delia, so I knew I was missing something.

William looks up. "Did you find what you needed?"

"Um . . . there are some pretty good ones in there," I say. I hold out the few I've chosen.

I'm staring at the mug, dark blue enamel with green glaze drips, brown fizzy liquid and melting ice cubes inside. Five seconds, that's all I need. Four if I'm quick.

"Could I have some water, please?"

"Yes, of course, sorry. Rude of me not to offer."

He stands up and goes to get me a glass. Now is my chance. My heart is on fire.

I walk toward the table, pretend to be interested in his magazine. My hand is over the mug, the bag in my palm. But I'm sweating, so scared, and suddenly I feel the tiny bag drop and land in his drink, cupcake side up.

Shit.

"Ice?" William is in front of the freezer, back to me.

My hand is shaking. "Yes, please." My voice is shaking too.

He's going to notice. He's going to turn and see what I'm doing. And then what?

William puts a couple of cubes into a glass. I reach into the mug, pinch the tiny bag, and shove it back into my pocket. Ice clanks. William is coming back with my water. There are Diet Coke drops on the table. I mop them with the edge of my sleeve.

He is next to me now. I feel my face turning red. He is staring at me, icy glass gripped in one fat hand.

Oh God, he saw. I should turn. I should run.

"You know," he says slowly. "I think there might be some older albums in the basement. Would you like to see those, too?"

Safe. For now.

I remember what Delia once told me, about how he wouldn't let her mother put most of their old stuff out around the house. "That was your old life," Delia said she'd overheard him telling her. "You shouldn't be thinking about it anymore." Delia said the worst part was that her mother didn't protest, didn't even fight back. She just agreed.

He turns and gives me a smile, friendly and warm. My stomach turns.

"Let's go have a look." He picks up his mug and takes a gulp.

And suddenly I desperately do not want to go down those stairs with him into that basement. What he did to Delia, he could try with me. Are my teeth as sharp as hers? My hands as quick? But it doesn't matter. Because if I don't go, he'll get away with what he did to her. And I want that even less.

"Good idea," I say.

He opens the door and holds out an arm. "After you." There's no room. When I squeeze past him, our chests brush. At the bottom he flips on a light. There aren't any windows down here. There are cheap bookshelves lining the walls, a small leather couch, a big new-looking TV, and a pile of cardboard boxes in the corner. It smells like new carpet and earth.

"I think the albums are in one of those boxes, at the back," he says. "Feel free to poke around." He waves his hand like *go on, then*. So I lean down, aware of his eyes on my ass. I feel sick. I need to do this, to get this over with. But how?

I grab a box. It's heavy, not too heavy for me to lift, but . . . I have an idea. I tug at it, let out a little *mmmmph*. I stop, then pretend to try again.

I turn toward him, giving him a sheepish look. "Um. This is embarrassing, but it's so heavy. Could you maybe, um . . ."

"Oh, of course," he says, and gives me a disgustingly indulgent little smile, then holds out his mug. "Would you mind . . ."

Delia promised he'll never guess that I'm to blame for what's to come. "He has more than enough enemies," she told me. All the interns he fired, hospital staff members he pissed off, it could be any of them. But for a moment I almost hope he figures it out. I want him to look back at this moment, remember how he smiled at me, and feel like a fucking fool.

I reach out for his mug. *No, William, I would not mind at all. But you might.*

He lifts the first box. I fish the soda-sticky bag out of my pocket, open it up, and sprinkle the yellowish crystals into his drink. I stick my finger in and swirl it around until they've all dissolved.

Meanwhile William has moved three of the boxes, four of the boxes. He is grunting, sweating a little. "Ah-ha!" he says. He bends down and pulls a box out from the back. ALBUMS is written on the front in green. He turns toward me, face shiny. He is smiling, pleased with himself. Pleased with himself for pushing around a few boxes when his stepdaughter is dead. I want to vomit. I want to punch him in his fucking head. "Found it," William says. He puts the box on the couch. "They're in here."

"Thank you," I say. And I hand him his mug, smiling back.

I open the box and pull out an album. Then watch as he brings the mug to his lips and takes the first sip.

Before we plant Tig's stuff on him, Delia said, *we have to plant it in him . . .*

He motions to the small sofa. "Sit down, if you like." He sips again.

My insides are lighting up, I feel a crazy rush, as though *I'm* the one slurping down a mug full of meth.

He is standing over me, watching me. I try not to smile as he gulp, gulp, gulps the rest of his drink. He puts the empty mug down on the arm of the sofa. Then he walks to another little room off to the side. He flips a switch and a harsh yellow bulb lights up a new-looking white refrigerator. He pulls out two brown glass bottles. Then he comes back to the couch, sits down, and holds one out for me.

"Technically I'm not supposed to even *drink* beer because of the diabetes. But, I guess, neither are you," he says. "Right?" And then, "I won't tell if you won't."

There's that smile again. I want to reach out and take the bottle and break it across his nose. I imagine the thunk, the crack, the blood pooling over his thick dry lips.

"Thanks," I say. And his fingers brush mine when he hands it to me.

The album is heavy on my lap. The beer is cold in my hand. I can smell his breath. He's close to me now. I wonder how long I need to sit here. I stare at a picture of Delia, age five or six. Her hair is dark and curly, her smile wide, both arms thrown up in the air like "ta-da!"

William is looking over my shoulder. "God, you see a picture like that . . . It's so awful to think how the story ends." He sounds so genuinely sad, so very heartbroken that for a second I could almost pretend that he was a real human being with real feelings. "You have to wonder, what the hell happened?"

And I think, *You know exactly what happened, shitbag.*

"We were never very close. I think she kind of resented me for being with her mother, for not being her father . . ."

For trying to fucking rape her.

"We didn't agree on a lot of things, I guess. But I always felt she was like a daughter to me, even if she didn't feel the same way. She was family . . ."

I don't know who he's trying to convince, me or himself, but I can't listen to this. And I'm struck, suddenly, by a memory, something I'd long since forgotten: It was the middle of eighth grade, and I was sleeping at Delia's house. I went to get a glass of water in the middle of the night, and William was in the kitchen. I was only wearing a nightshirt, one of Delia's—bright red with black stars. My legs were bare, and even though it was longer than the dresses lots of girls wore to school, I suddenly felt very naked. It was the first time we'd been alone in a room together. I remember him smiling at me, saying something like, "Fancy meeting you here . . ." and I remember how I'd awkwardly laughed.

"I'm just getting water," I'd said, self-conscious.

And he'd shrugged, and then, for some reason, winked. And I thought, even then, even at that moment, how I was probably supposed to think he was nice, that he was a cooler stepdad than Delia gave him credit for. But there was something in the pit of my stomach, a hard little stone.

Their glasses were all up on high shelves, and I felt her nightshirt riding up as I reached for one. I started to blush, tried to pull it down over my butt. And then I went to the sink and turned on the faucet. My skin was tingling. When I turned around, he was just leaning against the counter, staring right at me, hands in his pockets. I'd been planning on getting a snack, too, but suddenly I wasn't hungry anymore. I just wanted to get out of there. Like I want to get out of here now.

"I think I have enough photos," I say. And I stand up. I blink as though blinking back tears.

"You don't want any of those?" he says.

"No," I say quickly. "I have plenty already, from upstairs, I think."

"I can show you some more of her things," he says. "We're getting rid of a bunch of her old stuff, clothes and whatnot. Her mother wanted me to deal with it, thought going through it would be too hard. It's all in the garage, if maybe you want to take some mementos, or . . ."

He sounds desperate. He doesn't want me to go. His wife is away, his stepdaughter is *dead.* And the sick fuck wants me to stay here with him, reminiscing, having a beer.

"No," I say. "Thank you. I'm going to . . ." I point toward the stairs. I can barely look at him. "I'll let myself out."

"It was good of you to come by." His voice sounds muffled and strange. Almost like he's going to cry, but I'm not close enough to see.

I walk slowly until I get to the top of the stairs. I turn back, and the album is on his lap now. He's staring down, and I swear to God, he is stroking one of the pictures.

I put the bottle on the table and then I'm out of that house. Back in the cool clean air, I breathe deeply, so glad to be away from him.

I imagine William still in the basement with all those photographs. Doing who knows what with them now as the drugs spread through his system.

He deserves to be in jail for what he did to Delia. Soon, maybe he will be.

Chapter 39

Delia

I'm pacing by the door, buzzing white-hot. I bounce on my toes, kick my legs, run in place. I am burning up. "Sit down with me, baby," Ashling says.

She comes up behind me, puts her hands on my shoulders, and tries to rub them. I don't mean to *ugh* out loud, but I do when I shrug her hands away. Ashling gets needy when she's jealous—clingy. It disgusts me.

She stops, goes back to the couch, and pulls her long legs up under her. Her cheeks are pink. She's hurt but trying to pretend she isn't. *You don't scare me,* she said when I met her. *You're not too fucked up for me. I can handle you.* She said this like she was proud. I let her believe it was true.

"What are you still worrying about? Seb texted. She's back in the car. It went perfect. It's all happening. The fuse has been lit. . . ." Her voice sounds strained and her sweet berry mouth is pursed into a pretty little pout.

It's all happening.

I go over to her and kiss her like I mean it. "I'm sorry, babe," I say to her. I'm not sorry. But it's easier this way. She can go insane when she's jealous or insecure. I've seen her do it. I can't deal with it now.

She resists for a second, then wraps her thin arms around my neck and nuzzles me. And I force myself to sit still even though it is physically painful to do so.

I remind myself that I owe her, I always will. I remember that night at Tig's party, fucked out of my mind on who even knows what, her face like ever shifting liquid, quicksilver eyes swimming slowly back and forth. The words rolled out of my mouth. I heard them as I said them, amazed that I could still speak in sentences anyone could understand. *My fucking step-father,* I said. *This is what happened,* I said. I thought I'd surprise her; I wanted to. But she didn't gasp and her jaw didn't drop. She nodded like she understood. And even as fucked as I was, I realized then that those big gorgeous eyes had seen some really ugly shit.

What she said back then was, "I can help you, maybe." But she didn't elaborate at the time. I thought she was saying for the night, that she would bring me water and more of whatever pills it was I'd taken, because I wasn't ready to come down yet.

I couldn't have begun to conceive of what she really meant

then. Even later when she explained it all, I barely could. She has given me everything, I always must remind myself. I can't ever forget it.

So now, sitting here on this couch when all I want to do is stand at the door and wait for my Junie, I make myself hold Ashling's lips against mine.

Ashling is like a goldfish, or a puppy. She remembers only what you did to her last. The kiss is what counts now. But she has a core of electric hot wires. She is not—none of them are—to be fucked with.

I stroke her back, lean against her. Close my eyes and feel the adrenaline buzz until I hear the cars pull up. And I fly up to the ceiling and stick like a balloon filled with black smoke. *POP!*

"They're here!" Evan says. And he runs into the living room. He is excited too, but for different reasons. He's proud of what he's done.

A few seconds later they walk inside. Sebastian gives a tiny silent nod. June's eyes are bright, brighter than usual even. And her face is flushed.

"He's disgusting," she says. "I could barely stand to be in the same room with him, thinking about what he . . . I wanted to fucking kill him."

I wanted to fucking kill him.

Inhale, exhale, time stops. I hold my face still. Inhale exhale inhale exhale. In out. Whoosh. Time starts again.

I feel a rush of relief and joy and a tingle of something else. "Thank you, Junie," I say. "Thank you, thank you, thank you."

She shakes her head. "I . . . my God." She holds out a stack of photos. "I got these for you, if you want them. I mean, I had to take them, but if you want to keep them here . . ."

I look down at the pictures of me as a kid, my mom and I, our old house, everything from before. I feel nothing. I reach for them anyway, then put them on the table.

But I am already on to the next thing. Now it's time to tell her what I'm most excited about: the present.

Sebastian gives June a quick look, again, different from any I've seen before.

"Can I tell her?" Evan says. He is nodding and grinning. "Let me tell her."

Evan was the one who came up with the idea. When I first met him, I thought he was so sweet and innocent. I later learned that was only on the outside. Because inside he'd collected up all the evil that was directed at him—he stored it all up. Held it clenched between his jaw, let it condense and harden. Underneath his sweet smile he is a tiny demon. And although I'm not scared of him, there are moments when I wonder if I should be.

He also happens to be a genius at hacking, pixels, computers, stuff about which I know nothing and do not give a fuck but is useful to know about if your goal is mayhem, as his often is. It was his idea. The execution was his too. But I'm the one who said we should do something for her, and I'm the one who picked the target. So this is her present, wrapped up in a gold shiny bow. A present for her, for me. For us.

"Go ahead," I tell Evan. Because I guess the thing is, I owe him, too.

"While you were fucking with William, we were fucking with someone also. For you," he says.

June gets a funny look on her face. "Who?"

"Ryan."

She opens her mouth in a little O.

"We take care of each other," is what Evan says, which is the perfect thing to say, even if he doesn't know it. "And besides, it's fun."

I understand my Junie. I understand how desperately she always wants to be part of a we. Even when it was just her and I. And now there's more of us. *You can be part of us,* is what I think but do not say.

"So what did you do?" she asks.

"Remember how Ryan was always really into farm animal porn, like the super weird stuff, but was really embarrassed about it and didn't want anyone to know?" I say.

"Wait, what?" June looks so confused, it's adorable. "What are you talking about? No he wasn't."

"Oh really?" Evan says. "He *wasn't*?" He raises one caterpillar eyebrow. There's a big angry zit in the corner.

June is shaking her head. She still doesn't get it. I can feel

Evan's excitement vibrating through the air. He is about to burst open, let it all spill out. He looks at me, I nod. *Go ahead, you tiny, insane monster.*

His voice comes out high-pitched and squealy with no space between words, just talk talk talk talk talk like he's on speed. Guess he sort of is—fucking with people is its own kind of drug. "Well, then how come he *accidentally* tweeted a link to his own user profile on his favorite clandestine online forum—where he had been posting for two entire years, mind you—specializing in a certain type of, how shall we put this, *very animal friendly* photograph and then deleted it an hour later after all those gossipy popular bitches, who previously wouldn't have minded sucking his dick, saw it and clicked and barfed up the lunches they didn't eat? And also how come, lest anyone think that RyRy99 is not really Ryan Fiske, he had only recently posted a very, very dirty picture featuring his face, as well as other parts, hmmm? Riddle me that, Junie?"

Evan's eyes are glowing with the intensity of the demon inside him. I want to say *Stop it, don't scare her, you little shit.*

Junie opens and closes her sweet mouth like a fish. I want to shove my fingers in there, to stick them all the way down her throat until I reach her heart. I take a deep breath and hold my hands at my sides.

"But I don't understand, is that true?" she says finally. "Did he do those things?"

"Define 'true,'" Evan says. "Because it sure as hell is true *now.*"

"How did you make it so that he'd been posting for two years? And the picture . . ."

"Oh goodness, that was easy. A *child* could have done that." But I can tell he's excited by June's confusion. Sometimes the impossible is possible. We die, we burn up, we come back to life. We can travel through fucking time, making the hard cold steel of the past melt, then bend.

"Oh my God," she says. But she doesn't look happy.

I want her to smile. I expected her to smile! This is *funny* after all. She takes a few seconds, and then, I see her mouth cycle through every formation and finally settle on a tiny little unconvinced smirk. But I know her better than she knows herself, and the truth is, she loves it. She's sweet *almost* to the core, but *not quite*. "That's . . . that's . . . How did you even . . ." She is shaking her head. But inside I know she's imagining Ryan's blandly handsome face, twisting in horrified embarrassment, the way he deserves.

"Evan is a genius," I say.

Evan shrugs and grins.

June's face twists again. "It's funny but . . . does he deserve that? I mean, all he did was hit on you a bunch. And . . . who can blame him, right?"

I feel my eye twitch. I force myself to breathe, in, out, in, out. She doesn't like it. She doesn't understand. I was so excited. I feel sick. I can feel Ashling staring at us. *Stop fucking staring.*

"He almost split us apart, Junie," I say. I try to keep my

voice calm even though my insides are *bzzzt bzzzt bzzzzt*. I am short-circuiting. "He's lucky this is all he got."

"Besides," Evan says, "it's already too late. The rumor ponies are out of the pen. They're galloping along. I couldn't stop them now even if I wanted to."

June's face is bright red.

"He deserves it," I say. And in my head, I fill in the rest, exactly *what* he deserves and *why*. And then I force myself to smile, twisting the corners of my lips up in a grin I don't feel at all now. "Let's not think about it anymore. Because there's another ex-boyfriend to deal with." I hold up the letter for Jeremiah. This one I actually wrote myself, full of private details that only he would know. And then Ashling wrote a little note explaining that I'd sent it to her, asking her to pass it on.

"We'll drop it in the mail today; he'll get it tomorrow. And all will be fixed."

June looks overwhelmed, like too much is happening too fast. She needs me to help her know what to think. And so I do. I nod slowly—*This is okay, this is okay,* my head says. And finally she nods back. I keep my face calm, hiding my huge grin blooming on the inside now.

Oh, my sweet Junie, just you wait . . .

Chapter 40

June

Sometimes there's so much to think about that you just can't think about anything at all. Sometimes, all there is to do is sit and wait. So we wait.

For what? I don't ask. Maybe I'm scared to.

Sebastian is at the kitchen table typing on a laptop. Evan and Ashling are playing Go Fish. And Delia and I are sitting on the couch together and she is braiding and unbraiding my hair, the way she always used to. My eyes are closed. It has been so long since someone has played with my hair like this, because Delia was the only one who ever did. It is so relaxing, it is lulling me into some kind of trance, that place right before sleep. She gives a tendril a sharp tug. "A knot," she whispers in my ear, like always. But there never really was one.

A little *beep-beep-beep* starts sounding. Delia inhales sharply. I open my eyes. Everyone looks up. And just like that I know that what we were waiting for was this.

Evan takes a phone off the table, one of the three he has in front of him. He pokes at the screen, and nods. "All right, Willy is on the move now," Evan says. He points to the screen where a tiny red dot is moving across a map. He looks at me, because I'm the only one who doesn't know what's going on. "RFID chip," he says. "While you were inside, Seb stuck it to his car."

I turn toward Sebastian. He shrugs.

"He's heading southeast on Ridgefield . . ." He turns toward Delia. "Any idea where he might be going?"

"His gym, I think," she says.

Ashling grins. "Perhaps he suddenly has a lot of extra energy he doesn't know what to do with . . ." She looks at me, her lips spreading into a slow smile. "Wonder how that happened."

I smile back.

"He doesn't ever stay there very long," Delia says. "Mostly spanks it in the sauna, I think." Her voice is hard, but under that there is fear.

But suddenly I'm not afraid at all anymore. I feel strong enough for both of us.

"Well," says Sebastian, "then let's do this."

A few minutes later we're in the van, pulling into the parking lot of Brentwood Fitness. No one is talking; there is something steely serious about all of them now. All of us.

We make one lap around, driving slow.

"There." Delia knocks her knuckle on the window in front of a silver Audi, which I recognize. William's car. Ashling parks a few spaces away.

"We stay here," Sebastian says to me. "Keep watch, create a distraction if needed. But it won't be needed. This'll barely take a minute."

Ashling reaches under the seat and takes out a thin strip of metal and a crowbar. Then Delia pulls her scarf up high over her mouth, and her hood down low over her brow. Then she, Evan, and Ashling get out. The parking lot is mostly empty, the after-work crowd not yet arrived. My heart is pounding. After this there is no going back. Maybe there never was.

I watch through the dusty windows. The vinyl seating is cold, but my palms are sweating, sticking to it.

Sebastian reaches out and puts his hand on my shoulder.

"Relax," he says. And he reaches into the front seat, turns the key in the ignition, and starts up the heat and the radio. He flips through the stations until quiet classical comes on, tinkling pianos. Then he sits back and closes his eyes. "Just listen." I turn and stare at him, at his jaw, his lips. He takes my hand in one of his, like it is completely normal, like he's done this before. He squeezes it. I squeeze back. With the other hand, eyes still closed, he is playing imaginary piano keys on his leg.

"You play?" I say. My heart is pounding so hard.

He opens one eye and looks at me. "You're supposed to have your eyes closed, but yes." His face is calm and still as the music rises.

He squeezes my hand again. His is so warm.

I watch as Ashling takes the thin length of metal, wedges it in the crack between the window and the door frame, and slides it down. She jiggles it, and a second later, the Audi's door pops open. There's a sudden high-pitched blast—William's car alarm. But Evan pokes a couple buttons on his phone and the sound stops.

Delia opens the driver's side door then. She takes the brown paper bag from the pocket of her coat and stuffs it under the front seat. She shuts and locks the door. Evan pokes his phone again, re-enabling the alarm, maybe.

Evan offers the crowbar to Ashling, then Delia, who holds her hand out like, *Be my guest.* And Evan smiles—a sweet, almost giddy smile—winds up his tiny arm like he's about to hit a softball, and smashes the thick plastic of the taillight, over and over until it shatters and falls to the ground in pieces.

Ashling kisses Delia. Evan puts one end of the crowbar on the asphalt and does a little jig around it. Then the three of them start heading back toward us. Ashling takes out her phone and makes a call.

Sebastian runs his thumb over my knuckles. "You're still watching," he says, eyes still closed.

"Maybe," I say. And then, "What are they doing? Who is Ashling talking to?"

"The police, probably," Sebastian says. "Letting them know about the car with the broken taillight, and something hidden under the seat. But it's better not to know everything. You'll learn that. . . ."

Ashling hangs up the phone and smiles. Then kisses Delia again. I close my eyes, finally. A moment later, the car doors open. Sebastian drops my hand. Ashling and Delia get in up front, Evan slides into the back next to me. For a moment no one says anything at all. Ashling starts up the car. Delia turns slowly and looks at me. She smiles, reaches out, squeezes my knee, and I know what this means—it means thank you. My heart fills up.

Delia leans back against the seat.

"Bye-bye, Willy," she says. To all of us, to herself, to no one. Then she cranks the radio.

Chapter 41

June

It takes my brain a few seconds to figure out what that strange, grunty, snorty sort of sound is, is supposed to be, and then I realize—it's a neigh. Adam Bergan and his friends are neighing at Ryan.

It's the next day at school, and everything is happening.

In the entire time we were dating, I never once saw Ryan uncomfortable, not even a little. He sailed easily from place to place, party to party, with the self-assurance that comes from being rich and tall and handsome and athletic with a normal family who loves you, a level of self-assurance which is almost *unfair* for *anyone* to possess, given how few people get all those advantages. But now, Wednesday morning, standing in the hallway, I hear a chorus of neighs. And Ryan looks like he's about ready to drop down dead of embarrassment.

A few ballsy freshman girls are wiggling their tongues at him. And then, clip-clop, clip-clop, clip-clop, Chris McGimpsey gallops up and stops right in front of him. "Do me hard, you naughty, naughty farmhand, I nee-ee-ee-eeeeed it."

How quickly things can change; how quickly everyone can turn.

"Screw you," Ryan says in a tone that's supposed to sound light. And then he shakes his head in what is meant to be a casual way. But I can tell he doesn't feel casual at all. He thinks by not denying it, he's not giving fuel to the fire. The thing is, some flames don't need any, they will just burn and burn all on their own.

"Screw me? Nah, you wouldn't like that," Chris says, deadpan. "I'm the wrong species." And then he gallops off.

Ryan shrugs like he doesn't care, but when his eyes meet mine, I see what's in there—fear, embarrassment, confusion, genuine pain. And I feel that twist of guilt.

But what can I do? I didn't ask for this, and I can't stop it. And besides, whether Ryan deserves it or not, far worse happens to people who deserve it less. Terrible things happen every day.

I go to homeroom and sit alone. Krista is trying to get my attention. But I avoid her gaze, put in my headphones, don't look up.

Homeroom ends. My phone buzzes with a text from Ashling's phone.

too good not to send. Delete!!! Xo D

Attached is a photograph of the TV screen, news channel 7. There's William's official headshot from the website of his hospital. And underneath, a caption:

Respected local surgeon arrested for methamphetamine possession, suspended from surgery, out on bail

Holy shit. It worked.

For the next few hours I float. English, art. It's lunchtime. I want to leave school now, go back to the house. I'm only here at all because Delia said it was important that I keep acting normal. But really—would it look so suspicious if I skipped just one day? I hate the thought of what I'm missing now. I want to be part of it, to be there with them.

Because—and my stomach lurches when I have this thought—who knows how much longer they'll be around for?

Screw it, I'm leaving. Delia will understand.

I start heading toward the door. I hear my name. I turn.

Jeremiah.

"Why did you and Delia stop being friends?" His eyes are rimmed in red. He looks like he hasn't slept since the last time I saw him. "You said you hadn't been friends in a while, but you never said *why*."

Considering our last conversation, this question feels like a trick. I answer carefully. "We grew apart."

"Nope! Try again. . . ." A muscle twitches in his jaw.

"That's what happened," I say.

Jeremiah shakes his head. "You stopped being friends because she banged your boyfriend."

"No she didn't."

"Oh, but she did. Must have made you pretty mad, huh? Your best friend and your boyfriend, humping . . . So my question is, when did you find out about it?"

"Never," I say. "Because it didn't happen."

"Don't play dumb," he says.

I take a deep breath. I have to stay calm.

"Delia and Ryan were banging for months right before I started dating her. She told me herself. It was like she was proud or whatever, got off on telling me about it until I forced her to stop."

"She told you she had sex with Ryan?"

"She said there was a swimmer, rich and pretty. She told me when she was drunk, wanted to rile me up I think. I tried not to let myself think too much about who it was—I didn't *want* to know who it was. But then you told me about her and Ryan. And the pieces snapped together. That's who she was sleeping with. Thing is, I guess they never stopped . . ."

"They never started! I was wrong about that. I was jumping to conclusions and . . ." I'm shaking my head, a tiny tornado is inside my stomach swirling faster and faster.

He keeps going. "So here's the thing. At first I thought you were covering up for Ryan. Maybe she got pregnant, he didn't want to be a father. He went nuts, but like an idiot you still loved him and didn't want him to go to jail. That story kind of works, *kind of.* Except that Delia would have had an abortion in a second. But then I thought about it and I thought about it and I realized, wait . . . I have this backward." Jeremiah pauses, then tips his head to the side. "Because, actually, *Ryan* is covering up for *you.*"

I keep my face still, but inside my entire body is vibrating. He is waiting for me to react. He starts talking again, more slowly, gently almost. "When you told me about Ryan, you were hoping I'd go beat him up, weren't you? You were *using* me, June. Free muscle. That's obvious now. The question I had, though, was *why* would Ryan cover up for you? He clearly didn't care about you that much or he wouldn't have been cheating in the first place. No, he didn't give a *crap* about you. But I think now I get it. He was covering up for you because you knew about his dark secret, this freaky farm stuff. You blackmailed him and then you let this leak, maybe to show him you were serious. I'm assuming there's more. You're too smart to play all your cards at once. . . ."

I stare at Jeremiah. Holy shit. He actually believes this crazy story. He actually believes all of it. "That's not what happened," I say. "You're completely wrong, about everything." I want to tell him about the letter that will be arriving in the mail for him any day now. But, of course, I can't. And now I'm realizing it won't even help. It's not enough; it's coming too late.

"You can tell it to the police," Jeremiah says. "I'm sure they'd love to discuss it with you." And with that, he shrugs, then turns and walks away.

I stand there, my insides on fire. I want to scream and shout, tell him he's wrong. But there is nothing left for me to say, nothing left for me to do. Everything is going to come crashing down.

Chapter 42

Delia

Once upon a time there was a boy named Trevor who did something bad but for very good reasons. To the wrong people, those reasons didn't even matter, they just did not give a *fuck* about the why. So instead of sitting around waiting for the serious trouble that was coming, instead of waiting for them to *kill* him, Trevor drove off a cliff. And his body sank down, down in the water, so deep that no one could ever find it.

Trevor loved music, played a half-dozen instruments, and was a DJ. His old friends played songs at the funeral, a string quartet came, an electric guitar player. Then an urn with his name carved on the outside was buried in a hole in the ground. But it was only symbolic—there was nothing in there. "It's as empty as my heart is now," his mother said.

Now that boy's name is Sebastian.

And today Sebastian has made a remix on his laptop.

Prominent surgeon, prom-prom-prominent surgeon. Meth-meth-methamphetamine. The news anchor's voice has been auto-tuned, and there's a video of William tipping his head down away from the camera, over and over and over. We've been watching it on repeat. The tune is really quite catchy. We are giddy, all of us. Ashling is dancing, arms up over her head, shaking her perfect ass. I reach out and smack it. She giggles. We are high on power and rightness.

"Does it ever get old?" I say to none of them, to all of them. But I don't need to wait for them to answer. This is the fun part; I'm nervous for what comes after. *But the reasons are everything. The reasons are what matter.*

It didn't take much convincing for them to understand what the next part must be. Ashling agreed right away—she wanted to claim it as her own idea, even. Evan, too. Sebastian was the holdout, but I put it in terms he could understand. What he did in his own life was hardly different at all. "What if the baby is a *girl*?" I said. "What *then*?" And that was enough.

But we don't need to think about it now.

The song stops. "AGAIN!" Ashling says. And Sebastian smirks, almost smiles. He is watching the door. I know he's waiting for Junie too. Well, get in line, pal. Get in the god-damn line.

And then it happens. I feel her before I see her, the bright blue light of her inside my chest, lighting up the dark parts. She walks inside earlier than expected. "Junie!" I call out. My voice loud and rough. I could overwhelm her so easily—I need to not do that. I don't throw my arms around her the way I want to, and Ashling is watching, anyway.

But when Junie turns, her face says everything and I feel a flickering inside, something flaring up in the bad way, in the scary way that I cannot always control.

She stands in the middle of the room, she takes a breath. "Jeremiah thinks . . . he thinks I killed you."

Her voice is low, hollow, terrified. I feel a flood of relief. I thought it was going to be something bad for *real.* Jeremiah is a pigeon, a donkey, a fly. A tiny candle so easily blown out.

"It's okay," I say to her. I want to pull her toward me, to stroke her like a sweet little rabbit.

"No, you don't understand," she says. She is looking at me, saucer eyes vibrating back and forth. She is more freaked out than I realized at first. I am feeling her feelings inside my skin. "He says he's going to the police." I pull her to me, and she's shaking. She feels cold. I let the fire inside me warm her up. "He's out of his mind. He told me . . ." She pauses then, like she doesn't even want to say what she's about to say.

"What is it?" And now I'm scared too, scared I know what's coming, and scared I don't.

"He told me that you were sleeping with Ryan before you and Jeremiah started dating. He said you were sleeping with a swimmer who was rich and pretty and that you told him that, and he decided that must be Ryan. But is it true you did that? With a swimmer, I mean?"

Her words come out in a jumble. But here's the worst part, what terrifies me: She says Jeremiah is crazy, only she doesn't think so, not completely. What she's scared of isn't just the police, an investigation. She's scared he might be telling the truth.

The flame inside me grows bigger, hotter. I can't let myself breathe, the oxygen will only feed it. I close my eyes. I wait for the blood to pound in my ears, for my body to scream out, to beg for air. I've passed out like this before, trying to starve that inside fire. I feel it going down, shrinking. When my vision starts to cloud, I finally open my mouth again.

"He's lying," I say, and my voice sounds almost like a regular voice coming from a regular mouth. "You must know that. If he thinks you did something to me, maybe he's just trying to get you upset. He's hoping you'll crack and then reveal things without meaning to. But I will *take care of it.* Jeremiah can't hurt you." I don't even bother saying "we" this time. Me. I will do this. No one else, all on my own. I will do what I have to do.

I put my hands on her cheeks. The fire comes right back, greedy and starving, I feel the sickest I've felt in a long time. "It's okay. It will be okay. I *promise.*" I hold her face and look deeply into her eyes until I feel her coming back to me.

I nod slowly. She nods too. We have to get out of this house, to go do something else, somewhere normal.

"Let's go out," I say. "Shopping. I need clothes." I turn to Ashling. There is a bag of cash in the closet, so much of it, it looks like play money. Ashling dumped it all out on the bed and made me fuck her in it once. We laughed the whole time, because it was so ridiculous. "Some pervert would pay a lot of money for a video of this," she said. "But we obviously don't need it." And she shoved fifty in her mouth, and then, because she was drunk and she could, she ate it.

They get it all sorts of ways. Evan's skills come in especially handy for that. There's so much of it, it almost doesn't mean anything. Money is only as useful as what you can buy with it, and for a while there was nothing I could imagine wanting. But there is now.

We have to pretend we're normal people living in the regular world, but better. We have to show her how good all of this is, can be. If we don't, I will lose her completely.

Chapter 43

June

It's three hours later, three hours since I got back to the house, sick and scared of everything. And now we're at a fancy shopping mall two hours away, playing dress-up. It's so insane and so surreal, but somehow this weirdness is calming me down. It's like any other day, except suddenly there's this bag of cash and I don't know where it came from, and we had to drive for hours so that Delia won't be recognized. Since she isn't supposed to exist anymore.

Delia nods at Ashling's reflection in the mirror. "Get it," she says simply. "It would be criminal not to."

Ashling is trying on a dark brown leather jacket, snug fitting to the waist, made of smooth leather with brass zippers on the sides and at the chest. She looks stunning in it. She faces the mirror and then turns halfway around. I look at the price tag. It costs half as much as my car, and I saved up for over a year to buy that.

"I'll get it, then," Ashling says. "Definitely don't want to be *criminal.*" She sticks out her tongue. She's trying to be playful, but something about it feels forced. All of this feels forced, I think.

There are five bags at Delia's feet already. Jeans, shirts, dresses, shoes, boots, bras, everything. Enough stuff for a brand-new life. Delia paid in cash for all of it, slapping stacks of bills down on the counter, smiling too widely, too brightly. I know this Delia, the charming one, making friends with everyone, talking fast. I missed this girl, but I'm also scared of her. She can do anything. She has. She does.

The dressing room is covered in piles of clothes; Delia brought them in by the armful. I'm sitting on a bench, near the mirror. Delia reaches out and grabs a cream-colored wrap dress made of lacy sweater material. She tosses it at me.

"Try that on," Delia says.

"That's okay" I say. I shake my head.

"For fun," says Delia. And she has that look on her face—a wheedling smile, a come-on-out-to-play smile. I know I have no choice.

I slide my own sweater and shirt over my head, suddenly self-conscious to be half dressed in front of them, though I don't know why. Putting on the dress is like putting on a bath-robe. The fabric feels so soft against my skin. But the belt is confusing and I can't figure out how to tie it. Delia is watching me, still smiling. She comes over and takes the belt and fits it through a tiny hole in the side of the dress. She pulls the two ends around me and ties it at the back, tight. Ashling is staring. I feel myself blush.

"You look like a milkmaid," says Delia. "The kind that might make a guy like Ryan consider stopping boning cows."

I feel a tightening in my stomach. I try to force a laugh. I don't want to think about any of that right now. So I focus on this dress.

"Doesn't she?" Delia says to Ashling.

Ashling nods vaguely.

"Yup," Delia says. "You're getting it."

I shake my head. "I was trying it on for fun. I don't need it. This isn't my money. It's yours."

"It's no one's," Delia says. "But we happen to have it, and we share. And you're with us. At least look in the mirror."

I slowly turn to see the girl in the creamy white dress, whose skin looks pink and fresh, whose curves look soft and warm.

"It's yours," Delia says. "Don't fight me. You know I'll win."

I shake my head. "I look like someone else," I say, finally.

"So be someone else for a while." Delia's lips spread into a slow grin. "Who knows, you might like it."

The house is beautiful at night, lit from within, orange and gold against a dark sky. We take Delia's many bags out of the trunk, and

Ashling's jacket, and the dress, which I guess is my dress now.

We walk into the house.

"Honeys, we're home," Delia calls out.

"Hello, dears," Evan calls back from the kitchen. Music is playing, trumpets and piano over beats. The lights are down low. The kitchen island is covered in platters of food. The air smells sweet and warm, like butter and garlic and other things I cannot name. I am filled with a wave of happiness, how lucky I am to be here. And then a squeezing in my chest, because I do not ever want this to end.

But it will. Soon, even. They will leave. This will be over.

And I will be alone again.

And this thought is followed by all of the other things I'm trying not to think about—Jeremiah and what he said, what he might do. Ryan and what they did to him.

But I'm here now. I remind myself I have to focus on that. I have to at least try.

Dinnertime.

The table is set—thick white plates on the gnarled wood, chunky glasses made of wavy bubbled glass. There are three thin candles, flickering in the center. I'm wearing the new dress, because Delia made me. No shoes, no tights, because I don't have those things. It's cold outside, but warm and cozy in here.

And when I walk into the kitchen in that yellow light, wearing my cream-colored dress and bare feet and no tights, and Sebastian looks at me, eyes sliding up and down before settling on my face, I feel fluttering in my belly and energy shooting up my spine.

I know Delia has arranged this, all of this, for me.

"You look pretty," Sebastian says. And I feel myself blushing, embarrassed at how happy these three words make me. And then I try to find something to keep myself busy, because everyone is being useful around me and suddenly I do not know what to do with my hands.

Evan and Delia carry the food out to the table—roasted orange carrots, potatoes crispy and brown around the edges. A creamy soup, colored with saffron. Grilled salmon, flecked with dill. Ashling fills our glasses with wine.

Sebastian takes something out of the oven—a pie oozing with fruit—and sets it out to cool.

They're moving together like a machine, like a single being, and there isn't anything for me to do, so I straighten the shiny hammered silverware until it's time to sit down.

"This looks awesome, bud," Evan says.

"Yeah, thank you," Ashling says.

And I realize that Sebastian has made all of it. I look at him, at his serious face. He shrugs, but I think I see a flicker of a smile.

We are all around the table now. Delia raises a glass. "To family," she says. She looks me straight in the eye.

I stab my fork into a potato. I take a bite—the edges are crusty and the inside is perfectly fluffy. It is the most delicious thing I've ever eaten. And so is the bite of salmon I take next, and the other dishes after that.

I am ravenous. My stomach growls. I don't want to drop anything on this dress.

I take a sip of the wine just to slow myself down. But I'm surprised to find that I like it. It tastes rich and round as it swirls over my tongue. I look up, and Sebastian is watching me.

And so I take another sip, and then another one. I feel my face flushing red and I am starting to smile. The rest of them are smiling too. We are all smiling. We are all happy and here together. The world outside of here, the things I do not want to think about, they're all so far away.

"So," Evan says slowly, "that stuff we've been expecting . . ." Something about his tone makes me feel like he's been waiting to say this, waiting for the right time. "It's almost ready. Will be here by Friday at the latest."

Ashling smiles and Delia glances quickly at me, then nods.

I take another sip of wine. The more I have, the better it tastes. "What stuff?" I say.

"Some stuff we've been waiting for," says Ashling. She shrugs. "For Delia."

Sebastian is watching Ashling. He doesn't look happy.

"We can finish off now," says Evan. "Because then it will be time to go."

I feel a jolt of panic. "What's next?" I say. I try to smile, to make my voice sound light.

And I want to ask more questions, the ones I haven't allowed myself, that have been on the tip of my tongue since I first came to this house. They're being loosened by the wine; they're going to start making their way out of my mouth soon. But I keep my lips clamped shut. This moment is too perfect. I don't want to ruin it. It will all be over too fast, then they will go wherever they're going. And more than anything, I want to hold on to this to fill my heart up with it so that when they're gone, and I'm alone, floating off in space with no one, I'll at least have this night to keep me tethered to earth.

"So, who wants more salmon?" Sebastian says. He's trying to change the subject. He doesn't want me to ask more, to know more.

Delia looks me in the eye. She winks.

Later. We're outside in the backyard and I know it's cold, because my breath is fogging up the air around us, but I can't feel it. I am warm, cozy, the very opposite of lonely. This is the very best feeling in the world. I think maybe I'm drunk.

Evan is rubbing his hands together while Sebastian lights a fire in the fire pit. Ashling passes the bottle of wine to Evan, who swigs and passes to Delia, who swigs and passes to me.

"I can't believe this bottle has lasted all night," I say.

And Ashling gives me a funny look and lets out a little

cough of a laugh. "June, that's, like, the fifth one we're on now."

"Hmmm," I say. "I guess that explains it." Then I smile and half laugh without meaning to. I take a gulp. It tastes like the inside of my mouth. I look at the others, lips stained purple. Sebastian's purple lips are perfect.

He is standing over the iron fire pit, twisting newspaper and adding sticks. He flicks a match, tosses it in. There's a crackle and a whoosh as the flames flare up.

I wonder if this is what Delia's fire looked like. I wonder if Sebastian was the one who lit it.

There are chairs around the fire, big ones made of logs. It seems weird to have wood chairs around such a big fire—it would be so easy for them to burn, I think. So many things are so flammable! It's amazing everything is not on fire all the time, considering how it spreads.

We all sit down, lean back, and soak in the heat. Delia isn't scared. We're sitting around a fire, a big one, and she's leaning up close to it.

I feel like I'm floating. I look up at the stars. I imagine I'm soaring up, up, up, and through space. I look back down at the people in front of me, warm on this cold night. Out here in the dark I feel like I could say anything. All those questions I've had stuck inside, I can open my mouth and let them out and it will be okay. So I do.

"How did you do it?"

They all turn to look at me.

"How did we do what?" Delia says slowly. But she's watching me watch the fire, and I know that she knows what I'm asking.

"Who was burned in the shed?" Even now, through this haze of dark and smoke and wine, I'm surprised to hear myself sound so casual, to say these words like they're nothing. For a long time everyone is silent.

And then, finally, Delia speaks. "I never found out her name."

The wind is blowing and the fire flickers, but still it burns strong.

"She was around my size, around our age. She'd had cancer, I think. She was supposed to be cremated."

"But how did you get . . ." *It? Her?*

"It was easy," Delia says. But there's something in her tone . . . I don't think it was easy at all. "Connections at the morgue and a bribe. Oh, and a blow job." I think maybe she's kidding about the last part. But when I look at her face I have no idea. She is half smiling; then her smile is gone.

"Tell me more," I say. "Please."

"You really want to know all of it?"

"Delia," Sebastian says. But she ignores him.

I nod.

"We went where we were told. A body was loaded into the back of the van. A girl. We dressed her up in my clothes and my jewelry. I put that titanium necklace around her neck, that one I always used to wear, because titanium won't melt. I touched her skin. I thought it might be weird touching a dead body, but I didn't feel anything. Nothing bad. I just felt grateful."

"And then what?" I say. I am whispering now.

"Then there was a lot of gasoline, and the shed was already full of firewood, so the fire was pretty enormous . . . and by the time it was out, there wasn't enough of her, enough of *me*, left for an autopsy."

"What about dental records? DNA?" I say. All the questions I've been cooking up for days are tumbling out into this cold night air with the flames, the smoke. I barely know what dental records even are, except from TV.

Delia just shakes her head. "No one checks for those things unless they have reason to doubt," Delia says. "And there was no reason for them to. I left a note . . ."

I watch the fire, the logs, crackling, slowly shrinking. Through the flames I can see Evan's eyes shining in the dark. Ashling's too.

"And all of you did something like this?" I ask. "What in your lives was so bad that you had to leave them and let everyone you've ever known believe you're dead?"

And now I know I've gone too far.

"We did . . . different things," Ashling says carefully. Then she is quiet.

Evan takes the wine bottle from between his knees, raises

it to his lips, and takes a long swallow. "I shot myself in the head . . . supposedly."

Sebastian stands. "Stop," he says. "That's enough now." And then, "It's not safe for her to know so much."

I am drunk, but even drunk, I feel that shame again, that hurt. Her as in me. I'm not one of them. I turn back to Delia.

"I still don't understand," I say. My voice sounds funny now. Forced. "Why did you have to do it? Why couldn't you just run away?" I am suddenly desperate and words are pouring out. "Maybe you can come back, say it was a prank. And then . . ." I know she can't, she won't. But for the fifteen seconds between when I ask and when she answers, I let myself believe she could. She could stay with me, she could stay forever and never leave me.

"And then what?" She shakes her head. "No, if you run away, they never stop looking for you. You still exist, trapped in your life. But if you die . . ." Her voice is soft and sweet. She turns toward me. She smiles. "Junie, you're free."

Chapter 44

June

I thought that fire would last forever, but eventually it shrank, and smoked and burned itself out. We're back inside now, sprawled out on the couch in a row—Sebastian, then me, Delia, and Ashling, with Evan halfway on top of them. Some amount of time ago—an hour? A half hour? A hundred years?—Evan said, "I'm getting in on this," and tried to squash himself into the space between their bodies. And that is where he now lies, eyes slowly closing. He is so small, he looks like a child.

We sit, watching some dumb movie on the giant TV. More wine. It slides so easily down our throats. And Sebastian is sitting far away from me on the couch. And I can't stop thinking about what he said. *It's not safe.* Like I am a danger, could be a danger to them. I turn. Delia is watching me watch Sebastian. I think she is drunk too. "You can have anything you want," she says. "With us you can have all of this."

There's a soft snoring noise. We turn. Evan is asleep, curled up, leaning on Ashling, who is now sleeping too, her arm over his shoulder.

I smile at them, because of how cute they look. And I look over at Delia, expecting her to be smiling too, but her face is blank.

She reaches out and strokes Ashling's hair—sleeping Ashling's sleeping hair. Ashling makes a quiet "mmm."

"Babe," Delia says. "Baby, time to go to bed."

"Thanks, sweetheart," Evan says. He smiles, cheeks flushed. Then he stands up and stumbles off down the hallway. And I laugh, and Delia laughs. She leans in again.

"Anything you want," she whispers.

Then she helps Ashling up. "Good night, kiddies," Delia says louder. And she leads sleepy Ashling out of the room, and I sit there, looking out at the night sky through the dark windows. Sebastian is next to me on the couch, staring straight ahead.

My entire body is tingling. I turn toward him and look at his profile, his eyes, straight nose, his mouth, which hardly ever smiles. His lips almost unbearably beautiful. And suddenly I'm angry, angry that he thinks I would ever, could ever do anything to hurt any of them. I love Delia more than life, and the rest of them—I'm starting to love them, too. Is this true? Is this the wine in my brain? Or is this the boundaries of my brain melted by the wine. I could open my mouth; I could say any words at all. I want to tell him that he can trust me. I want to know him. To actually know who he actually is.

Sebastian takes the bottle off the table and holds it up to his beautiful mouth. He tips the bottle back for a long time. Then hands it to me. Our fingers brush. The room is hot, so hot all of a sudden. I put the bottle in my lap.

I open my mouth, I take a breath. Sebastian is staring straight ahead.

Finally, he turns and looks at me.

Chapter 45

Delia

I wanted them to do this. I set them up to do this. A gift to my Junie, something I knew she wanted and needed. I close my eyes. This is a good thing. It's what I wanted. This is a good thing.

But now my insides are on fucking fire.

I close my eyes, and the backs of my eyelids are a portal to the world behind the door.

I don't want to watch it. Please, fucking brain, don't make me fucking watch it.

I can't stop.

Sebastian and June are kissing, softly at first. Even drunk they are so gentle. A little shy, because of how badly they've been wanting this. She is thinking, *I can't believe this is happening*; he is thinking just *holy fuck.* Lip against lip, soft and sweet, activating the lizard parts of their brain, circuits *lighting the fuck up*. This is what we are meant to do. This is how we *survive.* Without it we would all just *up and fucking die*.

Someone lets out a heavy breath, a tiny moan, and neither of them knows who did it. That sound is *trapped* like a *small animal* in the hot damp space formed between their open lips. It echoes, travels down to their guts. A jolt. His arms are stronger than she realized. His hands slide up the curve of her back under her dress. Her skin is hot and so smooth. She buries her face in his neck, inhales deeply. It is like a hit of a drug, that smell of his neck. Biology, science, art, magic, *pow-pow-pow!* Everything speeds up, their hearts, the blood through their veins, teeth and tongues, crashing together now. It *hurts* to want something this much, and it cannot be *stopped.* Clothes are *melting off.* Their bodies collide, the soft places and the hard places. Lights off, but moonlight coming in through the window, their skin *glows*. They are *glowing*, barely human, and they levitate and float over to the bed. A swirling storm starts around them, right there in that room. *Clouds and thunder and lightning!* The walls vanish—they are floating in space, rushing past stars into nothingness, tethered only to each other. He is on top of her. She is crying out. His fingers are around her throat. She sinks her teeth into his skin. They are wild animals. They are ravenous fucking beasts and they are going to devour each other. He will devour her *and there will be nothing left.*

I cannot breathe; I cannot stand this.

"Babe?" I am jolted out of my trance. I hear Ashling's voice, sounding so small, calling me through the open door of our bedroom. When she wakes up in the middle of the night, she is a scared infant child. And I'm supposed to be getting her some water. I tiptoe into the kitchen, take a glass off the table, rinse it, fill it from the sink. I gulp the water down, cold and clear. But it doesn't help. I am thirstier than I've ever been in my life. I drink glass after glass until my stomach is bursting with it, and only then can I go back to bed.

Chapter 46

June

Before I even open my eyes, the memories come rushing back—lips, hands, skin, sweat. But when I roll over, the bed is empty. I am alone, mouth dry, head pounding.

I go out into the hallway. I feel suddenly scared, and I don't even know why.

"Seb?" I whisper. I don't call him this, Delia calls him this. I feel strange now, saying his name at all. The clock on the microwave blinks 4:06. It is pure black velvet out the window. I see the glow of a laptop on the low table in front of the couch, a celestial screen saver, rushing through stars. It's lighting up Sebastian's face. His jaw, those lips.

He is curled onto his side. I sit down, my back against his belly, and put my hand on his warm bare skin. "Hey," I whisper. But he doesn't stir. Why is he out here? What was he doing? I reach out and tap his laptop's track pad even though I know I shouldn't. Maybe I'm still drunk. Maybe that's an excuse. His computer wakes up to a website. At the top is a banner, a digital photo collage—there's a row of kids at camp, a boy in a canoe, a baby and a mom, and a picture of . . . Sebastian? He has long-ish hair with green streaks and a skateboard. He's a few years younger than he is now. He's standing with his arm around a skinny girl with tan legs and a big smile. She looks like him.

We miss you Trevor, it says below the banner in a swirly green font.

And under it: *Memorial Page for Trevor Emerson.*

On May 21st the world got darker, and heaven gained an angel of light.

The rest of the page is messages people have posted for him. I start to scroll down.

I miss you buddy, always will. —FM

Don't forget: Rainbow slippers.

Trev was the absolute best, everyone who met him loved him. He was gentle and funny and kind.

I miss this kid so much, but I know he's up there. Say hi to my granny if you see her, pal.

The world makes no sense.

I first met T at a party where he was the DJ and I was a drunk girl flirting with the DJ . . .

And on and on, page after page of messages. There must be hundreds.

At the very bottom are the most recent ones. One from just last night.

It's been almost two years, but not a day, not a minute goes by when we don't think about you. Love you, Mom

I feel a stabbing in my chest and raise my hand to my lips. I look down at his sweet sleeping face. I think of all the people who miss him. Some have gone on with their lives. Some never will.

I shut the laptop and slide into the space between him and the couch, pressing my cheek against his back, holding on to him like he's about to fly away. And this is how I fall back to sleep.

Chapter 47

Delia

Every day thousands and thousands of people die.

Some know it might be coming—they're sick or old, or their lives are dangerous. Some don't have any idea at all.

They wake up and don't even bother to think, *this is a day*, because it is the same as the thousands that came before it and the thousands they think will come after.

None will come after.

Sparks fly, a fuse has been lit, it's burning down the wick. Then *kaboom*.

I am not religious. I am not a spiritual person. But there is something sharp and beautiful about this. It feels like it *means* something. I close my eyes and say good-bye to those who know it is coming, and especially to those who don't.

This is what I have to do. And I thought I might be scared, but I only feel excited.

And then I feel Ashling's hand on my tit.

"Kiss," she says, groggy, eyes puffy, half opened. Ashling is hungover. She nuzzles up against me. I close my eyes, imagining things. Then I kiss her hard on the mouth. "Later," I say. Then I lean in, and I whisper into her neck. I remind her what happens now, what today means, all the things we have to do. And Ashling doesn't mind, since half of it is a secret only we know about. She wants more secrets, just for us. "Secrets link you forever," she said to me once, as though somehow it was possible I didn't already know that.

Chapter 48

June

I'm alone again, in a bed this time. On the nightstand next to me are a glass of water and a bottle of aspirin. Someone has left them there for me. Who? Sebastian?

Last night.

Everything comes rushing back, slamming me in the face—gulping wine, the fire, *the other fire*, talking to Delia, Sebastian turning toward me, leaning in. Then just me there. Looking for him. The laptop. What I saw. Curling up behind him. *His real name is Trevor.*

The others have real names too.

Soon Delia won't be Delia anymore.

The feelings rush in after the thoughts, one by one by one. This morning I feel absolutely everything.

I stand up. The room spins. I sit back down. Breathe, in out in out. I'm wearing someone else's T-shirt. Big, gray, it reaches halfway down my thighs.

I hear a door slam. I walk out into the hallway, into the kitchen. Sebastian is in front of the stove, flipping pancakes. I watch him, heat climbing up my cheeks.

Our eyes meet.

"Last night," I start. But I have no idea what I want to say, even. "It was . . ." Fun? Sexy? Strange, terrifying, amazing, sloppy, ridiculous.

"I think it was kind of everything," he says. Which I realize, after he says it, is exactly right. "Listen," he says. His voice is low. "There's something I need to tell you. I shouldn't tell you, but . . ."

The door from the hallway opens and Evan walks in, sleep rumpled, in a Superman T-shirt and a pair of red-and-blue plaid pajama pants. He glances at me, at Sebastian, at me again.

"Oh God. Really? Now you guys too? Yeesh!" But he's grinning. "Where are the other *lovahs*?"

Lovahs. Delia's word. I smile.

"Left early for some kind of errand," Sebastian says. He shrugs, then flips the final pancake onto a stack. Then divides the enormous stack in two, gives half to Evan, and half to me.

"None for you?" I say.

Sebastian shakes his head. "Maybe later. I'm weirdly not that hungry."

And for a little while, it is the three of us, me and Evan

wolfing down pancakes, Sebastian sipping coffee. It's just after eleven. If I were at school, I'd be in bio. I'd be in bio, closed off in a bubble, all alone. But this is bliss. Nothing outside of this moment matters. I look up and Sebastian is staring at me. I smile. He smiles back.

A car pulls into the driveway.

Chapter 49

Delia

Ashling parks and turns toward me. "You're sure you're okay," she says. "No second thoughts?"

I shake my head and reach out for her hand. "None. We protect the people we love."

"We do," she says. And then she nods. I can tell she's trying to keep her smile small, keep the full glow out of it, so I won't be freaked by how easy this was for her. Thing is, I'm not freaked, I'm *impressed*.

We sit there for a minute, in out in out, breathing together, air in my lungs and her lungs and my lungs. I can feel her trying to suck me in, to absorb me. And then she brings my hand to her lips and kisses it. "And you definitely don't want to tell her first?"

Love drains away. Hot anger, a sudden flash, deep in my gut like a lighter flicking fire. She knows the answer. She's only asking because she's jealous. She's asking because she wants me to tell first, and she thinks Junie will say no, will flip out, and then she won't come. And Ashling will have me all to herself.

I turn toward her. *Don't even try,* I say with my eyes. *Try, and you will regret it.* But with my lips I say. "I'm sure, baby." And then, "I love you." Because I never say this, and I know it will shut her up.

Now her smile is the brightest thing I've ever seen—it hurts my eyes. It makes me sick.

"Baby," she says. "I love you too."

Ten minutes later, I'm inside the house telling June what I was planning on telling her, as she blink, blink, blinks her big bunny eyes. She is confused. She is scared. And that makes me nervous. "But for what? I thought the whole point of what we did was so that what needed to happen would happen. He would go to jail like he deserves."

"The problem is"—I pause—"we already have reason to believe this isn't going to work. He's going to get off."

"How do you know?"

I shake my head. "Just trust me. We have . . . information. So now we have to let him know we're watching him, that I'm watching him. That he has to be on his best Boy Scout behavior from now on or he won't like the results."

"You mean you'll come see him, too?"

I nod.

"But then he'll know you're alive. . . ."

"He won't tell anyone. I can promise you that."

June shakes her head and bites her pink lip, skin pudging out around her little white teeth. "I don't understand. He'll want to tell your mother. How could he not?" I can feel the little wheels spinning, spinning inside her brain. I can feel them in mine, too. I want to wrap my arms around her, cradle her, pull her to my chest like a baby.

"We'll convince him not to," I say.

"How?"

It's time to tell her the rest of it. "There are other things you don't know about, things he did." I look at her meaningfully. "He has secrets he wants to keep."

"Like what?" Her voice is barely a whisper.

I shake my head. This is where I have to stop. "You don't want to know. I won't burden you with that. But they're awful things, illegal things."

"Then why can't we send him to jail?"

"The justice system is fucked," I say. "No, she's safest if we're the ones in control. The baby is safest if he knows we're watching, and will always be. We have to protect the people we love." I pause. It's time to do it. This is it. This is everything. "But we need your help again."

And June stares at me. She is nodding slowly. She understands. "Okay," she says.

We have to do it before she changes her mind, because we need her.

"And it's got to be today. . . ."

Junie's sweet little face goes bright white. She looks like an angel. She *is* an angel. For a second I almost feel bad for what I've told her. But I remind myself that loving someone doesn't always mean telling them everything. Sometimes the kindest thing you can do for a person is to shield them from that which will not help them. Make the decision and then carry the burden yourself, bear that weight so that they don't have to. I know she will forgive me.

Chapter 50

June

We're standing in a circle, huddled together, our breath fogging up the frigid air around us.

"Ready?" Evan says.

"Ready," I say.

Delia leans in and gives me a hug. Her hair tickles my cheek. "I love you, Junie."

When she turns away, I feel Sebastian's hand on my back. He comes in close so no one else can hear. "You don't have to do this," he whispers. "You know that, right?"

The sun is starting to make its way down the gray slope of the sky. My pulse is beating in my ears. But I'm not scared anymore.

"I know," I say.

* * *

When the numbers on my phone roll from 4:04 to 4:05, I go down Delia's driveway and up the slate steps to the big gray house. I push the bell with one frozen finger. The chimes chime; the door opens.

William looks like he hasn't slept in a month.

"Hi," I say. Inside my sleeves, I squeeze my hands into fists. "Sorry to bother you again. But I was just wondering about the pictures. I mean, how you said there were more of them that I could look through. I was hoping I could still do that? I should have done it before. I was . . . kind of overwhelmed."

He licks his cracked lips with a dry tongue. "I understand that feeling," he says. "Perhaps you heard what happened."

I nod.

"I didn't do what they're saying I did." He is speaking so slowly. I think maybe he's on something, something he prescribed himself to relax.

"Okay," I say.

But I wonder what else he really did do, what they're going to use to blackmail him. From the way Delia was talking, I think maybe I have an idea.

He stands there staring at nothing; he is not here anymore. He snaps back. "But, yes, the photos. Of course. Come in."

He steps aside as I walk through the door. He shuts it

behind me and locks it. When he is up ahead, his big back to me, I reach out and twist the lock in the other direction.

He leads me down into the basement. The albums are out and open on the sofa, like maybe he was looking through them on his own.

"When's the memorial at school? Maybe I should go to it. Maybe her mother would like to hear how it went."

"Next week," I say. I sit down then—I don't know what else to do. I pick up an album and slowly flip through the pages. My hands are sweating. My heart is about to escape from my chest. William sits next to me, heavy on the couch.

I hope they come soon.

I don't have to wait long.

Now there are sounds coming from upstairs, voices, footsteps.

William stands. "Do you hear that?" He goes to the foot of the stairs. "Hello?" He starts walking up them.

I count.

One-two-three.

I look down at a picture of three-year-old Delia on a tricycle. She looked like herself, even back then—the slant of her smile, something in her eyes.

Seven-eight-nine.

When I get to fifty, I stand and walk up the stairs too. I don't know what I'm going to see when I pass through the door. But I need to be brave now.

The world is only fair if you make it.

"Well, goodness," I hear Evan say. "You're a feisty fella, aren't you." I enter into the kitchen. William is facedown on the linoleum, bucking and grunting like an animal, a broken blue mug on the floor next to him, a brown Diet Coke puddle spreading out. Evan is sitting backward on his back, wrapping a rubber cable around his wrists. Ashling is kneeling on his legs, which are already tied.

Sebastian stands above, quietly watching.

"June!" William shouts. He cranes his neck to look at me. "Call the police!"

He is red faced, terrified, trying to shake them off. I think how terrified Delia must have been when he was on top of her.

"I'm not calling anyone," I say.

He deserves this.

They finish tying him. Ashling and Evan get up and step back. Then the three of them stand there staring down at him.

"What do you want?" He manages to roll himself over onto his side. He kicks his legs, tries to stand but he can't. "There's no cash in the house, I don't keep any prescription pads here . . ."

Ashling pulls out one of the kitchen chairs. "Let's lift him, boys."

The three of them pick him up. They put him on the chair, his arms behind him. And that's when I notice the gloves, baby blue latex. They're all wearing them.

"Your hands," I say.

Evan reaches into his pocket and tosses a pair to me. “Here. We’ll clean up your prints before we leave, don’t worry.”

My prints? I put the gloves on. The latex feels powdery and smooth.

William is wheezing now, moving his mouth wordlessly.

She crept up so quietly, I didn’t even hear her. “Surprise,” says Delia.

“Oh my God.” William pitches forward. Ashling holds him back.

“Going upstairs for a sec,” says Delia. “You stay here.”

“Delia, wait!” William shouts. And then Delia is gone. “She’s alive?” William’s eyes are filling with tears. “How is she alive?” He turns to look at us. “I have no idea what’s happening right now, but you’re making a mistake. You don’t have to do it . . .”

“You’re the one who made the mistake,” says Ashling. “Did you think you could try to rape her and then, what? Nothing would happen?”

“There are *always* consequences,” says Evan. He is smiling, a different kind of smile than I’ve ever seen before. All sweetness gone.

Sebastian shakes his head. “You stupid fuck.”

“I didn’t do that! I would never! How is Delia still alive? How are you alive?”

Delia is back now. She’s holding a little glass bottle and

a syringe. LEVEMIR is printed on the bottle in black, and underneath, INSULIN DETEMIR. Delia puts the needle into the tiny hole at the top of the bottle, then pulls the stopper until the syringe fills up.

"Delia," William says. "Whatever you think you're doing, this is insane. Please stop."

Delia shakes her head. "It's not insane." She sounds so calm. "It's medicine. You take it every day."

"Wait," I say. But no one looks at me. I take a breath. I need to calm down. I remind myself that this is all part of the plan. The plan to terrify him, show him that we are powerful and in charge. After this he will have no doubt.

"Delia, whatever kind of trouble you're in, I can help you. We can talk about this."

"It's too late to talk," Delia says.

"Do you need money? I can get you as much as you need, I can wire it anywhere."

But Delia shakes her head. I look at the two of them together. An image flashes in my mind—her struggling under his bulk, him smiling, pressing himself against her, her desperately trying to get away, sinking her teeth into his skin.

"Shut up," I say to him. They turn then, all of them, surprised to hear me speak. I'm surprised too. "Don't talk. Just listen, you rapist piece of shit."

Delia looks me straight in the eye. She smiles.

"Exactly, Willy. Now is the time for you to shut up."

Delia holds up the syringe. Ashling reaches out, grabs the bottom of William's shirt, and untucks it, revealing a line of pale pudgy belly.

Delia puts the needle to his skin. "Where do you usually do it?" she says. "Where do you like to stick it in?"

"Don't," William says. He is shaking his head, leaning far back in the chair to try to get away from her. But there is nowhere to go. He is really panicking. Just like we want him to. "It's not too late to stop."

I look at Delia.

For a moment no one moves.

Now is when she'll tell him what she knows. Now is when she'll tell him what she wants. I stare. I wait.

But Delia doesn't say anything at all, just slides the needle into William's stomach and presses down on the plunger.

William's face goes from bright red to stark white. He starts to struggle again. Ashling pushes him back, her hand at his throat.

"Don't move," she says.

"Don't bruise him," says Evan. "He's like a big fat peach. We have to be careful or it won't look right."

"Please," William is begging now.

Delia fills the syringe again, injects him again. *What's going on?*

"What won't look right?" I say. "Delia?"

"They say sometimes at the end, people get very wise," Evan says. "Any life lessons for us, buddy?"

"Shit," I whisper. "What's happening?" I think I'm starting to understand something. The gloves. The talk of fingerprints.

Evan turns toward me. "Insulin lowers blood sugar," he says lightly. "That's important if you're diabetic and your body doesn't produce any insulin. But if you take too much and your blood sugar gets too low, you go into shock, and then you fall into a coma, and your breathing slows and your pulse slows. And then eventually . . . you are not breathing or pulsing at all anymore."

"Wait," I say. "You're actually planning on killing him."

At those words William lets out a cry, but he doesn't sound surprised. I look up. I was the last to understand this.

Ashling and Evan are watching William. Sebastian opens his mouth like he wants to say something, but he just shakes his head, closes his mouth back up. I lock eyes with Delia.

"Junie."

"You said you were just going to threaten him."

She shakes her head. For a moment all that fire is gone. "Please don't be mad at me, Junie." She is speaking so quietly I can barely hear her.

Our eyes are locked. I feel her reaching into my heart.

"You didn't know," William says. His voice is suddenly very calm. "I understand that you didn't."

I turn. His mouth looks wet. "Please." His eyes are pleading and desperate. I can't look away. He is digging his finger into the cracks of my doubt and trying to pry me apart. "Just get me some orange juice from the fridge. That's all I need. And we can pretend like none of this ever happened. I'll forget this ever happened . . ."

"Shut up," I say. But I don't feel powerful at all anymore. "Dee Dee?" I am weak and small. "I'm scared."

Delia hands the syringe to Ashling. She wraps her arms around me. "This is okay. I promise, this is okay." She pulls me to her, her body so warm against mine.

"Don't listen to her," William says.

"Shut the fuck up," says Ashling. "Shutupshutupshutupshutupshutup."

"I'm sorry I couldn't tell you before," Delia says. "I couldn't. I . . . But this is what has to happen. He doesn't deserve air, he doesn't deserve life. The entire world will be better off if he's not in it . . ."

"I didn't do anything," William says. "June, she's lying to you. Whatever she said . . ."

Delia turns toward William. "You think I'm going to leave you alone in this house with my mother? With her new child? What if that baby is a girl? Will you rape her like you tried to do me?"

"None of this is true," he says.

"So here's an idea," says Evan. "Maybe instead of a bunch of bullshit, your final words should be real." Evan shrugs. "Come on, Willy. I'd say you have, oh, I don't know . . . ten minutes left? Surely there must be something you want to say. You haven't even begged for Delia's forgiveness yet. Don't you even want to try that?"

"Just get me something from the kitchen," William says. He sounds sleepy. "Anything with sugar."

Delia walks across the room and disappears into the kitchen then. I hear the fridge door slam shut. She comes back a second later, holding a jar of maraschino cherries. Maybe she's changed her mind. Maybe this really was the plan all along.

She opens, dips her fingers in, and pulls out a glistening cherry, chemical red. She holds it up. "You mean, like this?"

William is nodding. "Yes, just like that. Please. Thank you, oh God, thank you, Delia." He opens his mouth. Waits like a baby bird to receive it. She holds the cherry up above him, then pops it into her own mouth and crushes it between her teeth. Tears are running down his cheeks. "If you let me die, you'll get caught." His voice is quieter now. He sounds more drugged than before.

"I don't know," Delia says. "I think being dead is a pretty good alibi, don't you?" She grins.

"There'll be an investigation," William says. "They'll figure out what happened. No one will believe this was an accident."

Delia shakes her head. "Well, they don't need to, because it *isn't* an accident. Your stepdaughter killed herself, then you were arrested for your drug habit. You're a prominent surgeon with everything to lose. Surely no one would be too *shocked* that you killed yourself too."

"The drugs," William says. "My car." His words are slurring. "That was you . . ."

"Look, you even left a note." She pulls a sheet of paper out of her pocket, unfolds it, and holds it up in front of him. "That is your handwriting, isn't it?" It's a long letter, the words *To my darling wife* written at the top.

Delia goes to Ashling and kisses her on the lips. "Thank you for being brilliant, babe," she says.

"June, please," William says. "Youcan stopthis. Please helpme."

I look at Delia, my best friend who I love more than life, at William drooling in his chair. Both of them are staring at me now. I have no doubt about who is lying and who is not. This time, it is easy to tell. The question is what happens next. I think of Delia, alone in this house, alone in that room. I think of Delia's mother. I think of that sweet tiny baby who hasn't even entered the world yet.

"Get me when it's over," I say. And I turn and walk into the kitchen. I stand in front of the refrigerator, scared to touch anything, scared to move, scared to breathe. I just stand there listening to the voices from the other room. I am dizzy. I crouch down onto the floor and press my face against the tile, trying not to pass out. I close my eyes. And after a while I hear Delia's voice, so soft above me. "Junie, you can come back now."

Chapter 51

June

We are silent. And we are still. And my heart slows down, and everything in the room slows down, and I am not sure if I am breathing. I force myself to turn and look at him. I thought he'd look like he was sleeping.

He does not look like he's sleeping.

Ashling brings her hands together in a muffled latex clap.

"Okay," she says. "Let's finish this off." And suddenly everyone is moving again.

Ashling unties William, and his body slumps forward in his chair. She takes the syringe from Delia and positions it in William's hand, then she curls his fist loosely around it, lets go, and it drops to the floor.

"I've got the basement," Evan says. "Junie, what did you touch down there? Just the albums?" But I can't even open my mouth. "Don't worry," he says with a grin. "I'm very thorough." And he leaves.

"I've got the doorknobs," Sebastian says.

And I want to ask them what I'm supposed to do now, but I just stand there. And they are all moving, and I am not moving. I'm watching William's face. And he is not moving either.

Time passes, I think. Evan is back in the room.

"Shit," he says. "His shirt." He points to a dark stain on William's back.

"His drink," Sebastian says. "From the floor."

"Hold on." Delia runs back upstairs and returns a few seconds later with a button-up shirt, baby blue like her gloves. "He loved this one," says Delia. She sounds almost tender.

She reaches out and unbuttons his shirt. Evan and Sebastian hold him up while they work together to slip it off. His chest is pale and soft, clammy-looking, dotted with more dark hair, puckered around the nipples, a jiggly belly.

They take the stained shirt, ball it up, and throw it in a trash bag. They slip his arms into the new shirt, button it up over his body, gently, gently. Delia smooths it. "There," she says.

I am not here anymore. I'm in another world now. I feel motion all around, and then Delia comes over to me. She removes one of her latex gloves and stuffs it in her pocket. Then she reaches out and takes my hand, but I can't feel it through my own glove. She squeezes. "It's time to go now," she says.

They walk toward the back door, carefully. I follow. They

push through it and I follow, onto the porch. The sun is starting to set. The world looks unreal in this light. Evan holds the door, and one by one we make our way through it and down the stairs. I'm last. I turn back and look at the porch, at the rocks lining the edge, at the house where I spent so many days with Delia, so many nights with Delia. And then I look away.

What the fuck have we done?

Chapter 52

Delia

My mother always wanted me to love him. "He's family!" she would say, begging, desperate. I couldn't, I couldn't . . . not after every fucking thing he did.

But he has paid for his sins now. He has sacrificed himself to give me what I need. I watched him, his eyes closing, his face growing slack, drooling, helpless, sweet like a baby. For a moment I almost felt sorry. And when he floated away, leaving only his meat lump of a body behind, I felt a surge of something, maybe it was love, maybe I do love him now. Just a little.

When no one was looking, I leaned over. I kissed him good-bye.

Chapter 53

June

We make our way up through the woods, quickly, quietly. Nothing is real. I am floating and sick.

Through the fog I feel something hot poking me at the base of my skull. A tiny thought egg that hasn't hatched yet, but the thought is trapped inside, scratching and scratching its way out.

"Come on," Delia says. And I realize she is still holding on to my hand.

Hot acid swirls in my stomach, I wonder if I'm going to throw up. I try to take a breath, but my lungs have forgotten what to do. I have to fight to get the air in.

And we keep walking, down the street, toward the reservoir.

No one is talking, and then we are back at the cars, Ashling's and Sebastian's. The air around me is vibrating. We can't undo this. It can never be undone. "You'll ride back with us," Delia says.

"Back?" I fight my way through that fog. Hear the words.

"To the house," says Delia.

She smiles at me. Evan, Ashling, Sebastian. They all smile. Who are these people? Who is Sebastian? Who is Delia? What the fuck have we done?

"I need to go home," I say.

"But home is with me," Delia says quietly.

"I want to go to my house." I imagine my bed, my dark sad house, my mother.

Delia is watching me. I can't look at her now.

Ashling and Evan exchange a glance. "She can't," Evan says.

Ashling shakes her head. "Later," she says.

Sebastian turns away from both of them. He puts his hands on my shoulders, turns me toward him. "The thoughts that come won't be good. You shouldn't be alone with them."

He stops, and his words sink in. He has done this before.

He squeezes me. "We did a good thing."

"June," Delia says, "please." But I don't know what I'm thinking now, what I'm feeling now.

"I have to go," I say. And I force myself to look up at her. "I'm so sorry that everything that happened before happened." I hear the coldness in my voice. I mean what I'm saying. But I can't get my tone to match. I can't pull forth anything but frozen fear. "I'm glad you got out of there."

"I really do not think you should go now," Delia says. Each word so slow and careful. The light is fading. I can barely see her anymore. The moment stretches into infinity.

But I shake my head. I break free.

"I'm sorry," I tell her.

Evan is staring at me. He starts to reach out toward me. *"Don't,"* Delia says. "Not now."

Sebastian leads me over to his car then and puts me in front. I think Evan is yelling now, but I can't make out the words. Ashling kisses Delia on the lips, but Delia doesn't move. I watch them until we drive away.

The sun is going down. I watch the road and trees and cars in front of us.

He pulls up to my house. He is shaking his head. "I told you you didn't have to," he says quietly. "Didn't I tell you that?"

He kisses me softly on the cheek. His lips are burning hot. I can still feel the heat of them as I take my key from my pocket to let myself inside.

Chapter 54

Delia

She wasn't supposed to leave me. She wasn't supposed to leave me.

She won't.

Chapter 55

June

I dream of rotting fruit, bruised, sticky, sickly sweet. Evan and Ashling are on all fours, shoveling it into their mouths, the juice dripping from their chins. They ask me to join in. And then there is Delia, telling them I already ate it, that she fed it to me when I was asleep. I feel myself start to choke then, choke on what I've been fed. I wake in the middle of the night, gagging, and it takes me no time to remember yesterday. What we did. I close my eyes, and everything is right there waiting for me—his skin, the way his face was transformed when he was no longer inside his body.

It's still pitch-black outside. I pull myself out of bed, make my way toward the bathroom. And that's when it happens—the egg lodged at the base of my skull bursts. This is what comes pouring out: Delia's words when she told me the story of that night, what he did to her.

I bit until I tasted fucking blood.

I remember William, heavy body. And his skin, waxy and pale . . . But what about the bite mark? I close my eyes. I cannot, suddenly, remember seeing one. Did I? Was there anything there?

I bit until I tasted fucking blood.

I need to talk to Delia, to talk to her so she can make me understand. We did what needed to be done, he deserved it. The world is a better place without him. I didn't even *do* anything, I just didn't stop it.

I just didn't stop it.

I throw on clothes, choke back bile. I'm running down the stairs, stomach churning.

I bit until I tasted fucking blood.

My mother is in the kitchen, standing in front of the stove. "Do you want some dinner?" she asks. "Or maybe we'll call it breakfast. I just finished my shift." She never asks this, hasn't in years. She flips a grilled cheese onto a plate. She cuts it in half and steam rises up.

My mouth is dry, my spit thick. I can feel the acid burning in my gut.

She looks at me; our eyes meet. Our eyes never meet. "Are

you okay?" She sounds actually concerned. "What are you doing up? And dressed?"

I shake my head. I don't remember words. I have to get out of here.

I bit until I tasted fucking blood.

"Jesus, I mean, the world is really crazy sometimes," she says. She shakes her head. "I'm assuming you've seen the news."

William. Already.

I try and keep my face calm. I breathe.

She goes on. "I mean, what are the odds, two students at your school in less than two weeks, but I suppose only one of them was an accident."

"What accident?" I say.

"A car accident," she says.

"Wait, what?"

"I don't remember the boy's name. He wasn't in your grade though, he was a senior. I'm surprised you haven't already heard about this."

Something inside me is sinking, floating, spinning. I have to get out of here. I put on my jacket.

My mother looks at me again, tips her head to the side. "Where are you going? It's five in the morning."

"I have to be at school early," I say. And I'm out the door before she can say anything else.

I'm in my freezing car, hands shaking. I take out my phone.

Search for Breswin, car accident, North Orchard. What comes up is this:

A Breswin teen has died after his vehicle struck a guardrail earlier today. Investigators believe brake failure may have been the cause.

The victim, Jeremiah Aaronson, 17, was declared dead upon arrival by emergency personnel at 1:46 this afternoon. This is the second tragic death this year for the North Orchard High School community . . .

I raise my hand to my lips. I have a bad feeling, a terrible feeling. I'm no longer on earth. But this was an accident, right? A horrible coincidence, that's all. That's the explanation. That's it. It has to be.

Chapter 56

June

I do not scream, I do not think. I am nothing but pure motion, a bullet, shot toward that house.

I pull into the driveway. There are lights on inside. The air is silent and still, and in the distance I smell the faint hint of smoke.

I get out, shivering, stones crunching under my feet. I am afraid to stand there, to walk forward, to move at all, to be on this earth. I am shaking and shaking for I don't know how long. I look up at the sky, at all that empty blackness, and know there will never be enough of anything to fill it.

I hear footsteps behind me.

And Delia's voice, "Junie, you came."

I turn. She is standing around the side of the house, walking toward me. I can see her face now, lit by the glow from the windows. Our eyes meet. She is inside me, in my body, in my heart. We are staring, and for a moment there is nothing but this.

"I knew you would," she whispers. "But you scared me."

There is someone else there now, Evan coming around the side of the house too, squinting in the dark. "Is that her?"

Delia coughs, turns, and answers. "I told you she would come."

"Good," Evan says. "It's much easier this way." But he doesn't look at me, he walks back in the direction he came from.

"I need to talk to you," I whisper. There is so much to say, to ask. I am so, so scared.

Delia shakes her head. "Not now, Junie. Please. Just wait."

She grabs my hand. She starts to run and won't let go. We stumble across the grass, following the scent of smoke around the side of the house. There's a bonfire down by the river, glowing bright against the slowly lightening sky. Ashling, Sebastian, Evan. They are tossing things into the fire.

There's a pile of papers in the center of the flames, and fabric, maybe a shirt. The fire is much too big for this backyard. But there is no one around for miles. No one to even see the smoke.

"What's going on?" I say.

"We're getting ready to go," Delia says quietly.

"It's good you came back," says Ashling. There is a flicker of something in her tone.

The sun is beginning to rise. There's a thin line of dark red at the horizon. A razor slash in the sky.

I catch Sebastian's eye. He looks away. "So, she knows then?" he says. But not to me.

"What is . . . ?" I start. My entire body is buzzing.

"I'm taking care of it." Delia sounds almost angry. And then she turns to me, her tone softens. "Let's take a walk." She still hasn't let go of my hand.

She leads me away, along the river, out toward the woods. We make our way in silence. She stops. I turn around. We are far from the others; it is just the two of us now. My head is spinning so fast, none of this is real.

I remember what I came here for.

She wants to say something. I don't let her.

I take a breath. "What happened to Jeremiah?"

Delia stares at me blankly in the early morning light. Maybe she really doesn't know. For a second I feel so strange and sorry to have to deliver this news. For a second I have hope.

"He was in an accident, a car accident. It was really bad."

I wait for my words to sink in, but her expression doesn't change.

"Did you hear me?" That feeling is back in my stomach. This was her boyfriend. "He didn't survive."

"You protect the people you love." She is speaking too slowly.

"I don't understand what you're saying."

"Junie, you protect the people you love. No matter how you have to do it."

"What do you mean protect, what are you . . ." I stop. I can't breathe. My heart is pounding so hard. "William's chest, I'm not sure . . . I don't think I remember seeing a bite mark."

She is shaking her head. "So?"

"When he tried to rape you." My voice doesn't sound like my own. "You said you bit him till there was blood. But when his shirt was off . . . I can't remember if I saw anything."

"Well, I don't know." Delia says. "Did you?"

I am sick with fear now.

"*Listen*, June," Delia says. "Junie, J, my heart, my love. That is not even important. It is just totally beside the point. It's time to go. Do you understand what that means?"

The red line on the horizon is getting thicker. The sun is coming up fast. I can smell the smoke in the wind. I turn. The fire grows and grows.

I feel heat in my belly, rising. "We did . . . what we did because of what you said he did . . . *Did he actually?*"

"I can't believe you're even asking me that," Delia says. Delia shakes her head. "Let's stop talking about this now. It's not what you came here for."

I feel something happening behind my eyes. William. Jeremiah. Even Ryan. I have no idea what is true. "What did I come here for?"

"June," she says. "You came here for me."

I am rushing through the air, spinning, floating.

"I came here to find out what happened. The bite mark. Jeremiah. Delia . . ."

"NO." She's shouting. She stops then, takes a breath. "*You came here for me.*" She motions back toward the fire. "And it's time to go now. We're leaving."

"You're leaving," I say. I feel my heart float up outside my body and beat between us.

Jeremiah. William's chest.

Delia shakes her head. "No, *we* are. They agreed. You'll come with us. They know you can . . . deal with real shit. They know how much you love me. We take care of each other, you and me. We always have."

"You're asking me to go with you?" I grab her shoulders. I am squeezing them. I need to make her look at me. "Delia, listen, do you understand what I am saying?" I say. "I don't know what's going on, and I'm really scared." I sound desperate. I am desperate. "Did he actually try to rape you? Did he do the things you said he did?"

She isn't breathing.

I feel the cool air against my skin. I imagine myself floating off into space. No one and nothing is holding me now.

She leans in. She is whispering. "Or it can just be us, just the two of us, if that's what you want."

There is something in her eyes—I see it. In there she is every age she's ever been, every age I've ever known her.

"Why did you bring me there? Why did you bring me to your house to kill him?"

"Because I needed you there," Delia says.

"For *what*?" I say. But suddenly I know. And under the fear, under that otherwordly terror, I feel the loneliness sucking at my insides, the black hole threatening to pull me in.

"I almost killed myself for real, you know," she says. "Once, a hundred times, a thousand times. I almost killed myself every day. And you know what stopped me?" Her eyes are filled up now. "You." Tears fall. She reaches into her jacket.

I think I'm crying too. And for a moment nothing at all matters but us here in this moment, the two of us, my best friend. Oh God, what have we done.

I start to wrap my arms around her. But she doesn't lift hers. And I realize Delia is holding what she pulled out of her jacket. And I am understanding something. There is just one thing I forgot about.

But now I remember. Tig. What Delia stole. She never returned it.

"I won't tell anyone. I promise. I swear. I would never. This never happened, any of it."

"Every day since I met you, you stopped me." She is not looking at me anymore, the tears sliding down her cheeks as though they are someone else's tears and someone else's cheeks. She sounds so far away. "Even when you weren't my friend anymore, you kept me alive. Because I knew, I just knew, somehow one day . . . I'd have you back." She holds it out in front of her now. "I stole this for *me* to use on *me*. Before I knew what was possible." She holds it up. "Do you understand what I'm saying? You need to make a choice now."

"Between what and what?" I say. I am whispering.

"Please, Junie. Please." She is begging now. "Because I can't let you leave me."

"Delia," I say.

"Junie," she says. "I love you."

Chapter 57

5 years, 3 months, 15 days earlier

Later Delia would explain to June that finding a best friend is like finding a true love: when you meet yours, you just know. But the truth is, that isn't quite how it happened.

It was the third week of sixth grade when Delia, brand-new to the school and angry as fuck, stood up in front of the room and was introduced to the class. Her mother had just married a shitbag and moved them in with him. Delia wasn't sad to leave her old school behind, because things had gone wrong there in ways she'd rather forget about. But she didn't want to be at this new school either. In fact, she'd have preferred to not have to exist at all. It was *painful* living like this, burning angry anxious fire inside. It *hurt all the time.*

But then, that first day, she spotted June, and the hot fizzy flame subsided. And it turned to a bottomless starving wanting, still painful, but in a different way. What did she want?

She didn't quite know. Not to fuck this girl exactly, or to be her, really, either. No, more like she wanted to *eat* her. Delia was suddenly *ravenous* for the blond wide-eyed bunny-looking thing three rows back. She wanted to take this girl, gulp her down, even her *bones*, just gulp her down whole.

Of course, that isn't the kind of thing you could say to someone, a brand-new maybe friend at a brand-new school. So instead, she did what she knew was normal—because she did *know* that, at least most of the time! She invited that girl, whose name was June—it was the perfect name for her!—over for a sleepover.

And June opened up her sweet blue eyes in delighted surprise and said yes.

The night of the sleepover Delia's stepfather was working late because that shitbag always did, and Delia told her mother they were ordering pizza and eating it up in her room. And her mother didn't argue because her mother never argued with her anymore, which was upsetting in its own way, because it was like her mother *couldn't*, didn't even have it *in her*, since shitbag arrived in their life. But it also meant Delia got to do what she wanted.

Upstairs in her room with June, Delia could barely eat at all, couldn't even sit still. She was full of manic insane energy, walking around the room, pointing things out like some kind of cracked out tour guide—there was a tiny painting of a winter scene that Delia had stolen from a thrift store, there was a cherry stem that she'd knotted using only her tongue, there was the pill bottle containing her secret escape plan, assembled bit by bit from the medicine cabinet in her mother's bathroom when no one was looking. Late at night sometimes, she would empty them into her hand. Once, she held them all in her mouth, even. She lied and told June they were breath mints.

June looked at everything with such sweet awe, radiating pure goodness and light.

Just after eleven, shitbag came home and started yelling at her mother behind their closed bedroom door. Delia felt the hot fizzling inside of her, but she made herself breathe in and out three full times, and then she smiled like everything was fine and told June it was time to sneak out.

She climbed out her window and then dropped down into the grass. June was trying to pretend not to be scared—it was so cute!—but she followed. They walked up and down the block a couple of times. They snuck dandelions in people's mailboxes, which was June's sweetly innocent idea of something naughty they could do. They peeked into the window of Delia's seventeen-year-old neighbor. They watched him changing out of his clothes, but when he got down to his underwear, he shut the curtain. "Damn it!" Delia said. And then she grinned, like this was just fun, like she hadn't actually offered to suck his dick the day before (he said no, looking pretty freaked out by the offer, actually). But it was okay. Standing there with June, she didn't give a fuck about that or him at all, anymore. She wanted to do something to bond the two of them together. What did normal people do? What would be okay to do?

Delia had an idea. She took off her bra. Then she convinced June to do the same, taught her how to get it off without taking her shirt off. June's bra wasn't even really a bra, and she seemed embarrassed about it. June's little tiny raisin boobs were poking through the thin fabric of her T-shirt. Delia had a sudden fierce urge to reach out and pinch them, hard, make June wince and squinch up her sweet little face. Instead she forced herself to look away and said, lightly as though they were just having some silly fun, "Now we mark our territory." She grabbed June's hand, and then Delia snuck around the front of the house, opened up the boy's family's red-barn mailbox, and tossed both bras inside.

"There," Delia said. "And now we have a secret. Having secrets together makes you real friends," she said. "Secrets tie you together." Delia was imagining all the future secrets they'd have, each one a thin rope wrapping around the two of them, binding them up.

They went inside after that, and Delia could feel the connection now, could feel those ropes when they got side by side into her bed, when Delia combed June's hair so gently. She wanted the ropes tighter, more of them. An infinite number.

This girl was going to change everything. And she would never, ever let her go.

Dear Delia,

When you died, part of me died too. Now I'm finishing off the rest, so we can be together.

You once told me you wished we could leave this world behind and go into space where nothing bad had ever happened. I think eternity will be something like that: just you and me, floating in infinite blackness, tied only to each other.

I never used to believe in heaven, but now I know I was wrong—heaven is the feeling of home. Home was always with you.

I'm coming.

Yours always,

June

Acknowledgments

Infinite thank-yous to my amazing agent, Jenny Bent, for being an incredible editor, brainstormer, adviser, and advocate. And also hilarious. Working with you is an absolute joy every step of the way. I am so happy that I get to.

I am very grateful to the extraordinary people at Simon Pulse, including Mara Anastas, Mary Marotta, Lauren Forte, Sara Berko, Carolyn Swerdloff, Teresa Ronquillo, Jodie Hockensmith, Michelle Leo, Christina Pecorale, Rio Cortez, and the entire Simon Pulse sales team. An enormous thank-you to Regina Flath for designing the gorgeous US cover. And special thanks to Michael Strother for the brainstorming help, including figuring out things like the temperature at which titanium melts, and the best drug to sneak into someone's drink.

Thank you to the lovely Victoria Lowes and Gemma Cooper at The Bent Agency.

My gratitude, and Swedish Fish, to the fabulous Nicola Barr at Greene and Heaton.

I feel so very lucky to get to work with all the outstanding people at Egmont UK's Electric Monkey imprint. Very big thank-yous to Alice Hill, Charlie Webber, Denise Woolery, Laura Grundy, Laura Neate, Lucy Pearse, Sarah Hughes, and Sian Robertson. Much appreciation to Andrea Kearney for the beautiful UK cover and interiors. And extra, extra thanks to my fantastic UK editor, Stella Paskins.

Thank you so hugely much, Robin Wasserman, for reading the manuscript and for the amazingly smart, astute, and helpful notes, not to mention very appreciated encouragement. Thank you, Brendan Duffy, for the brainstorming, terrific suggestions, and for asking just the right questions. Thank you, Micol Ostow, for the excellent notes on the final manuscript, and for being so very supportive throughout.

Big thanks to Siobhan Vivian for, among other things, that very pivotal phone conversation. To Paul Griffin for all the help when I first started working on this, and to Aaron Lewis for the help with that bit at the end. Thank you to Martin Arrascue for saying yes every time I said "Wait, but can I read you just one more thing out loud?!" Thank you to Mary Crosbie for reading things, brainstorming, and sending me all those cat pictures.

Massive thanks to Melanie Altarescu for very many things, but specifically in regard to this book, for dropping everything to read it in a mad dash right at the end. (And I'm sorry for the nightmares!!!)

Thank you to the entire staff at the Cocoa Bar, and to my delightful Cocoa Bar writing buddies.

And thank you to my wonderful parents, Cheryl Weingarten and Donald Weingarten!

Thank you to my Internet pals, some of whom I've never even met in real life, but all of whom I adore. Giant thanks to all the bloggers who've written such thoughtful reviews. Thank you so much to anyone who has taken the time to read this book.

And finally, my endless appreciation to my editor, Liesa Abrams Mignogna. Thank you for being brilliant; for being tons of fun to work with; for your incredibly insightful notes, thoughts, and suggestions always delivered with so much kindness; and for your deft guidance on issues huge and tiny. For always just getting it.